ALSO BY
MICHELE ZACKHEIM

FICTION
Violette's Embrace
Broken Colors

NONFICTION
Einstein's Daughter: The Search for Lieserl

LAST TRAIN
TO PARIS

Michele Zackheim

LAST TRAIN
TO PARIS

Europa
editions

Europa Editions
214 West 29th Street
New York, N.Y. 10001
www.europaeditions.com
info@europaeditions.com

Library of Congress Cataloging in Publication Data is available
ISBN 978-1-60945-179-0

Zackheim, Michele
Last Train to Paris

Book design by Emanuele Ragnisco
www.mekkanografici.com

Cover photo © Linda Steward/iStock

Prepress by Grafica Punto Print – Rome

Printed in the USA

For Jane Lincoln Taylor

Get your facts first and then you can distort 'em
as much as you like.
—MARK TWAIN

LAST TRAIN
TO PARIS

Author's Note

A German citizen named Eugen Weidmann abducted a distant cousin of mine in Paris in 1937. For more than two years in Europe, Britain, and the United States, it was a flashy headline news story. The case fascinated me, so I set out to write a nonfiction novel. I did all the requisite research. I traveled to Paris and Berlin. I had done this kind of writing before. But I became far more interested in my fictional characters and less in the "real" people. Except for a few. The lawyers Renée Jardin and Moro-Giafferi are real. Colette is real. Janet Flanner is real. Aurora Sand is real—and indeed, they were all part of the real story. The rest are from my imagination.

Some days, I'm too angry for words. Those are the days when I can't get to my writing table. When I don't bother to dress. When I stay in my ratty blue chenille bathrobe and shuffle around the house in my slippers. Those days I eat yogurt out of the container, and drink too much coffee—sometimes too much whiskey. I read the newspaper and carry on conversations with myself about the dismal state of the universe. Over the years people have tried to assure me that as I grow older I will become less angry, more accepting of the stupidity I see on our planet. This has not proved true. Sometimes, to ease the tension, I'll read a mystery, hoping to be fooled; often I waste time daydreaming. But I have a job to do, a column to compose, so eventually I'll hunker down and begin writing. Then it gets interesting. There is a shift in my mind and my body. Love takes over. My pen begins to tickle my passion for words and I squirm with pleasure. I still love to use a fountain pen—love the way the smoothed nib pushes the stream of blue ink across the paper, making letters, making words—trying to make sense of the world. I write for a short time and then remove my pen from the paper, put on the cap, and place my fingers on the keys of the typewriter. As if by magic, I write my weekly column for the *New York Courier*. But, really, it's not magic. It's a facility with rhythm, language, and ideas that comes with age and hard work. And I do have to admit that I still get a thrill when I turn a newsprint page and find my byline: "R. B. Manon."

I love my old house in the rolling hills of upper New York State. Made of wood that's gray with age, it has a peaked roof, ornate gables, and faded red window frames that sag toward the south. It reminds me of the Victorian houses that dotted the mountains of Nevada. And although I'm loath to remember my childhood, the architecture remains in my mind as calming and pretty.

The back of my house has a screened-in porch and faces the southeast. Ten years ago I planted wisteria, a climbing vine, on the south side. Now it snakes around one porch pillar, curls itself around the crossbeam, winds down the other side, and then climbs up again, twisting and turning back and forth. I can no longer tell if it's the woody wisteria holding up the porch roof or if it's the pillars. What I do know is that in the spring, the flowers drip from the vines, creating a gossamer fringe of lavender.

A reminiscence. Spring in Paris. Overnight, shops moved their wares out onto the sidewalk. Fresh-cut flowers, especially modest bunches of violets; potted pink and red geraniums; lovebirds cooing, baritone pigeons, squawking hens, soprano canaries, even small green turtles whose shells were painted with *J'aime Paris*. The streets became alive with the new season, just like my splendid twelve acres of rolling hills and blooming wildflowers.

It's the spring of 1992. Except for a lip of charcoal-colored cloud peeking over the horizon, the weather's clear. Here I am, an old woman of eighty-seven, on my knees pulling weeds in the cool morning. I hear the phone ringing in the house. Blast it!—it always rings when I'm out here. I know there's no chance of standing up, climbing the steps to the porch, going inside to the kitchen, and getting to it before the answering machine does its job. So I don't bother.

As the afternoon approaches, I'm getting hot and tired and cranky. Finally, achingly, I stand, walk to the porch, climb the three steps, and lower myself into a faded green rocking chair in the shade. Looking out over the hills, I think about the horizon, that mysterious threshold between earth and sky—and I remember the Eiffel Tower. My God! It's a little more than fifty years since I worked in Paris. I remember how I used to long to see over the horizon to the other side. Whenever I was feeling stifled, or more angry than usual, I would go to the top of my urban mountain—the Eiffel Tower. Resting my arms on the railing, I would gaze west across the imaginary sea to the mountains in Nevada where I was born.

One early morning in 1940, it all changed. The French surrendered Paris to the Germans. The city was eerily silent, bereft of many of its citizens. My instinct was to get to my mountain. As I walked toward the Seine on the boulevard St. Germain, I saw Parisians sneaking around corners, hugging walls, slinking past windows painted with ugly methylene blue. The SS were everywhere. Their gray field blouses, cinched with thick black leather belts and closed with shiny silver buckles, were inscribed *Gott mit uns*—God Is with Us. I was frightened. I knew firsthand how rough and unforgiving those conquerors could be. But I persisted, turned left along the river, and after a short while, turned left again. I walked over the Pont d'Iéna, seeing before me the Eiffel Tower and beyond to the Parc du Champ de Mars. The park was dotted with ancient lime trees casting their shadows, creating umbrellas of coolness. I looked up. The catastrophe was clear. Flying from the top of the Eiffel Tower was a huge red flag with a black swastika in a white circle.

I needed to get to the summit, but all the elevators were out of order. Sabotage. I wasn't sure if the guard was German or French; he wasn't wearing a uniform. I spoke in French. He didn't understand. I switched to German and he did. He told me that someone had removed crucial parts from the mechanisms. So I climbed. It took a long time. The metal steps were treacherous; they could be slippery, the handrails thin. By the time I reached the second deck, I was exhausted—and relieved to see a chain blocking the rest of the stairs. Still, I was high enough to look out and over the wide expanse of Paris. I was struck by both the city's astonishing beauty and the crushing undercurrent of fear. Rather than taking a deep breath and imagining what brightness was over the horizon, I felt paralyzed by the disaster at hand.

Now, many years later, on this pleasant summer day, I look over my peaceful green hills and feel safe. My only enemy is time.

It isn't until the afternoon that I remember to check the answering machine. It's a message from the delivery company, informing me that they will arrive tomorrow morning.

A few weeks ago, I was informed by the *Paris Courier*'s office that the newspaper was moving to new headquarters and the staff was cleaning out the basement. Would I like the crate that they had been storing for me since the beginning of World War II? I said yes, of course, curious about retrieving whatever ancient fragments of my old life still existed. But I was also surprised. I had heard that the newspaper's basement had flooded during the war. Oh well, I remember having thought—there go my notes.

For years I had been avoiding the task of organizing my archive, using the lost notes as my excuse for doing nothing. Now I couldn't avoid it. And what a job it threatened to be! I dreaded it. Like most journalists, I never throw anything away. After all, one never can tell. I might be sued—a researcher might need information that I have—I might need to refer back in time for a story I'm writing. Everything after 1940 is here in my house, roughly tossed into boxes, sometimes labeled with the year, sometimes not.

The next morning is cloudy and the sky a mottled steel gray. I've become melancholy, like the weather. Then there is a loud clap of thunder, and just as it begins to rain, the delivery van arrives. What bad luck. But the man wrangles something onto a hand truck and delivers my young life to my elderly house.

I'm astonished. Standing before me is my old red-leather traveling trunk, not a box. "What the hell," I say aloud, and have to sit down.

I eye the trunk as if it's an ogre in repose. Get on with it, Rosie, I say to myself, don't be such a coward. But the latches are glued shut with the passage of time. It rankles me. I get a chisel and hammer from the pantry and begin to tap my way lightly around the edges. Before long my hands ache, yet I'm persistent. And I'm fascinated. Soon there is a small pile of rusty dust, but the latches still won't open. I place the chisel in a logical spot and whack it with the hammer. Then I do the same to the second latch. They are both open.

I wait.

I pour myself a glass of whiskey.

I open the trunk.

Out wafts the fragrance of cloistered time.

There, sitting on top, alongside George Sand and Balzac, is my Freud—still stuffed with notes. Oh, no, this isn't mine—it's Andy Roth's. I don't want to open it, afraid it will release old demons into my beloved house. Ah, here's my copy. Just as old and tattered, but filled with my own typed notes and underlines and many, many exclamation marks. Everything then was so important, so dramatic, so tragic. I put Freud aside for the moment, not wanting to be detoured. The next layer is a collection of newspaper articles that I had written in Europe. Careful. They are yellowed, flaking—disintegrating. I save them for later.

Next is a pile of handwritten notes on onionskin paper. They are now so delicate, so fragile—the ink has faded but they're readable. These notes were my witness to the world going mad. I remember a friend telling me that when he came across his old journals, he opened one to an arbitrary page and remembered years of searching and confusion and anger. In one fell swoop, he gathered them up and threw them into a passing garbage truck. "It's good the truck was there at the right moment," he said. "Otherwise, I might have read them and jumped off a bridge!" But I see it from a different perspective. It will be interesting for me to read my old self. I'm curious. I wonder how honest I was? As a reporter I've always been interested in the truth. Was I really determined to tell the truth when I was young?

It's raining hard—the tin roof is protecting me, while at the same time making a huge racket. No matter. I'm wrapped in words and memories. Here are the remnants of my early life. I wonder who I was. Making myself comfortable on the sofa, I begin to read.

* * *

In 1933, I had just traveled across the sea to the second floor of the *Paris Courier*'s editorial office. It was midnight. I remember entering bedlam. It reminded me of a George Bellows painting of an action-packed boxing ring and arena—ochres, grays, an occasional spot of color. Cigarette, cigar, and pipe smoke was hanging in the air, adding its aroma to a miasma of damp paper and stale ink. It made my eyes water. The reporters were working at several large, scratched, coffee- and beer-ringed oak tables that made a square in the middle of the room. Over the tables dangled bare light bulbs that were swaying in slow motion to the noise and the bustle. There was too much smoke and too little bright light. The rewrite men were sitting at battered desks haphazardly placed around the room, banging away at rackety typewriters.

Even though it was a blazing hot summer night, most of the men wore fedoras. They had their shirtsleeves roughly rolled up, some with their cigarette packs stored in a fold, the top buttons of their shirts undone, their ties loosely knotted. Cigarettes were burning in ashtrays or hanging from their mouths. My unremarkable black trousers were sticking to my legs and my wilting white blouse was a mistake. The sweat made it stick to my back and stomach, making my brassiere and breasts obvious, and my feet were swollen and sweating in a new pair of flat-heeled black shoes. I stood transfixed—actually, scared—at the top of the stairs, and scanned the room.

Some of the newsmen looked out through the tall open windows onto the street. Others faced the damp interior walls. The walls were decorated with discolored newspaper clippings, water-stained foolscap, and beautiful, but faded, engraved maps of Europe dating back to before the Great War. Scattered on top of a carpet of scrunched-up balls of paper, ripped from typewriters in frustration, were cigarette butts, slimy cigar ends, and empty beer bottles. Tucked into dark crevices were grimy-looking brass spittoons. A few men were talking, but most were yelling at each other across the room; there was the sound of the Teletype machines, and the insistent, nerve-shattering noise of honking taxis outside. It was familiar—reminding me of my previous newsroom, in New York. As I glimpsed my first Parisian cockroach, I also realized that I was the only woman there.

"What can I do for you?" asked one of the men, drinking a beer while reading a galley.

"I'm looking for Mr. Ramsey, the managing editor. Name's R. B. Manon," I said, and we shook hands.

The beer-drinking man gestured toward a glass-enclosed cubicle. "There he is," he said, "the master of chaos. Good luck to you."

Mr. Ramsey was a short, heavyset man with tiny hands and feet and short arms. He had straw-colored hair with a distinctive cowlick at the top of his head. His nose was small and red and pimply; his eyes were blue and quite pretty. He was wearing a bow tie with blue polka dots on a white background. "Well, well, they've sent me a young lady," he scoffed. "I thought you were a man with a name like R.B. Was wondering why they assigned a guy to the social desk. Assumed he was a queer," he said, and shook my hand, trying to show me how strong he was.

I kept a straight face and looked him in the eyes. "My name's Rose Belle Manon. You can call me R.B."

He looked at me strangely. "Well, it's good you're not a looker. It'll be easier to work with you."

My new home was on the Left Bank, the Hôtel Espoir on the Place de la Sorbonne. The name of the hotel was deceptive; it was a sad-looking fleabag with blistering gray paint over gray stone. My room cost fifty cents a day. The hotel had five stories, with two dormer garrets on the top floor. The rooms opened off long corridors, dimly lit with cold blue bulbs. There was no elevator. Fortunately, I lived on the second floor. Few of the locks on the doors worked—it was like a ranch bunkhouse. I wasn't used to people barging into my room, and at first found it disconcerting. The rooms were almost identical, and people joked that after too much drinking, you shouldn't be surprised if some morning you woke in the wrong bed. My room had one of the few sinks, although no hot water, and the sink was decorated with unpleasant mineral stains that were impossible to clean. Above the sink was an old, golden-clouded mirror. The rooms were long and narrow and each had one tall French window that opened out onto either the street or, as in my case, the trash-strewn courtyard. An old woman, who I called Madame Canari, lived across the way. She was always wearing a starched pink apron with a flowered red kerchief on her head. "Good morning," she would yell across to me, no matter what the time of day. She had pet canaries that never wearied of filling the courtyard with their lovely song. They would flutter about, reminding me of a forsythia shrub whose yellow flower petals were being blown by the wind. I was grateful for a touch of nature and the woman's neighborly ways.

Having inherited a narrow and rather lumpy bed, I covered it with my Indian blanket, brought from Nevada. There was a ratty, dull-brown armchair whose arms were encrusted with ancient dirt, but it was comfortable. Between the chair and my bed was a brown fringed lampshade that shimmied when people walked on the stairs. My favorite piece of furniture was the Técalémit radio that I bought at Marché aux Puces, the flea market at Porte de Clignancourt. As time went on, and the world was on the brink of war, I needed music more and more. Above the bed I hung a poster, of the turn-of-the-century dancers, *Bal Musette,* which I had bought at a green metal bookstall along the Seine. I also bought four pots of red geraniums, which I placed on the narrow wrought-iron balcony outside my window.

A reporter, Andy Roth (originally from Golden, Colorado), whom I'd known since my stint at the *New York Courier,* welcomed me to the hotel. "I live two doors down from you. I know this is a dismal joint, but you'll get used to it."

Wherever I looked, there was fodder for stories. Having come from a small town, I was amazed at the variety of people. "I could write forever here," I told Andy. "The entire world's represented under this roof."

Quickly I learned that the hotel was a haven for émigrés. They were living under assumed names, carrying false papers, vulnerable; they were hiding from hatred and the constant threat of death. They were Jews, communists, homosexuals—

people living on the edge of the political knife. The concierge and her husband, Madame and Monsieur Pleven, called themselves Marxists. Although they had a picture of Marx hanging on their wall, I never had a conversation about Marxism with them—though I certainly tried. Perhaps they thought it was fashionable to belong to the movement. I don't know. But I do know that they managed the hotel well, and took great pride in protecting everyone from the authorities. Whenever the police arrived to conduct a raid (a monthly occurrence), Monsieur Pleven alerted the residents and they would quietly go to the basement and leave by a nondescript door that led into another building. If I happened to be in my room, I didn't bother to hide. My *étranger résident* card, American passport, and newspaper credentials were always in order.

Besides a few other newspaper people, whose typewriters were clicking away day and night, there were three prostitutes, one with hennaed hair, one a peroxided blonde, and one with coal-black dyed hair; a wealthy, generous, and serious female drunk from London who loved young boys; a Polish communist who sold Persian carpets on the boulevards; two German Jewish lesbian couples who came from the same village near Berlin; a Romani bookbinder who spoke only Yiddish; a Russian cellist who practiced six hours a day, and his wife who worked in a Russian bookstore at the *Exposition Internationale*; two male Serbian exiles from Belgrade who often hid in the dark hallways and always greeted me with a whispered *"Dobra dan"* (good day); an Italian Jewish maker of fashionable shoes who sent money in shoeboxes to his family in Rome; a Pole and his wife who were so frightened that they rarely left their room; a male dancer with Les Ballets de Paris who lived in the hotel with his wife and two children; the Finnish gardener at the Jardin du Luxembourg, who tended the English-style gardens; Mademoiselle Ruska, *Voyante Médium, Hindique* (originally from Ohio, and stranded in Paris for lack of money), who often tried to convince me that she could show me the destiny of my "fractured soul"; and a French taxidermist and cold-weather hand-muff maker, whose specialty was household cats. "Look, Miss Manon," he once said. "If you rub yourself with this cat-fur mitten, it will keep you warmer than those ridiculous, useless coal stoves that we have in our rooms." Facing the park on the second floor was Mr. Hin, an exiled Chinese poet of note and an earnest member of the PCF, the French Communist Party. We became friends. There was also an elderly woman who had lived there since the beginning of the Great War. She wore only black and owned a wool shop around the corner. Arrayed on her shelves were pasteboard boxes filled with skeins of yarn in every color—lively vermilion, carmine, vibrant orange, emerald, ultramarine, Indian yellow. Her establishment reminded me of my Aunt Clara's button-and-trimmings shop in Brooklyn.

There were no toilets in the rooms, but each floor had one at the end of the hall. I didn't like this at all. I've never liked sharing such an intimate room with anyone and his brother.

ABSOLUMENT AUCUNE CUISSON DANS LES CHAMBRES, the black-on-white enamel signs warned on each landing. No cooking allowed in the rooms—but most residents had spirit cookers and locked larders, both to keep the mice away and to hide the stoves. The aromas of food wafted through the hallways; nothing was a secret. If someone was in the money, the halls smelled of frying meat. Otherwise, there was an abundance of cabbage. Every morning, if a tenant had paid a small extra amount, Monsieur Pleven would bring him or her a steaming cup of coffee with a small pot of hot milk and a freshly baked croissant from the bar at the corner of the boulevard St. Michel. I liked that amenity. I would buy the evening newspapers and save them for the morning's coffee in my room. Every once in a while, when Andy and I missed the American breakfasts of our youth, we would go to a restaurant run by a former

Pullman porter near the Eiffel Tower. The Chicago-Texas Inn specialized in fried eggs, corned-beef hash, and thick griddle-cakes dripping with butter. It also had a private stash of American-made bourbon, saved for special customers. On occasion, there was genuine maple syrup. As soon as the syrup arrived, the word would go out to the American newspaper community.

Fifty steps away from the Hôtel Espoir's front door was Henri's Café, the local bar, with the nearest public telephone. All the newspaper people who lived in the area would check each day to see if any messages had been left with Monsieur Henri, who was the owner, the waiter, and the bartender too. If so, the message would be written on the back of an old receipt in Monsieur Henri's spidery nineteenth-century handwriting. He would place it at the end of the wine-stained bar with a shot glass on top.

Outside the café was a dingy green kiosk selling French and international newspapers, and it also had the tobacco concession for the neighborhood. On the upper part of the kiosk, directly below the dull bronze, pineapple-shaped dome, each day's headlines were printed on cheap paper and applied with thick wheat paste. The French bought between three and five newspapers a day, more newspapers per person than any other country in the world; this was one of the characteristics of France that I loved. Each time I approached the kiosk, the newsagent, Monsieur Villières, was there with the same greeting. "Ah, Mademoiselle Manon. *C'est la fiction! C'est toute fiction!*" (It's fiction, all fiction), he would say as he handed me copies of *Paris-Soir*, the *London Times*, and the *Berliner Morgen-Zeitung*.

I hate to sound like a curmudgeon, but today's newspapers aren't written as well as the ones from that time. Before the war there were more choices, more published differences of opinion, more column inches to tell long stories. And I miss my print-stained hands and that heavy, wonderful smell of ink.

When I first arrived in Paris, I thought it would be thrilling to have a chance to go to China as a correspondent for the *Paris Courier*. In Simon's Creek, Nevada, where I was born, there were many Chinese people who had come to work on the railroad and then settled there. Having learned Mandarin as a child from my nanny, I had many people to practice with. But in Paris I had met only one Chinese person, my new friend Mr. Hin. If the weather was nice, Mr. Hin could be found in the morning sitting on a bench in the small square just outside the hotel, reading a newspaper or a book, or writing, his wire-rimmed glasses perched on his nose. Tall and thin, he was a straight-postured man with his long hair worn in a braid. His face was ancient, reminding me of an ivory Chinese figurine. He wore the robin's egg blue, heavy-cotton clothes of a French laborer, but interrupted that look with a faded red-and-orange embroidered cap.

Andy had introduced me. "Mr. Hin, please meet my friend R. B. Manon. She's new here and lives on the second floor, two doors down from me."

"Happy to meet you," I said. "What are you reading?"

"Glad to meet you too. Cigarette?" I was happy to take his offered Gauloise Bleu. Although I had to force myself to inhale the heavy Turkish tobacco, I felt more French than American, which pleased me no end.

"I'm reading *Les Fleurs du mal et oeuvres choisies* by Baudelaire."

"I'm impressed!" I said.

Then I felt embarrassed for implying that it was unusual for a Chinese man to be reading in French, and Baudelaire to boot.

Mr. Hin smiled at my discomfort. "No, don't worry, Miss Manon," he said. "French is my second language, too."

"Please," I replied. "Call me Rosie."

Meeting Mr. Hin had made me homesick. How odd, I mused, that to me the American West felt Chinese.

I don't like admitting it, but I'm still smoking. And to tell the truth, I love it. I don't know if it's the pure delight of taking the first puff, or the shock on my friends' and colleagues' faces when I light up. I'm not stupid—I know it's not good for me. However, I appear to be one of those people for whom smoking has no lasting ill effects. My doctors simply shake their heads. I think they're envious.

But I do know that the smell of old cigarette smoke is quite unpleasant to many people. While I was still in Europe, I stopped smoking for more than a year because tobacco was so hard to come by. It was then that I understood the awful odor of stale cigarette smoke. It was everywhere. There was always, no matter what season, a sweet-and-sour smell of sweat and cigarette smoke that permeated Parisian cafés, public buildings, and the Métro and city buses.

Mr. Hin had wryly informed me, "It's an old Parisian adage that you will wreck your eyes if you read too much—and wear down your skin if you take too many baths." Every three days—more often if I could afford it—I would go to the public bath on the rue de Vaugirard. The proprietors provided me with a thin piece of soap, a gray, threadbare towel, and a tin tub of warm water. It was never enough; I never felt fresh when I left. I had been brought up breathing the crystalline air on a mountaintop. When I first moved east to work at the *New York Courier*, it took me a long time to become accustomed to the new smells.

In Nevada, an old, scarred, red-leather trunk sat closed in the corner under a window in my childhood home. It smelled of mountain dust and memories. In the trunk were tarnished nineteenth-century silver teapots, sugar bowls, and creamers from Russia and England, marked with cryptic stamps and the etched names of artisans. As a child I used to play a game with myself, closing my eyes and running my fingers over the etched names to try to feel out the letters.

Then one day I dug deeper. I discovered a pile of yellowed linens wrapped in tissue paper, which had begun to flake like a thin layer of dry spun sugar. Under another layer of tissue were crocheted doilies and Victorian lace collars; the insides of their rosettes had turned from ecru to umber. Under all of this I found a pink satin-covered candy box filled with letters. Most of the letters were from my mother's sister, Clara Silverman, who lived in that mysterious place, Brooklyn. Her handwriting was scratchy and hard to read, already fading with time. Finding the letters boring and almost indecipherable, I put them aside. It was then that I found a telegram from Clara congratulating my parents. *Mazel tov on the birth of your daughter*, it said, and I had no idea what it meant.

"Mrs. Cheng?" I said, moving my nanny's arm back and forth to wake her.

"What, Rosie, do you need?" she said.

"What does this mean?" I handed the telegram to her.

"I don't know, sorry."

"But this doesn't even look like English. Perhaps it's English for a Chinese word?"

"No," she said as she looked at it again, "sorry, Rosie, not Chinese word."

I replaced the telegram and closed the trunk.

I loved my Aunt Clara. Every other year she would travel from New York City on the Atchison, Topeka, and Santa Fe for a visit. I can still see her stepping down from the railway car with smoke billowing around her while she held onto a hat decorated with colorful bird feathers or splendid silk flowers and carried a lumpy, stuffed handbag. Clara wore dangling earrings and the kind of clothing that I never saw in my town. Her brown-leather trunk, bound with a thick strap and closed with a heavy brass buckle, would be put on the cart and then towed into the wagon, and in later years, the trunk of the car. I learned early on that it was filled with amazing gifts: toys and books for me; art supplies and sophisticated big-city clothing for my mother that she never wore. Also in the trunk were books; whiskey for my father; and all kinds of salami, fat loaves of dark bread, and large chunks of hard cheese wrapped in cheesecloth, waxed paper, and then newspaper.

My parents would unpack every last thing, and then carefully smooth out the pages from the *New York Post*. They put the pages in order and savored every word, reading them time and time again. Some of my later love for newspaper work must have come from watching my parents peacefully reading. Those were rare instances when there was no tension in the house; my parents, for the moment, were in harmony.

Unlike my schoolmates, Aunt Clara never teased me about my shortsightedness, about being an oddball with my tightly curled black hair, about being funny looking. Even when I was very young, I could read in her eyes that she loved me. And Aunt Clara, my father, and Mrs. Cheng were the only people I allowed to call me "Rosie"—otherwise I was Rose, without the "i."

The year I found the *mazel tov* telegram, Clara made another visit. During a Sunday dinner that included a family friend, Father Patrick Maloney, I asked my burning question.

"What does *mazel tov* mean?"

For a pregnant moment, there was silence at the table. "Why, it means 'good fortune,'" Clara said easily as she looked around the table at the shuttered faces.

My mother was staring at her older sister with a "don't you dare say another word" look on her face. My father was looking down at his plate. Father Maloney took a larger than usual gulp of wine.

"My God, Miriam," Clara exclaimed, "doesn't Rosie know she's Jewish?"

All hell broke out.

My mother was screaming at Clara, my father was trying to calm my mother, and Father Maloney was intoning to his friends, the angels.

"Listen, Clara," my father said, "this wasn't my idea."

"Well," my mother answered, "all of a sudden my milque-toast of a husband is being a man!"

My father's face crumbled.

"You can't talk like that to him," I said.

"Oh, shut up, you horrible brat," shrieked my mother, and struck me across the face.

"Stop," shouted Clara, "leave her alone!"

Finally, Father Maloney had had enough. "Holy Mother of Jesus. Stop!" he said, and he slammed his wine goblet down on the table, splashing red wine on the white tablecloth, on Clara's crisp white blouse, on my mother's black dress, on my father's collarless white shirt. He missed me altogether. Silence.

Then my father began clearing the table and cleaning up. Clara came out of the kitchen with a dishcloth and went to work. Father Maloney looked about the room and said, "Obviously, this is a family matter." He got up and left, his black cassock billowing behind him. I stood in the doorway, holding my burning-red cheek and glaring at my mother; she was seated at the table, staring at a mysterious horizon.

It is more than seventy-five years later, and I can still recall the slap of her hand. The humiliation I felt was profound. Experiencing it in front of my beloved Aunt Clara was the worst part. Over time, I got over the embarrassment—but it was translated into fury. I nurtured that fury, embracing "poor me" with a stern, unrelenting, unconscious delight. Although, over time, there were many slaps, many spankings, many cruel words said to me, that was the first public slap. It taught me to hate my mother from the inside out.

* * *

It had taken a little more than two years of good hard work in Paris to convince the guys in the New York office to move me from the society page to the foreign desk. I became a political correspondent, somewhat rare for a woman. Silly as it may seem now, I had to be careful about the way I dressed. I put together a uniform. Black trousers. A dark-colored blouse. Sensible shoes. I wore my hair pulled back with a barrette at the nape of my neck. Sometimes to amuse myself and be contrary, I would wear the round brooch that had belonged to my grandmother. Clara gave it to me—and I still have it. It's an enamel painting of a sweet, idyllic scene in the woods. Leaning against a tree trunk are a couple holding hands. They are dressed in eighteenth-century attire, with ruffles and pointed shoes. The young woman is holding a fan edged with lace; the young man is gazing at her. They look comfortable and a bit naughty, too.

Whenever I wore the brooch, I felt mischievous, daring the men to look at my cleavage. But it was a waste of time. It was obvious that I was completely without glamour. I got used to it. It didn't matter, for I was as excited as a schoolgirl to be working in Paris.

It was the summer of 1937, and I had just returned to Paris from an assignment in Berlin. I was sitting outside under a café's canopy reading the *Paris Courier* and having a cup of coffee. As I scanned the "News of Americans in Europe" column, I read at the bottom of the page: "The actress Stella Mair and her aunt, Miss Clara Silverman, arrived in Paris on the *SS*

Normandie. They are staying at the Studio Hôtel on the rue du Vieux-Colombier."

Soon after I began working at the newspaper in 1933, I had become familiar with this column. At the desk next to me was a day-staff man whose task was to gather arriving ships' manifests and compile the daily list of passengers. The list was then handed over to Ramsey before being sent down to the Linotype machine operators. Ramsey put most of the names in alphabetical order, but he put the Jewish-sounding names at the bottom.

"Why?" I had asked.

"Directive from high up," Ramsey said, and stuffed a cigar stump in his mouth, ending the questioning.

I had known that Clara and Stella were coming, and had asked Ramsey for permission to return to Paris from Berlin. "Sure," he agreed, "but no more than two weeks."

The idea of my family being on my patch of the planet was disconcerting. Although I adored Clara, I worried that they might be a burden. I would have to spend time with them and take them sightseeing. I knew that I would feel responsible for their having a good time. Clara would be easy, but I wasn't sure what I felt about Stella. Stella—the family beauty, the family success story. I was jealous. She was inclined to be dramatic and there was no telling what trouble she could get into. Besides, I couldn't understand why Jews would want to visit the *Exposition Internationale, 1937.* It was an open invitation to the Germans. Paris was crawling with soldiers of the Reich. The city was being seeded with spies. The soldiers, with their clean, sharp haircuts and trim uniforms, were enthralled with its beauty. They strolled along the boulevards of the Right Bank, side by side with American tourists, all thumbing through their *Guides Bleus.* It was impossible for me to walk to and from the newspaper office without seeing them. I heard more German and English spoken than French.

At the same time, thousands of German Jewish émigrés, without official residency permits, were hiding from the authorities while trying to eke out a living on the Left Bank. The Emergency Rescue Committee in Paris helped as much as it could, but its efforts were meager and the human needs overwhelming. Émigrés were forced to move from one cheap hotel to another; they were forced into dealing in the black market, along with stealing, counterfeiting, cleaning offices in the middle of the night, selling safety pins and shoelaces—living hand to mouth. The trick, everyone quickly learned, was not to behave like émigrés or they would certainly be caught. But try as they might not to, the émigrés gave off an odor of fear, easy to distinguish.

I knew the drill. The Café Maurice had become one of the main haunts for displaced persons. The owner, who had a soft heart, allowed people to sleep on the floor at night. Once I saw the French police sweep into the café and line everybody—men, women, and children—up against the wall.

"*Carte d'identité d'étranger*," they politely demanded. Of course, nobody had them. Arrest. Deportation. And yes, even back to Germany. Wander. Find a safe boardinghouse. Wait for the waning of the moon. Slip back into France under the cover of a black night. Know you will be caught again.

I was curious about the café and would make a point of occasionally walking past. One day I had to force myself to keep my mouth shut. A scraggly band of wanderers was being herded toward police vans. The men and women looked lost, anxious. Some stumbled and were helped by their fellow unfortunates, and some looked stoic, straight ahead, obviously planning their next move. All of a sudden, a painfully thin elderly man, dressed in black with a yarmulke and sidelocks, ran for the door. One of the policemen nonchalantly put his foot out and the old man tripped and fell flat on his face. No one laughed. A young man asked for permission to go to him and was allowed.

"Come, old man," he said, "let me help you." I saw that the old man's bewildered face was wet with tears.

This behavior made me sick. I knew there was no way to help. When I saw this kind of harassment, I would coil into a tight ball, like the doodlebugs I used to collect as a child and keep in a jar. The bugs had an armored exterior and would roll up into balls when threatened. I understood that in this atmosphere in France, it was dangerous for me to have Jewish blood. I quite consciously took on the demeanor of a serious atheist, letting my colleagues assume that I was a lapsed Catholic.

I was still afraid. Every couple of weeks, whether in Paris or Berlin, I was stopped and asked for my papers. I showed all my credentials. And even though they were in order, each time this happened I thought it was the end. I knew that, if someone did a little research, I would be identified as a Jew. I felt soiled and ashamed after each encounter—like an imposter. No surprise; I had been pretending to be someone else all my life.

But I don't feel I'm pretending any longer. Time has eased the ancient pain of feeling different. It's like my garden. Some varieties of plants flourish. Others struggle to be happy. It's the sad plants that I work the hardest for. I'm convinced that if I'm more solicitous toward them, they'll strengthen their roots and begin to thrive. But alas, I've learned that many of them simply don't belong here. They're not nurtured by the soil. But I've learned where I can flourish.

I walked to the Studio Hôtel where Stella and Clara were staying. This would be the first time in four years I had seen them—although Clara had kept in touch with the crisp, short letters that I loved. She had been born in Russia, and had not come to America until she was fifteen. Although she spoke acceptable English, her writing was filled with misspellings and hilarious malapropisms. I kept them, planning someday to use pieces of them in my writing.

The hotel's entrance was dark and it took me a moment to adjust my eyes. As I approached the desk to be announced, I caught a glimpse of Stella. She was on her way out, holding the arm of a truly dashing man—oblivious to me and everyone else. Stella, the chatterbox, was trying to be demure and elegant. She was wearing a dark blue dress with a low-cut bodice, a matching blue hat with a white feather, and scarlet high-heeled shoes, carrying a small red handbag. She looked like an American flag. Stella was smiling at the gentleman with a flirtatious look that I knew well. I didn't want to interfere.

Waiting until they had gone out the door, I stepped up to the concierge's desk but was informed that my Aunt Clara was out.

Why did I have such a hard time seeing Stella with a handsome man? I could have approached her and said hello—she might even have been happy to see me. But I was envious of her. I can still remember how I felt diminished by the drama of the moment—longing to be Stella, wanting her confidence, her glamor. I felt homely, sorry for myself. What the hell, I thought, I would just embarrass her.

Now, I'm surprised that I harbored those feelings. After all, two years before, my life had blossomed.

* * *

In 1935, I had met a man at a bar. *Der blaue Himmel*, the Blue Sky, in Berlin's Wilmersdorf neighborhood, was a bar frequented by newspapermen, artists, political émigrés, communists. The man was sitting alone, reading a book and drinking. I was doing some reading and drinking myself. Indeed, that was all my acquaintances and I did in our spare time. Too much drinking was no longer something to joke about. We were drinking on purpose; as foreign correspondents, we knew too much. The left-wing German nationals who patronized the bar were part of the ten percent of the population who had not voted for the Nazi candidates in the March election. I watched them and listened to them and sympathized. I had thought that being an American would make me immune to their fear. It wasn't true. For everyone, seeking solace had become an obsession.

The man asked if he could sit down, and did so without waiting for an answer.

"You're an American?" he asked.

"Yes, how did you know?"

"Your friends told me. Name's Leon Wolff," he said, and we shook hands.

I struggled with my manners. At first I wanted to say something biting, but his face showed no guile, simply curiosity. I wasn't bothered by his straight talk. It reminded me of the shepherds I had known in Nevada who cut to the core of a conversation, having no time or inclination for chatter. I smiled at the memory.

"What's so funny?" he asked.

"Just an old memory, sorry. I've never seen you here before."

"Well, I've noticed you," he said, "but you've been too occupied with your friends or your books to look around. And I don't come often—just when I get restless from working alone."

His deep voice sounded like an echo. Perhaps he was nervous, but he kept using his fingers to comb back his thick, dark hair. And each time he did this, he revealed his beautiful blue eyes. I was infatuated. My hands were sweating; the waistband of my slacks was uncomfortable. My entire body felt awkward.

"I'm a journalist," I almost stuttered.

"I know you are," he said. "I know some of your colleagues."

"And, what do you—"

"I'm an artist—in the style of George Grosz. Now he's gone."

"Did he die?" I asked.

My question made Leon laugh.

"No, no, he's still alive. At least I hope so. Grosz emigrated to America. He was one of the smart ones. Anyway," he said, "like Grosz, I used to love drawing on location. Café life; singers—jazz musicians—fat, opulent industrialists out on the town." Leon had a faraway look on his face. "Now I make my living as an engraver. Jewelry, watches, baptismal cups, anything needing a steady hand and an exacting eye."

"I've never known an engraver. Is that why your hands are so dirty?"

Leon smiled. "Yes, of course," he said, "it's the silver tailings—impossible to keep them clean. And I can't wear gloves because they get in the way."

I thought Leon wonderful. Still do. I remember his smell. It was the odor of metal and heat, which came from his working with a soldering iron. One day, many years later, I walked past a man who smelled like this. "Leon!" I said, and a stranger turned to look at me.

At first, I tried to convince myself that my affair with Leon was a pleasant interlude, nothing more. He appeared to think the same. We were both curious about the world's problems—spoke about them, dissected them, came up with brilliant solutions. We had a good time together, in all ways. But I was fearful of love. I didn't think I could be in love and at the same time be a successful female foreign correspondent. And Leon? Well, he was difficult to read.

Why was I so fearful? I knew little about being in love. I

had no models, except for women in books. I think my parents had lived under the illusion that I didn't see their problems with each other. And there was no one else in their community whom I could learn from: my mother's best friend was a retired, unmarried prostitute, my father's best friend was a Catholic priest, and Mrs. Cheng's husband only returned home late at night after closing his shop, and I rarely saw them together.

But as time went on, I was seeing Leon more and more. The anticipation, the flushing of my cheeks, these were all new feelings to me. There was no hiding from it. I had fallen in love and didn't have a clue what to do about it.

* * *

But now it was 1937, and I was back in Paris. I had to deal with Stella and Clara. The next morning, as I was walking past Monsieur Henri's café, he beckoned to me. "R.B.," he said, "you have a message."

"Stella's missing! Call me. Clara." I didn't bother to call but went directly to her hotel.

I still had not seen her. Oh, no, I thought, what a terrible way to welcome them to Paris. Without saying hello, Clara said, "I can't believe Stella would do this to me. She's always been theatrical, but never rude. I just don't understand."

I hugged her, but she was somewhere else.

"Tell me," I said. "What happened?"

"We were sitting in the lobby," Clara said. "A handsome man approached and began a conversation. He spoke excellent English and gave us advice about Paris. We were grateful. There was a *thé dansant* happening at the bistro next door—a pretty bistro with a dance area with palm trees around it. He asked Stella to dance. His name is Bobby Hunter, and he's the son of an industrialist. He was charming. A perfect gentleman."

"How old?"

"About thirty, maybe a little older. I went off to do some shopping and when I returned they were still talking. Yesterday, early in the afternoon, after more sightseeing, we returned to the hotel to rest. Shortly before three Stella went downstairs to meet Mr. Hunter."

"Did she say anything to you before she left?" I asked.

"Just that she would see me later. I'm sorry, Rosie," Clara said, "I've overwhelmed you with this and haven't even really said hello. Let's go. I need to get something to eat or I'll faint."

We walked to a café on the boulevard St. Germain and sat at a table outside. I ordered for both of us—*paté maison*, salad, Camembert, and Vouvray *en carafe*.

"Oh, thank you, dear," Clara said, obviously relieved that I had taken over.

We were quiet while waiting for the food. Then, as soon as Clara took her first sip of wine, she said, "Rosie, I don't know if I should call the police. It's alarming that she's missing, but I wouldn't be surprised if she simply decided to stay with Mr. Hunter overnight. But I don't understand this kind of behavior. On the other hand, what if something has happened and the police could help? Oh, I wish she had your sense of responsibility."

I didn't consider that a compliment.

Then, all of a sudden, Clara yelled, "Stella! Stella! Over here." And Stella nonchalantly strolled over.

"Oh, oh—Stella, you're alive!" Clara shouted with relief.

I was furious. And before Stella could say a word, I stood and slapped her across the face so hard that some of the patrons jumped up.

"You bitch!" I screeched at her in English. "What did you think you were doing? Clara's been sick with worry. Are you trying to kill her?" And I raised my hand again.

"Don't you raise your hand to me, you ugly witch," Stella

said, curling her lip. "A homely girl like you could never have as much fun as I just did. So go to hell.

"Come on, Aunt Clara, let's go back to the hotel. I'm exhausted."

And Stella spun on her shiny, red high-heeled shoes, put her arm through our stunned aunt's arm, and they walked away.

I was staggered by her behavior. How could Stella be so inconsiderate? How could she say such nasty things? We had always gotten along. When I lived in New York we often spent time together. Now, four years later, this was a new Stella. I wondered if this was what happened when you became famous. I knew that she was well known for both her beauty and her sex appeal. And although she was a little old to be playing ingénues on the stage, she had received sterling reviews for her sophisticated, ageless talent.

And my behavior? I was startled by my rage. I thought I had cleansed myself—had banished my mother's behavior toward me to the clouds. But no. Now I was a mirror image of my mother. My own rage had been held up to the light—and there I was in the reflection, an exact replica of everything I detested.

Indeed, around Stella, I forgot that Leon thought me beautiful. Forgot that my Aunt Clara loved me. Forgot that I was talented in my own right.

Once, when I was in my late fifties, a yellow cab in New York City almost hit a friend I was walking with. I got so angry that I kicked the door of the car. The driver leapt out, yelling at me in Farsi and pointing to the dent in his door. I began to yell back when I noticed that I couldn't put weight on my foot without it being excruciating. "Oh, no," I said. "I think I've broken something!" After much commotion, the cab driver kindly helped me into his cab and drove me to the emergency room. He wouldn't charge me. I had broken a bone and had to wear a cast and use crutches. Have I learned to control my anger? I have to confess that I don't think so.

I paid the bill, not even bothering to taste the wine and the food that was placed so appealingly on the table. Bowing my head to avoid people's glares, I walked to the Jardin du Luxembourg, where I watched seemingly normal people taking a stroll. My mind was blank. I presume I was in shock. I was aware of a large flowerbed of Madame Pompadour pink roses directly in front of me. But I refused myself the pleasure of their beauty.

Slowly, I became uncomfortably warm from the full sun. I had to see Clara. When I arrived at the hotel, the concierge waved me upstairs to her room. She was lying on the bed with an ice bag on her forehead.

"Aunt Clara, I need to speak to you."

"Come in, Rosie," she mumbled. "Come in and close the door behind you."

I squeezed a small chair next to the bed, sat, and took her hand. "I'm sorry you had to go through this. I don't know what else to say."

"There's nothing to say, Rosie," she said, and she sat up and leaned against the headboard. "I feel betrayed and alone and I want to go home."

"I understand," I said, "but I don't know how to make this better for you."

"You can make it better," she said, "by trying to understand something that's important to me. I must support Stella." And she began to cry. Between wiping her eyes and blowing her nose, she said, "I can't abandon her—she knows I'm deeply disappointed in her—she knows I don't trust this Bobby person—but she can't help herself." And Clara threw herself into my arms and wept.

I realized that what Clara said was painfully true. Stella was family, and Clara was going to honor her, no matter what had happened. She had accepted the facts: Stella was impetuous, selfish, lost in her own world. And if I were going to continue to be part of the family, I would have to find a way to accept and forgive.

That evening I forced myself to knock on Stella's door. Bobby Hunter opened it. We stared at each other for a moment. He had obviously been told what happened. "Who is it?" Stella called out. "Oh, it's you, what do you want?"

"I've come to beg your pardon."

"Geez, you sound like a Victorian greeting card, Rose. But I accept your apology. And I'm sorry for causing everyone such worry. And I know you'll learn to love Bobby," she gushed, putting her arm through his and snuggling into his side. "He's such a gentleman."

The next day Stella told Clara that she was meeting Bobby Hunter for lunch and would be home in time to get ready for the opera, *Ariadne and Bluebeard*. Clara went shopping for ribbons and buttons for her store.

Early that evening I walked toward the Seine, thinking I would browse the bookstalls and have an early night. On the rue de Grenelle I ran into Andy Roth and we decided to have dinner together. My friend Andy was a wiry, quiet man with almost-orange hair, given to dreaming. He was married to a gorgeous woman; her name was Ruby and she seemed to be forever in London visiting her family.

After the first few drinks, we got into an intense argument about newspapers. Andy believed strongly in straight-shot writing—no flourishes, no embellishments. I felt, and still feel, that journalism could be more literary.

"Look, Andy," I said, "why can't we be more poetic, like Colette?"

"Oh, come on, R.B. She's a fiction writer for girls!"

"You're impossible," I said. "She's brilliant. Read her work carefully and you'll see. Haven't you ever read her essays in the papers?"

"Naw," Andy said, "don't have the time, and my French stinks. All I can manage is *s'il vous plaît* and *merci.*"

"Well," I said, not willing to give up, "how about Janet Flanner?"

"You mean the lesbian who writes for the *New Yorker*? The one who calls herself 'a gentleman of the press in skirts'?"

"Oh, for Christ's sake, Andy, so what! Not only is she a fine essayist, but also a true intellect."

"Listen, R.B., you're the one with the mind like a corkscrew. I'm Mr. Simplicity."

We talked and argued late into the night, primarily about writing, and about Freud and our favorite topic, our unbearable mothers.

"My mother threatened me with a knife and said she hated me," I said.

"My mother threw a can of beans at my face and gave me a black eye," he said.

Whenever we got into this conversation, we would try to laugh at the similarities. But when we had a bit much to drink, we would moan and groan and try not to cry and make fools of ourselves.

That evening, since we both lived at the Hôtel Espoir, we wobbled home together. As we were turning onto the boulevard St. Michel, a *Paris Courier* truck pulled up to the curb in front of the newspaper kiosk. The driver handed Monsieur Villières a roll of paper and then tossed down bundles of newspapers. "Hey, Mademoiselle Manon," Monsieur Villières said, "want the first edition of your paper?"

"No, thanks," I said. We were too bleary-eyed to care about reading, and kept walking.

As I tried to sleep, I couldn't shake my disappointment with myself. The evening with Andy reminded me that I might have come far geographically, but a small distance emotionally. I tried to push the self-doubt aside and think about something different: My home. Simon's Creek, Nevada.

Simon's Creek was a small silver-mining town that had been carved out of the crown of Moon Mountain. It had profoundly influenced me with its azure skies, the crisp thin air, the rocky barrenness of the mountainside. I loved the miles of trails sliced out of rock gullies by extreme weather, the copses of pine trees, the smooth-barked, claret-red tamarisk, and the remarkable horizon. The open spaces allowed me to escape the problems at home. Outdoors in the mountains I could be quiet and listen to the wind, listen to the stillness. The austerity of the land gave me a sense of being special, as if I were alone in the world.

Born in France, my father immigrated to New York with his parents when he was a young child. He met my mother at Brooklyn College; after graduating they eloped. A marriage between a Catholic and a Jew was not smiled upon in 1900. They had seen an advertisement: "Teachers Needed in Nevada," and applied—not caring a whit where Nevada was, as long as it was in America. My father was hired as a history and Latin teacher, and for a small extra stipend he served as the custodian.

Mother was an accomplished illustrator, who had paid her way through college with freelance commercial jobs. In Nevada, she was hired to teach biology and art, part-time. She supplemented her salary by taking jobs as a court illustrator in Reno, and less often, Carson City.

1905. I was born at home. There was a midwife and old Dr. Springer, who, I gather from family anecdotes, hung around, nipped at a bottle of whiskey, and chatted with my father, who stayed sober. My mother refused to breastfeed me. Later, she would laugh and claim that she was more evolved than a cow. She hired a local woman, Mrs. Cheng, as a wet-nurse. Two weeks later my mother went back to teaching.

Mother had the talent of an artist and the heart of a naturalist. Arrowheads, rocks, plant life, petrified wood—all interested her. It didn't matter that during a strenuous hike, she could be drenched from a downpour or sweating like one of the miners in the local silver mines; she loved being outdoors. Sometimes, when my father was drinking and things were difficult at home, she would slip out the back door with a tent, food, water, and her metal botany satchel slung across her chest. Depositing me with the ever-dependable Mrs. Cheng, she would stay away for at least a full night, sometimes more, depending on her mood and her job.

A self-possessed woman, my mother had to work to be accepted into the narrow confines of that rural Nevada community. Not only was her education advanced for a woman of the time, but she had cosmopolitan airs. She tried to combat the community's opinions with irony. When someone would say something about her leaving her child, about being away alone in the mountains, she would answer, "Oh, there's nothing to worry about. I've hung Rose on the forged hook on the front door. Mrs. Cheng will feed her," and they would laugh, smitten with what they thought was her sophisticated New York humor.

Although she was relieved to have left New York, from the moment she arrived in Simon's Creek, she longed to leave. The town was full of Italians, Ukrainians, and Chinese people who had come to work on the railroad or in the silver mines. All the women had one style of dress—long black shirtwaists, black stockings, and black laced-up boots. Mother would laugh and tell my father, "I'll dress the same, so as not to stand out—but I feel as if I'm wearing my shadow."

Used to being quiet in the mountains—not wanting to disturb a rattlesnake nest, a family of coyotes—my mother moved like a shadow. She slipped around corners; she shocked me with her sudden appearance in a room. She stayed hidden. She was never emotionally present, except when she was angry. I always felt like a lumbering fool, while she moved like a dancer. In the end, though—and I'm horrified to admit this—there are, indeed, characteristics that we share.

I know we all have many facets to our personalities. But my mother appeared to have only a few. One was the quick-witted, talented teacher and artist—a good friend to many women. The other was her doppelganger—the stranger, the mirror. I would often watch her when I was little and we were shopping in the Moon Mountain General Store. She was friendly and funny, asking questions that showed how she cared for the people she was talking to. Her ability to make new friends always surprised me. People liked her. Until we got home. Then she was spiteful toward them, calling them stupid, without imagination. And as for me—she either ignored me or was angry with me. To the day she died, I had trouble determining when to speak to her and when not to.

Father was of medium height, thin, with a chest that was almost concave. He had curly thick hair that began to be sprinkled with gray when he was in his early twenties. His face was oval and his nose was slightly bent, almost as if he had been a boxer. Walking like a crooked broom, he leaned to the left and swept his feet along with a shuffle-shuffle sound.

Most of the time he was a soft-mannered man, happy to let everyone else do the talking. But he wasn't perfect. He drank too much. Not all the time, but in spurts—and he hated this weakness. For no reason that he could determine, a terrible urge would grab him and not let go until he had passed out from his indulgence.

"I feel," he once said to me, "that the devil captures my soul and flings me into hell."

When he was on an alcoholic rampage, I was petrified. Even now I remember cringing at the way he hugged me, how he insisted upon my sitting on his lap and reading to me. He was disgusting. And I was often confused. I detested him for his weakness, for his slobbering behavior—and I never forgave my mother for abandoning me to him. Thank goodness for Mrs. Cheng. As soon as she saw what was going on, she would take me to her house. After a couple of days, my father would arrive to collect me—forlorn and groveling with guilt. My mother let him perform that ritual: his Catholic penance. Then we all three would pretend that everything was fine—until the next time.

At ten years old, I was already tall for my age, developing breasts, and quite outspoken. My classmates assumed I was strong. I understood this and postured as if it were true. One day a classmate said with a sneer, "You're a stinking kike. Your people killed Jesus!"

I shoved him. The boy came back at me with fury and threw me to the floor, holding my arms behind my back until the pain was unbearable.

"You dirty Jew," the boy yelled at me in front of everyone. "Go back where you belong."

"I give! I give!" I had to beg for mercy. Then the gang of children descended on me—kicking me, grabbing my hair, and finally in the most humiliating act they could conjure, pulling off my panties and ripping off my skirt. Then they ran, flying my skirt behind them like a kite. They left me there, naked from the waist down with nothing to cover me up. I curled into a fetal position and wept. A teacher found me and put his jacket around my body and carried me home.

I was delivered to my parents. Soon after my mother's oohing and tsk-tsking about the horrible thing done to me, the teacher left. "For heaven's sake," she turned on me and scolded, "can't you do anything right? I hope you had on clean underwear!"

"Leave her alone," Father said. "That's an awful thing to say to the girl. Imagine being attacked by a pack of animals."

"Oh, be quiet," she said. "And where in the world did this Jewish thing come from? I thought that nobody knew except us, and your drunken Father Maloney. What a blabbermouth he is. Does he tell you," she wheedled, "the good dirt he hears during confession?"

And she walked out and slammed the door.

It was always this way. My mother was impossible to please. My father was easy. I was caught in between.

Once I heard Father say, "Let her be, Miriam. You're too hard on her."

"Yeah, well, she's just like you," she said. "A dreamer who won't get anywhere. You both disgust me."

I thought I was plain. I loathed my long upper lip and the prominent Silverman nose. When I was a little girl I would sit and read with a finger holding up the tip of my nose, hoping to make it straighter. I wore my hair in thick braids. Like my father, I was terribly shortsighted. My parents tried to keep me in glasses, but I hated them. They always got in my way. I would lose them, bury them in the backs of drawers, leave them around until someone stepped on them. And although I didn't always appear to be paying attention, I had learned to listen keenly.

Even now, I hear well for my age, but I'm still losing my glasses.

It's become a habit. I remember when I first met Leon I kept my glasses in my pocketbook. For the longest time I didn't wear them. Then, once, when we were on an outing, he noticed that I was squinting through the train's window. "Have you ever had your eyes checked?" he asked. "You don't seem to see very well, and you're missing pretty scenery." And because I couldn't bear to miss seeing anything, I took them out of my purse and put them on. "This is why I don't wear glasses," I said. "They make me homelier."

"You're a silly woman," he said. "You look a hell of a lot better than when you're peering out with teeny, straining eyes. Actually, you have very pretty eyes."

I still think about what I've missed. What I haven't seen.

When I was eighteen I left home and moved to Virginia City, about ten miles west of Simon's Creek. I lived in an apartment over a bar on C Street. Taking classes in journalism by mail from the University of Chicago, I worked as a substitute reading and writing teacher in the Fourth Ward School. This was a hateful job. I had no patience, and absolutely no interest in children. I wanted to be a newspaper reporter—that was my passion. No marriage. No children. On this I was clear.

At night, if I weren't studying, I would head over to the *Territorial Enterprise*, the only newspaper in town. Sitting quietly in a corner, I would read back issues. The men all knew me. "Hey, Rose," the typesetter would sometimes offer, "want to set the headline for me?" And I would go downstairs to the composing table and the font cases and get to work.

Aunt Clara continued to visit every two years. One year, the year before I left Nevada for good, she brought my cousin for a visit to the "Wild West." Her parents had named her Stella. My Aunt Leah Mair, having read the name in the society column of a newspaper, thought it quite modern. "After all,"

Leah had written to my mother, "don't we want to be real, honest-to-goodness Americans?"

Stella dreamt of being a famous actress. She made exaggerated hand gestures, no matter the topic of conversation. And given the opportunity, she would throw her body into grand dramatic poses, as if she were on the stage. At first I was fascinated with her. But after a couple of weeks I grew tired of her theatrics. I did have to admit that she caused quite a sensation in town. The men were goggle-eyed; the women tried not to look concerned. But one of the things I liked about Stella was her unabashed openness about being Jewish.

At the beginning of her visit, in her ebullient fashion, Stella threw her arms around me and said, "We can be sisters! I only have a brother and he's a stick-in-the-mud—absolutely no fun. But you, well, you're a real cowgirl from the West! Isn't this neat?"

I was already nineteen years old and she was eighteen, and although I thought her silly, I had to admit that I was enchanted.

"Are you all Jewish?" I asked her.

"Of course I'm *all* Jewish," she said proudly. "What a silly question, Rose. You know that even though your father isn't Jewish, your mother certainly is. No one in the family understands what Aunt Miriam has against Jews. My mother told me that she became this way while they were all living in a tiny town, far out on Long Island. There were no other Jews in the town and Miriam was desperate to fit in. She could already speak Russian, Yiddish, and a beautiful French. But she struggled to learn English."

"How odd. I wonder why she became an English professor."

"It's obvious, Rose. Learning English was a challenge."

"That sounds like her!" I said.

I couldn't help but compare my Jewishness with that of my cousin. Stella was comfortable with being Jewish. She never questioned her situation. But being Jewish challenged the grandiose image I had of myself—the all-American girl who was above the petty labels of race and religion. I told myself I wanted to be a woman of the greater world. But honestly, what I really wanted was to please my parents.

I never got a university degree, nor did it matter. I accepted the offer to work as a printer's devil and jack-of-all-trades for the *Territorial Enterprise*—the newspaper for which Mark Twain had been a writer. My writing career began with hand-setting headline type, and learning the Linotype machine. Finally, I worked my way upstairs to the newsroom and writing. I loved everything about the newspaper. The smell of the ink—the smell of newsprint—the concentration required to find the right word. Once my boss reprimanded me for agonizing over every turn of phrase. "Listen, kid," he said, "you've got talent, but you don't have the same twang as Twain. You've got to find your own style. Your strength is in your descriptive observations of how people behave. Work on it. You'll be fine."

Early in February 1929, quietly, without saying anything to my family, I applied for a job at the *New York Courier*. In my letter to the personnel officer, I wrote, "I've been sitting in Mark Twain's chair and working at his desk for almost four years. Now I'm looking to move on. Also, I'm fluent in French, German, and Mandarin." I got a job as a social reporter. At first, I was furious to be put at "the women's desk." But I was so longing for an adventure that I would have swept the newspaper office's floors. It still amuses me to think about how my parents had longed to leave New York—and how I longed to go in reverse. The craving for change and adventure must have run in my family.

Although leaving my hometown was emotionally confusing, the bustle of preparing for the journey made it easier. My budget allowed for one steamer trunk and a knapsack. "You can take the old red trunk," Mother said. "If I ever get the chance to leave here, I'd rather a new case." I accepted. It opened with a key that I was petrified of losing. I wore it on a piece of twine around my neck. The trunk opened like a book. On either side there were six small drawers made of cardboard, each covered with faded red-and-white *fleur-de-lis* paper, which I took out to give myself more room. My clothes and an Indian blanket filled half the trunk, and the rest of the space was taken up with books, my shiny black Smith Corona typewriter, a stack of notebooks, and two reams of cheap onionskin paper.

My father drove me down the bumpy and dusty Geiger Grade to Reno in their first car, a used black 1930 Model A Ford. My mother claimed that she was too busy to take the time. When I said good-bye to her at the car, I leaned to kiss and embrace her. But she turned her body, as if she had seen something down the road. Saying good-bye to my father at the station was harder than I had imagined. Surprisingly, although we had lived under a resolute armistice for many years, we had become an odd triangle of a real family.

The journey to New York City's Penn Station took four days. It was torturous. I had to sit up all day, and recline ever so slightly to sleep in the same seat at night. When I finally exited the train, I was struck with a blast of hot, sooty, humid air. I had only ever felt the dry air of the West; this was an entirely new experience. And the noise! I had no idea.

A part of me felt foolish, like a bumpkin; the other part was awed and scared and excited. I placed my trunk in storage and, with detailed instructions from Aunt Clara, I haphazardly made my way on the subway to Brooklyn.

It was a relief to find her house. And there she was in the window waiting for me. Clara, forever a spinster, still smelled like faded mothballs, but also still had beautiful dark eyes protected by her black, untamed eyebrows.

On my first morning, as I was washing my face, I realized

that there was no mirror. I almost blundered and asked where it was. Then I remembered another Clara story: she had unscrewed the medicine cabinet's mirror many years before and stashed it in the basement. She didn't need one: she felt her hair into place—she sensed the cleansing of her face.

Mother had told me that Clara had felt she had been wearing a mask—and an unfortunately ugly one at that. But, over time, she began to see herself differently. The longer she didn't glance at herself, the better looking she felt. That pleasant feeling of self-approval took on its own visual persona. When she caught an accidental glance of herself, Clara didn't recognize the woman staring back. The charade had become a part of her life.

Clara lived upstairs over her button-and-lace shop on Havemeyer Street in Brooklyn. The shop was called New World Notions. "I named this," she said, "in honor of my becoming an American citizen and being free to have my own ideas." Running along three walls of the store were built-in cabinets with rows of drawers filled with buttons. On the front of each drawer was a white ceramic knob and around each knob were painted colors and shapes to denote the drawer's contents. Above these cabinets, secured to both sides of the long and narrow shop, were spools of lace and ribbon displayed on dowels that were balanced over the heads of the shoppers. The shoppers would point to what they wanted, and Clara would climb a wooden ladder with a cloth measuring tape draped around her neck and cut the desired lengths. Being Clara, she always added an inch or two.

"I've fixed the spare room for you," Clara said. "You can stay as long as you want."

I had been planning to stay at a women's boardinghouse on the Lower East Side of Manhattan until I found an apartment. Now, I wasn't sure. It was nice to be with family—but maybe a little too nice. I would have to think about it.

One Monday night when the theaters were dark, I saw Stella at Clara's.

"Oh, Rose, it's unbelievable! Two months ago I played Molly the whore in *Threepenny Opera*! I couldn't believe it! Now I'm rehearsing *The Mask and the Face* with Humphrey Bogart. It's so exciting!"

"Stella," Clara said, "calm down and act like a lady."

The next Friday night the family, five people, gathered for dinner at Uncle Saul and Aunt Leah's house. Leah sat at one end of the table, Saul at the other. Seated on either side were Clara, Stella, and me. The only Brooklyn relative who wasn't there was David, Stella's brother, who was on a business trip. It was the first time I had been around so much family, and I felt besieged. Questions and more questions. They couldn't get over the idea that I knew so little of my own family's history, while I sensed that they lived too much in the past.

When they lit candles, I asked, "Are we celebrating a special event? Is it someone's birthday?"

They were shocked. "Didn't your mother tell you anything about being Jewish?" Stella asked, laughing.

"Your mother," Leah said, shaking her head, "your mother —"

"Ma," Stella said, "let's change the subject. Come on, let's eat."

And then there was a great commotion about food. "*Es, es, mayn kind!*" Eat, eat, my children! Clara said in Yiddish.

Leah remained quiet. I found her cold and distant and felt as if she were passing judgment any time she opened her mouth. In the middle of serving the soup, Leah stopped, the ladle suspended in the air, and said, "Miriam has always hated being Jewish. Do you have any idea why?"

"None," I answered. "Why don't you ask her?"

"I never dared," Leah said. "Not with her temper!"

Well, I thought, this is indeed something we share. But I kept quiet.

"Can you answer another question?" Leah persisted. "Why did your mother leave us to marry a Catholic stranger? You know, it's a tragedy in our family. Nothing could be worse, except marrying a Negro."

I could see that everyone around the table was mortified.

"That's an awful thing to say," Clara said. "You should be ashamed of yourself. Paul's a lovely man, and Rosie's father, for heaven's sake!"

And I felt like tipping the food-laden table onto Leah's wide lap.

"Look," I said, taking a deep breath, "you know nothing about the circumstances of my father's and mother's lives. Only Clara and Stella have taken the time to visit them."

"Well," Leah said haughtily, "they could have come here."

"Yes, but how?" I asked. "First of all, they didn't have the money. And second, they're aware of your disapproval. And now," I said to their stunned faces, "excuse me, but it's time to go." I had made up my mind. I would leave Brooklyn and find a cheap apartment in the city.

Clara left with me. "I'm so sorry, Rosie, you didn't need to hear that. Leah can be so difficult—"

I cut her off midsentence. "Don't worry, Clara. Both Leah and Miriam are difficult. But now I certainly understand why my parents never wanted to come back for a visit." And putting my arm through hers, I said, "I wish you had been my mother."

Stella invited me to see her in the play. But neither I nor New York would get to enjoy *The Mask and the Face*. The play closed. Indeed, half the theaters were dark.

Stella, near tears, was sitting in Clara's living room. "Damn this Hitler character," she said. "He's making us all so nervous."

"It's a scary time, Stella," I replied. "I don't think any of us can find a context for what we're feeling."

"All I know," Clara said, "is that I'm reminded of the past—of Russia—of close calls."

* * *

For almost two years, I worked at the *New York Courier*'s main office on West Forty-third Street. I worked hard—did whatever I was asked, met all my deadlines, learned more about celebrities and wealthy people than I had ever wanted to know. I had a few friends, mostly colleagues who all went home to their wives and children. I went home to a five-flight walk-up, one-room apartment on Bedford Street in Greenwich Village. The bathtub was in the kitchen, the toilet in the only closet. Sometimes I had dinner with my relatives, but I stayed away from going there on Friday nights.

I was very busy—having sex, dreaming sex, and trying to stay interested in the boring job of covering social news. Many weeknights were spent in bed with lovers. I had two long affairs, concurrently, with married men I had met while covering stories. To this day, I can't remember their names.

Then I got my break. A society-desk job opened up in Paris. By then I was a pro at composing those stories. That ability, along with my fluency in languages, cinched the deal. And I sensed from my interview that if I did a good job, they would move me to another desk—if I were lucky, a political one.

My Aunt Clara, being as sweet as she was, gave me a bon voyage gift. A fur coat. A mink coat! She had bought it from the estate of one of her clients. The edges were slightly worn. I didn't care. It made me feel *très chic*! "Just look at you!" she said as I modeled the coat for her. "I'm proud of you, Rosie, I really am."

Summer, 1933. I sailed from America with the hope that I would charm and transform the world of journalism. That was one side of my dream. The other side was more like a nightmare: I felt inadequate, terrified that I would make a fool of myself. But I couldn't help marveling that I had set myself free—that I was no longer tethered to my native shore. Truly, but with trepidation, I was proud of myself for getting a writing job in Europe. Where I came from, the rest of the world was very far away.

Crossing the turbulent Atlantic, I shared a cabin with a young man and woman who had just been married. We were on a tramp steamer that was loaded with pecans, cotton, soy oil, and we three courageous passengers. We were all seasick. And even though I was miserable, I had a good time between the visits to the railing or the sloshing buckets. The poor newlyweds could hardly stay on deck for more than a few minutes. They were both poets and would scribble away between their battles with the sea.

* * *

The day after the argument with Stella, it was still humid and overcast. But my spirits had lifted. I had wanted to take it easy. Maybe have my hair washed, do laundry—get myself together before seeing Clara and Stella again. I was sitting at Henri's Café, drinking coffee and reading a book. But my attention was interrupted by the awareness of an unsettled feeling. Perhaps, I said to myself, it simply had to do with the drama of slapping Stella. I was afraid that Clara was angry with me— that I had disappointed her with my violent behavior—that I was an echo of my mother. I feared that now Clara would see through me, see that I was an immature, neurotic mess; see that I was a fraud, a two-bit hack, a nothing in comparison to the excitement of "our" Stella.

Then, without warning, a newspaper was slapped on my knee and I was rudely forced from my reverie.

"Did you see this one, R.B.?" my colleague Pete Grogan asked, sitting beside me. Pete, a British freelancer, worked at both the *Paris Courier* and the *London Times*. He was a short man with a rotund belly that hung between his red plaid suspenders. A protruding chin, accentuated by his dark hair, which was parted in the middle, set off his face. He was one of the few writers who seemed to have a stable home life. I liked him. Actually, I envied him.

"For Christ's sake," I said, "I'm not working until tonight. Please. Go home to your beautiful wife."

"Ha, I'd like nothing better," Pete replied, "but Ramsey sent me to find you and give you this morning's paper. It may be a sensational case," he said, stretching out the word "sensational."

"What does that have to do with me? I've been covering politics for the past two years."

"What's the difference?" he said.

"Oh, stop being a two-bit philosopher—leave me alone."

"Just read the article," he said.

"All right, all right—but I need another coffee. Give me a few minutes."

New York Actress Kidnapped. Just to the left of it was **Soviet Union Begins Great Purge**. *"The American actress Stella Mair is missing from her hotel in the rue du Vieux-Colombier, the Préfecture de Police announced last night."*

Oh, Stella! I thought, what have you done? With a sense of dread I rolled up the newspaper and put it in my pocket.

As soon as I was halfway up the stairs of the newsroom, I was assaulted by the awful smell of stale cigarette smoke, mixed with old food and the humidity of the summer. I wanted to turn around and go home. It was only nine in the morning and already I could feel sweat meandering down my back.

"Hey, R.B.," one of the reporters said. "Looks like you're our gal for the most melodramatic story of the year. Of course," he added, laughing, "now you can be assured of a long-running serial—just like the funny papers."

"Count me out," I said. "I have to be in Berlin next week. The news is getting seriously grim. Yeah, I know," I teased, "I know, it won't sell papers. No one wants to hear the truth."

"You might be right, R.B. But you'll have to tell it to Ramsey. He's in charge." He pointed with his thumb over his shoulder toward the glass wall of the office. Ramsey was rolling a cigar in his mouth, shouting into the phone, and beckoning to me at the same time.

"So, Rosie, what do you think of the *Times* story?" Ramsey asked in his raspy voice.

"I told you not to call me 'Rosie,' Mr. Ramsey," I said, trying to give myself some space to think.

"What's the matter, kid?" Ramsey asked. "You look as if you've been hit with a baseball bat."

"Nothing Mr. Ramsey, nothing, just thinking."

Was Bobby Hunter the kidnapper? Would I be able to give the police a description of the guy? Was this another of Stella's dramatic moments?

I had to be careful. I couldn't be assigned this story. It wasn't ethical. I had always avoided conflicts of interest, real or perceived. But then, what was more important—upholding the standards of journalism or finding my cousin? I voted for my cousin.

"Mr. Ramsey," I said, "you know it's not my kind of thing. Why assign this story to me?"

"For good reasons, kid. One's that the bosses in Chicago are complaining that your Berlin stories are getting too tough on the Reich. They think you need a break. And since it's about Jews, I thought you'd know how to approach the situation, you know what I mean?"

"No, I don't know what you mean," I said.

"For Christ's sake, Rosie—excuse the pun—you look like a Jew."

"I told you not to call me 'Rosie,' and anyway, you're wrong," I said. "I'm not a Jew."

"C'mon, kid, calm down. If you declare you're not a Jew, I'll accept it, but I don't believe you."

"But—" I tried to interrupt.

"Anyway," Ramsey butted in, "you have more imagination than anyone else in this newsroom."

I sat on my hands to remind myself not to react.

"Disappearances are the best," Ramsey said as if he were offering me a gift. "The higher-ups will be happy. Great for circulation. Perhaps you'll find her yourself! Just don't get fancy-dancy with your writing.

"Be careful," Ramsey cautioned. "You have to be sure not to mention that she's a Jew."

"Why not?" I asked.

"Don't be stupid, kid. Our readers want news about a young, sexy, beautiful American actress, not some Yid dame."

"But," I said, "her name is Mair, and her aunt's name's Silverman. They're both Jewish names."

"Yeah, yeah, I know," Ramsey said, "but people won't know the difference between a kike name and a kraut one. They all sound alike. So, this is the deal. If you refuse to cover it, I'll post you to China. That's what the main office wants. They say you're our best and they want to spread you around a bit. China will give you a shot at using your high and mighty Mandarin. Lot of war going on there. You'll love it. The Japs are fighting the Chinks and they need a hotshot correspondent. So, how 'bout it?"

I looked away from his ugliness.

"Jeez, anyway, it's a better story than the constant whining from those Yids about what's happening in Germany. If you ask me, they're getting what's coming to them from Herr Hitler."

Oh, how I detested him.

But I wasn't ready to lose my job—or go to China. I wanted to get back to Berlin and Leon.

"Mr. Ramsey, I can't cover this story. Stella Mair's my cousin."

"Your cousin!" he yelled, and I could see all the heads turning in our direction. "Then you're a . . . I knew it!"

"Calm down, Mr. Ramsey," I said between clenched teeth, my hands in fists. "Whatever I am, it's none of your goddamned business."

Ramsey sat down at his desk. All I wanted to do was to sock him in his wine-soaked, pockmarked nose.

"I propose," I calmly said, sitting down in front of his desk, "that Andy cover the story. I'll feed him inside information. But when it's over," I emphasized, "I want my Berlin beat back."

Ramsey leaned back in his chair with a smirk on his face.

"It's a deal, kid."

All these years later, I still wonder how I kept myself from punching Ramsey. I'm amazed. After all, I had slapped Stella. I guess I was afraid he would hit me back. If it happened today I would have reported him to a union official, and he, most likely, would be fired. And today, I wouldn't have hesitated to let him know I was Jewish. But back then—well, things were different.

Clara looked godawful. Her skin had turned yellow; her eyes were rimmed with red.

"Oh, Rosie, I'm glad you're here. I wanted to call you when Stella went missing last night but the police wouldn't let me contact anyone associated with the newspapers. Isn't this terrible? Do you think you can help?"

"I'll try, Aunt Clara. Let's sit down and you can start at the beginning. I have to take notes. The story's been assigned to my colleague, Andy Roth, who's a very nice man and a good reporter. But I'll interview you. I hope you understand that it would be unethical for me to cover the story."

"Of course I understand," she said.

"So, what happened this time?" I asked, unable to keep the rancor out of my voice.

"Stella told me that she was going to lunch with Mr. Hunter and would be back in time for the opera. I believed her. But she didn't come home and I could sense that this time was different. So I called the police. I knew that she had five hundred dollars in American Express traveler's cheques, her passport, her Exposition card, and an expensive camera. Why did she take all this with her? The police are convinced that she took everything on purpose. I don't know anymore what's going on. She promised me!"

A feature story had been cobbled together by ten that evening. Because Andy had been drinking, I quietly helped him write it. While we were working on it, we laughed at the idea that he was a bit inflated with the possibility of writing himself into history.

Andy reminded me of my father. He was a tall, skinny man with a very big heart and no idea what to do with it. I had met him in New York at the newspaper and liked him immediately. When he was overwhelmed by an emotional crisis, he'd take off on a long drunk—like my father. But when he wasn't drinking, he would be reading—also like my father. Indeed, I depended on him for books. His taste in literature was sophisticated. Even the penny novels he read were well written. I liked Andy, and I liked the way we could be friends without the silly boy-girl business intruding. I didn't like his wife, Ruby, though—and couldn't understand her attraction to such an egghead.

"Hey, Ros—R.B.," Ramsey said. "What's all this literary crap?" And he dismissively tossed our story on the desk. "This isn't a goddamned publishing house. Take out the flowery adjectives, or I'll give it to one of the copy editors to clean up." I wasn't about to confront Ramsey about acceptable styles of writing. Andy had disappeared. I went to a café next door and edited.

Five hours later: "Front page, smack on the top," Ramsey said. "It's perfect! Right next to the news that the Fascists are bombing Madrid."

I have to admit that I got a kick out of scooping the other newspapers. Also, it didn't hurt that Andy's story was the leading one—the first column on the right side, with his byline.

But the other side of me, the side I couldn't show to anybody, was hurting. My cousin was missing, and I felt responsible. If only I had interrupted her meeting with Hunter the first time I saw them together.

I returned to the Hôtel Espoir. Walking upstairs, I ran into Madame Pleven, who reeked of onions.

"Been cooking, Madame?" I said. "Smells like your famous stew."

"Yes, my dear, we're celebrating our thirty-fifth anniversary tonight. But I've just come from helping Andy. He's 'sick' again."

Andy was passed out on his bed. There was no rousing him.

I turned around and walked to the rue du Vieux-Colombier to see Clara. She was downstairs in the lobby speaking with a man and twisting a handkerchief on her lap. "Oh, Rosie, I'm so glad you're here. I'd like you to meet Inspector Pascal of the *Préfecture de Police*. He's in charge of the investigation."

Pascal was a short man with a belly that looked solid. His face, with its piercing blue eyes, was framed by white hair that was so thin that you could see his pink scalp. His manner was perfect for a detective: enigmatic—hard to describe. He was wearing a rumpled brown suit with a stained, ochre-colored tie, a bit askew, and brightly polished brown shoes.

"Inspector, this is my niece, Rose Manon. She's a reporter on the *Paris Courier*."

"Good to meet you, Miss Manon. I've haven't seen you around before. Are you new? No," he answered himself. "You're the reporter from Berlin whose columns are translated in *Paris Soir*, but you go by R.B."

"Yes, sir, that's right," I said. "I'm researching Stella Mair's disappearance. As you've most likely figured out, she's my cousin."

The inspector whistled. "My god," he said. "This must be very hard for you."

"Yes, it is," I said.

I told Pascal about seeing Stella with Bobby Hunter. I gave him a description.

"Your description's helpful, as was Miss Silverman's," the inspector said. "Now I wonder if you would do me a favor and work with our staff artist at the police station. Would that be okay with you, Miss Silverman?" he asked. "I don't want to make you come to headquarters—anyway, you need to stay here in case there's an attempt to contact you."

"Of course," she said.

"Miss Manon," he continued, "perhaps we can get a good portrait of Hunter. If so, we'll place it with all the newspapers in France." I looked at him and smiled. "Okay," the inspector said. "I'll release it to the *Courier* six hours before the rest."

We went to the police station. The task wasn't easy. I struggled to describe Hunter. First, the artist tried drawing him straight on. That didn't work. Then he tried drawing him in profile. That didn't work. Then he tried drawing all the parts of his face separately. But when we assembled the pieces on an illustration board, the portrait still wasn't right. Mr. Hunter had a deceptive face. We had to settle on a composition that I felt was inadequate.

"Listen, Mr. Ramsey," I said when I returned to the newsroom, "Andy's still sick, but he gave me this report."

"Read it to me, don't have my glasses. But, listen to me, R.B., you better tell Andy that if he doesn't show his face here by tomorrow, I'll assign this plum to someone else."

"Yes, sir," I said, and began reading aloud. "The clues have begun to pile up, as have the false leads. Once yesterday's article was published with Stella's description, she's been reported as having been seen everywhere in Paris. A headwaiter at a fancy restaurant saw her lunching with a famous Italian athlete. A psychic said she saw her in a trance by the Seine. And a man, who said he was a Russian prince in exile, rang Miss Mair's aunt five times at the hotel to announce that Stella was dead. The leads were all checked out and were found to be false."

"Put it at the top of Andy's story for tomorrow's edition," Ramsey said. "It's a good kicker."

A good kicker! I thought. Ramsey's really a gossipmonger at heart. He should be managing a tabloid.

Although I thought that Ramsey was a ridiculous man, he was as treacherous as a hyena. Sometimes I would work downstairs in a corner of the Linotype room, just so I didn't have to hear him expostulate. I was still the only female on the staff and most of the men were terribly sweet to me. Besides Ramsey, the ones who gave me the hardest time were the pup reporters. All male—all full of themselves—and all competing for a byline. I hope I wasn't that way. But I do think that I still came across as a tough broad.

The next day Andy appeared at my door looking terrible. "Sorry, R.B., for letting you down. Let's walk over to the office together. It'll do me good to get some air."

We checked in with Ramsey. "The police," Ramsey said, "have found a badly forged American Express traveler's cheque for a hundred bucks. The description of the check casher was a dashingly handsome man. He showed Stella Mair's Exposition card for identification."

"But Stella's a woman," Andy protested. "How did he get away with that?"

"A stupid salesgirl," Ramsey said. "Along with this guy being so suave and good looking. Probably put his thumb over 'Stella.'"

I had to sit down. "This means that Stella must be dead. I've got to go to my aunt."

"No, R.B.," Andy said. "There could be something else going on here—this doesn't mean she's dead."

"Yeah, it probably does," Ramsey said. "But, well—I guess she could have gone off on a toot, looking for publicity," he added and grinned. "Naw, she's kaput and we know it. Now the story's got to be about the manhunt for this guy Bobby Hunter and finding Stella's body. So get to it, Andy. And you, R.B., I want part of the story to be about your aunt's reaction."

"Forget it, Mr. Ramsey. Neither Andy nor I are that kind of sob-sister-story writer, and—"

"And—by the way," he interrupted, ignoring me, "this isn't a political story. Andy, you need to put more energy into the writing. Write to the masses, not the highbrows."

I swallowed hard, thinking: What in the hell's wrong with our writing, you imbecile? Before, you told us it was too flowery; now it's not dimwitted enough.

I was so angry, so upset, that I fumbled my way onto the Métro, then got off at the wrong stop and had to walk back to the rue du Vieux-Colombier. I found Clara sitting up in bed, staring out the window.

"Aunt Clara, I have something to—"

"Yes, I know, dear, the inspector was here—he'll be back in a little while. I think she's dead. I can just feel it."

"No, wait, Clara. Wait. Perhaps she's been kidnapped? Perhaps this is a publicity stunt? Perhaps—"

"Oh, Rosie, what's happening? I don't understand. Why this violence against our family? We left Russia to escape this—and now look what has happened."

I could see that Clara was too horrified even to cry. I held her hand. There was nothing to say. We had to wait to hear from Inspector Pascal.

A while later, his arrival was announced by the concierge. We went downstairs to the lobby and the three of us sat in the back near the garden.

"By any chance, Inspector," I asked, "do you think Stella could be alive?"

The inspector sighed. "There's nothing to substantiate the belief that the girl's dead. Then again, there's no proof that she's still alive. Last night we rounded up questionable characters and checked their papers. About a hundred men were arrested, most for being émigrés without identity cards, some for unsolved petty crimes. It's sad. But not a clue was found."

"What will happen to the men you arrested?" Clara asked, looking relieved to be worrying about something else.

"They'll be deported, probably to Switzerland. Within a few days, they'll be back." And the inspector turned and looked pointedly at me.

"What's the matter?" I said.

"Look, Miss Manon, I'm worried about all of you. I know you're Jewish. Take caution. Especially working in Berlin—you're playing with fire. And here in Paris, anti-Semitic pamphlets are being distributed all over the city. If you're ever arrested here, tell them to contact me. But be vigilant. These are dangerous times."

"I'm not worried, Inspector, but thanks for the warning. Maybe being half Jewish will let me off the hook."

"That's ridic—" he started to say, and then realized that Clara had a horrified look on her face.

"Sorry," he said, looking at me. "I'll check back with you as soon as I have more information."

Later, Andy called from the hotel's front desk. He had attended a news conference led by the inspector and written a good article. Watching his trembling hands, I knew what Andy's staying sober was costing him.

"Thanks, Andy, for writing this," I said, and I placed a hand on his.

"Another front-page, banner story," Andy said with sarcasm. "Ramsey will be thrilled."

After Andy returned to the office, I went back upstairs to Clara's room and insisted that we go for dinner. We strolled along the boulevard St. Germain. The street lamps gave off a pale yellow glow, blurring the evening like a painting by Utrillo. Even the voices of the pedestrians were soft, and we found ourselves almost whispering. We turned left onto the rue de l'Ancienne Comédie, meandering past a row of small galleries and antique shops. Displayed in one of the windows were three small charcoal drawings by Giacometti.

"That's what I feel like," Clara said, "a line that's disappearing into the horizon. Lost." I took her hand and we walked.

"Let's go to Deux Magots," I said. "It's late, and not so crowded, and I love to listen to that." And I pointed to an old tramp wearing drooping and patched trousers held up by a thick leather belt, a peasant's shirt, originally blue, but now black with grime, and a beret. He was clasping a battered violin to his chest. "He's remarkable. When you hear him play, you'll see what I mean." I walked over and handed him money.

For just a short time, we could forget our distress. The evening was transformed as the old man played Massenet's "Meditation."

I wish that I could rewrite this story. Go back to the beginning. Have Stella come bouncing through the door in her usual maddening fashion. But I would not be able to rewrite my anger at her—nor could I find a way to be sympathetic. I was too angry—too concerned for my aunt. And I was displeased with myself for not feeling more worried about Stella's well-being. Perhaps my mother had been right. I didn't care for anyone but myself.

The next morning I decided to retrace Bobby Hunter's trail. Maybe the police had overlooked something—and it turned out that they had. I went to Lancel's, a leather and jewelry shop on the boulevard des Italiens, where Hunter had bought a wallet with one of Stella's American Express checks. I found the saleswoman who had waited on him.

"Yes, I remember," she said. "A handsome man came into the shop. He spoke beautiful English."

"Was it British English?" I asked.

"No," she said, "an impeccable American English."

Ah—at that moment I remembered that I had heard a small snatch of conversation between Stella and Bobby Hunter at the hotel. For all this time, I had forgotten how surprised I was to hear him speaking English with an American accent.

As soon as I was on the street, I went into a bar and called Inspector Pascal. "Thanks, Miss Manon," he said. "This is important."

Three weeks of waiting. Nothing new. Clara was withering. "I'm going back to New York," she informed me. "I've booked passage for next Wednesday. It's useless. There's nothing more

I can do. Even Inspector Pascal told me that it's over. They've put the case in the icebox." And I had to control myself not to laugh. It was a fleeting moment's reprieve.

I accompanied Clara on the boat train from the Gare du Nord to the liner *Statendam* at Le Havre. We had a quiet journey. Everything had been said. It was a dark night. No moon to show the way, no stars to guide the wanderers.

Once we arrived at the quay, there were indeed large numbers of wanderers. Frightened-looking people were everywhere. I could see the anxiety in their eyes. I assumed they were Jewish—and we soon learned that I was correct. Clara and I watched them warily. One by one, each of the travelers went past the customs house, handing an official their precious papers: *Cartes d'identité d'étranger* and passports. I knew that most had been bought on the black market—forged, new-old photos carefully pasted in place, aged with fine dirt. Some of the émigrés looked as if they were holding their breath. I heard one woman say to her husband, "Eli, they're not going to let us on. I can feel it in my bones."

"Hush, Sarah, hush, it'll be all right." And her husband took her hand to lead her to the official. She turned her face away, not able to look while he stamped her papers. I watched to see if I could see a change on Sarah's face, but there was nothing. Her fear was too intense. Even the grandeur of the boat, decked out with its glittering strings of lights that made the moment feel like a celebration, wasn't enough for her. She had to pass one line of passengers, who were dancing up the right side of the gangplank. The line on the left, which included Sarah and Eli, was slowly trudging, the passengers knowing they might be leaving behind their villages, their countries, their families forever.

Clara looked stunned. "They'll never get the Jewish population of France to safety this way," she said. "It would take years!"

And I knew she was right, but didn't want to say anything to add to her anxiety.

I was ashamed to watch the American passengers. They were exuding cheer—carrying bottles of champagne, baskets of expensive foods, calling out to each other apparently without a care in the world.

"What are you going to do, Rosie?" Clara asked, interrupting my anger. "You know you can't stay. There'll be a war."

There was no answer. I agreed with her.

"Rosie," she persisted, "no matter how hard you try, you'll always have the Western twang in your voice and the ancient tribes of Israel on your face. Why can't you just accept that?"

"I'm trying, Clara. I am."

"Good-bye, my dear," she said. "I don't know what I would have done without you." And she climbed the gangplank with the refugees, not the Americans.

I waited until the ship sailed. It felt odd seeing Clara off. Should I be going with her? I honestly didn't know who I was anymore. Was I an American? Or had I so completely transformed myself that I had lost my identity? Ever since landing on the shores of Europe I had been trying to recast myself as a Frenchwoman. Because of my looks, I fit neatly into the Parisian community. And because of my ease with the language, I had almost begun to think that I was a different person. Now, having spent time with Clara, I knew I had to drop the French pretense.

* * *

Beginning in 1936, I had worked on the *Courier*'s foreign desk in Berlin. Every couple of months I would have to return to Paris to check in with my paper. It was nice to take a break from the unrelenting apprehension of living in the Third Reich—but it was also difficult. Leaving Leon made me nervous. His being a member of the Communist Party put him in jeopardy. I thought that if I were in Berlin, and he were arrested, I could use my contacts to get him released and out of the country.

But being in Paris, even though it was under the same threatening sky as the rest of Europe, was like traveling to the private planet of the sun goddess. No matter what the season, I was always struck by the subtle beauty of the gardens—by the wavering lines of ancient trees—by the variations in colors of the sky. Traveling though the countryside to Paris reminded me of Proust and his imaginary Balbec. The scenery was so delicate, so graceful—it was as if it had been lovingly embroidered into the fabric of the land.

It was this vast piece of embroidery that I have tried to replicate here on my land in the little mountains of New York State. My garden is planted in a landscape of lines and colors and shapes and shadings. I've always imagined that if I went up in a balloon, my garden would remind me of a quiet Vuillard painting. And I feel that then, high up in the sky, my heart would finally, peacefully burst, and I could die in bliss.

But bliss was in Berlin. I would take the dark-blue Nord Express back to Germany. The first time I boarded the train and we chugged out of Paris, it was as if I were entering a dream. We moved through such glorious country, passing by small villages whose lanes were lined with chestnut and lime trees reflecting each other in a dizzy pattern. The French architecture was delicate, romantic. Soft pink and yellow stone pillars balanced narrative cornices; houses were colored with subtle fading pastels; the scale of the buildings was pleasant, almost dreamlike. But once I was in Belgium, I began to notice gloom. And by the time I crossed the German frontier at Aachen and passed over the Rhine River, I had entered a different world. The cottages became squat, without a touch of elegance.

That first journey took almost twenty-one hours. Finally, riding through the dismal suburbs of Berlin, I arrived at the Anhalter railway terminus and stepped down onto the platform under its grand glass roof. But I couldn't see the sky. It was seven at night and already dark, with no moon, and dim streetlights. There was a light drizzle. I set out on foot, following written directions to the bureau's office. Soon I heard a vague sound and thought it sounded like a gathering of people. Then the noise rose in volume and quickly became thunderous. What I saw and heard marching down a broad boulevard were legions of soldiers of the Wehrmacht, Nazi youth groups, and members of the National Socialist German Workers' Party. The soldiers, with their steel-gray helmets matching their steel-gray uniforms, were carrying carbines on their left shoulders. Their right arms swung like metronomes in perfect cadence, while they slammed their boots against the cobblestones. The youth groups were carrying Nazi flags, hundreds of them, all drooping in the rain. The Workers' Party was carrying the banners. The rolling cacophony of voices became clearer and clearer: *Germans, awake from your nightmare! Jews have no place in our Empire!*

I was stunned. I simply stood there and shivered. Welcome to your new life, I thought. Is this what you wanted?

It was tragic, crushing, to observe what was happening in Germany. I needed to find a way to relieve the tension. After a few months, I wired my boss in New York to ask if I could write a column about what I was seeing outside the arena of my political reporting. With his blessing, I began writing a weekly column called "Berlin Journal." An elaborately painted sign that I saw in front of a clothing store prompted my first column. I used it as my lead sentence. GERMANS, DEFEND YOUR-

SELVES—DO NOT BUY FROM JEWS *read a sign in a shop window. There's no beauty in this city. I look at people's faces, trying to sense their moods, but I can't read an emotion. Their eyes are blank.*

Looking back, I wonder how I maintained my equilibrium. The signals heralding doom were everywhere. I saw them, tried to ignore them. But it was clear that Berlin was turning gray with fear. The apathy was palpable. Women shopping for food couldn't bear to look up at a clear blue sky. Instead, they looked at the sidewalk, or to the next line they had to stand in—but they were always looking down. I kept reminding myself that I didn't live in Germany, that I was a citizen of a faraway country. For the first time, I was homesick.

It was a long walk from my room on Mohrenstrasse to the press office on Wilhelmstrasse. I had to walk past both Ribbentrop's yellow palace and Hitler's stone residence. Once, I almost literally ran into the Führer as he was entering his car. I was daydreaming when suddenly a black leather-clad arm reached out and shoved me out of the way. "Hey," I said in English, "what in the hell do—" and before I knew what was happening I was roughly pushed against the building.

"Stay there," one of his guards demanded, and I had a quick impulse to run. It was a stupid idea, and I knew it at once.

"Papers," a guard commanded. He was short and muscled and had blond hair greased straight back from his impassive face. His eyes were like two black buttons and held me transfixed for a moment with their coldness. He wore a mustache. Just like Hitler's, of course.

I showed him my papers.

"Jew?" he asked.

"None of your business," I replied. "I have immunity through the American Embassy. Let me go or I'll report you!"

The impassive man, not surprisingly, sneered. Then, in one fell swoop, he turned, grabbed me by the back of my shoulders, and slammed me against his car—his shiny black symbol of power. My breasts received the brunt of the force and I cried out in pain. He got into the passenger seat, snapped his fingers, and the car drove off, causing me to fall to my knees.

No one helped me. The pedestrians kept walking, eyes staring into nowhere, as if I were invisible.

I kept my confrontations with the Reich from Leon. He had made it clear that the less he knew about my movements in Germany, the better it was for him. This suited me.

We correspondents in Berlin found ourselves in a rough spot. Censorship sliced out the real news. Press conferences were a joke. We were being fed propaganda and we all knew it. When the floor was open for questions, only certain reporters were chosen to address Goebbels, or whoever was giving us the news. If another reporter challenged the spokesman, he was ignored. And if a reporter was too nosy, too persistent, he was on the train back to wherever he came from.

Pete Grogan and I had been in yet another press briefing. Pete, having just been chastised by Goebbels for an article he had cabled the day before, was angry. I felt for him. It wasn't fair. I looked around the pressroom and all I could see were blank faces.

Pete sat back in his chair, flipped his notebook shut, and looked out a window. "Let's get out of here," he whispered. "Our job's a farce."

"Wait," I whispered back, "wait until it's over. We don't need to make more enemies than we already have." The truth was that I didn't want to be sent back to Paris. What I wanted was in Berlin—involvement in history—a chance to make a name for myself. And Leon.

* * *

I was assigned to cover the public meeting between Hitler and Mussolini. When the meeting was over, as we had planned, I went to Leon's place. I was exhausted and in a cranky mood.

To get to his third-floor apartment, I had to walk up a dirt-stained circular marble staircase with ornate wrought-iron railings. The building had once been a mansion for a wealthy Jewish family, and they had sold it just in time. They had moved to London after the 1933 elections in Germany. Now the building was a rabbit warren of poorly constructed rooms where more than fifty people lived. Leon's apartment consisted of a living room and a bedroom. There was a small niche for the simple kitchen that included a two-burner gas stove, a wooden icebox, and the only sink in the apartment. A cramped toilet was down the hall. The one original wall of the century-old house was in the living room, splendidly paneled in oak, made dark with layers of shellac. The bedroom was incongruously wallpapered with a joyful motif of light red and orange poppies and green leaves. It looked like a watercolor, although it had turned dingy with the dust from Leon's metalwork.

I found him sitting at his worktable under an ugly, cold blue light, bent over a magnifying glass. He was working on a silver plate. I knew not to move, but to stand still until he lifted his head. I liked to watch him engrave. His hands were enormous for such work. His fingers were long and thick, but he was meticulous with every line. I once knew a woman in Nevada who had hands like that. I loved watching her embroider with astonishing delicacy.

"It's good to see you, Rosie," he said as he polished the plate. Then he opened a cabinet door, placed the plate inside, and locked it.

"Why do you always lock your work away, Leon, don't you trust me?"

"Of course I do," he said, "but silver's valuable and I have to be careful."

"What about those other doors?" I asked, pointing to a row of them. "They're locked too."

He shrugged. "For the same reason. Silver's valuable and I have to be careful."

I didn't believe him, but sensed that I should drop the subject.

"They claimed that six hundred and fifty thousand people came out to hear Hitler and Mussolini speak," I said. "Everyone was jammed into the Olympic Stadium. I've never in my life seen so many human beings in one place. Like lemmings, they stood in the pouring rain. I was in the press box and could see it all. It gave me the chills."

"Would you like a drink?" Leon interrupted, and I shook my head no.

"Leon, it was so well organized! Perhaps, instead of lemmings, I should say that they were more like marionettes. Every time they were supposed to roar, they roared; every time they were supposed to salute, they saluted. When they sang that Nazi marching song, 'Horst Wessel'—I could feel a country going insane. There's something about Hitler's voice that mesmerizes. 'Today we own Germany. Tomorrow the world.'"

It was still dark when I woke the next morning. I reached for Leon, but he was gone. Seeing light coming from under the door, and without meaning to be so quiet, I entered the living room. Sitting at his worktable, he was wearing an old brown soldier's overcoat from the Great War. He had a jeweler's loupe over one eye, and was working on the same silver platter. The radio was softly playing classical music. Not wanting to frighten him, I watched quietly.

What's he engraving? I wondered. And I looked more carefully. Jeez, I realized, he was engraving a swastika. It was embedded in an elaborate background of oak leaves and acorns that decorated the platter. I gasped.

He dropped the tool, making a miserable "oh" sound. Then I could feel him gathering all his anger, and he cried out, "Rosie, why are you spying on me?"

"Ssh," I said, "you'll wake the neighbors," and he glared at me.

Leon threw a cloth over the plate, which he put in a cabinet and locked. "Get out of here, Rosie. Go away." He stomped into the bedroom and slammed the door. Then a moment later, the door opened and he tossed my clothes and shoes at me. I heard him lock the door.

I was horrified. He must be supporting the Reich. I had known he was a communist, and thought that he had voted against Hitler. At least that's what he had told me. Had he changed his thinking? Why did he always appear to be under pressure when doing certain engravings? I had taken Leon for granted, assuming that our conversations were in tune with each other—that our intimacy was something more than just a release of sexual energy.

A few minutes later, Leon entered the room. "What are you doing here?" he said. "I told you to leave."

"Leon—"

"What, Rosie?"

I couldn't help blurting, "What in the hell are you doing engraving that crap? You lied. You didn't tell me you were a Nazi."

Leon went to the front door and opened it.

"Go. Right this minute, go! This relationship is over."

What am I saying? I thought. How could I even consider such an allegation?

"No, not until you tell me the truth!"

"Oh, for Christ's sake, you're such an idiot, Rosie. You're

an honest-to-goodness fool. For someone so smart, you're really dumb. Of course I'm not a Nazi, I'm a *Jew*! Now get out—I can't bear to look at you!"

And my fury and distress flew out the door.

"Please, close the door, Leon," I said softly.

He closed the door, but continued to lean against it.

"Leon, my family lives in New York."

"You told me they lived in Nevada."

"My parents do, but the larger family's in New York."

"They're lucky," he said. "I would love to be living in New York."

"You know," I said, "there are lots of Jews in New York—"

Leon looked at me, puzzled. "Why mention Jews in New York? Are you trying to tell me you're Jewish?"

"Well, half-Jewish," I finally admitted, "on my mother's side."

"Really!" he said sarcastically. "I thought you were all Jewish. You look it!"

"What do you mean by that tone of voice, Leon? I don't understand."

"I've always known that you're Jewish, Rosie. We Jews have built-in antennas about who is one of us—and who is the enemy. Aren't you uncomfortable being in Germany?"

"Of course not," I said. "Since I've never considered myself Jewish."

"Are you telling me that you're detached from what's happening here?"

"No, no. I don't mean that I'm not sensitive to people's suffering. It's just that it all seems to be happening to someone else."

"Well, my dear," he said, "I'm one hundred percent Jewish, and I have to deal with more serious issues than your worrying about how I make my living. So I think it's a good idea that you leave and we not see each other again."

I didn't move. Leon didn't move.

"Then, if you're not a Nazi, why are you engraving this stuff?"

"I have no choice, Rosie. And I can't talk about it."

I looked at my watch. "I've got to go. Can I see you tonight? Nine o'clock at the Aldon?"

"No," he said, "I'm sorry. It has to be over. I need you to leave me alone."

"Please, Leon," I said, standing, "I—"

"Don't say it, Rosie, please don't say it. I honestly can't handle an emotional crisis. I must keep to myself. There's too much at stake."

"Please, just tonight, just a drink."

I walked through an opulent lobby, surrounded by square pillars of amber-clouded marble, up three steps and through the leather-covered and padded doors with two round windows, outlined with brass brads. I was relieved to see Leon sitting at the bar. The room was so dimly lit that the faintly moving shadows of the waiters formed a gray moiré. He was drinking a whiskey. I was nervous. I knew I was an intuitive woman; that was why I was such a good correspondent. But it could make me a bit paranoid too. My mind was racing. I wanted to turn and go out the door. I was terrified of his rejecting me again.

"I'll have one of those," I said to the bartender, pointing to his whiskey. "But make mine a double."

I was thinking. I could finally admit to myself that I had fallen in love—and had absolutely no idea what to do about it. I looked at Leon staring at the opposite wall. He had turned into the most handsome man in the world. I was afraid for him.

"Listen, Leon," I said. "I know you see me as cantankerous and moody. But it's just a cover-up."

"Then who are you, Rosie? I get the sense that you've no idea."

I laughed. "You're right!"

"Go ahead," he challenged, "try to tell me."

"Sometimes heartless. Often distant," I said. "But unintentionally."

"Well," he said, "I think you play at being a self-confident, tough newspaperwoman."

"It's a lie," I said.

"Is it?" he said. "Perhaps. But I suspect you think that you really are a romantic. Well, you're not. You're practical and determined to a fault. And sometimes I don't like you at all—and other times I think you're wonderful, but this can't go on, Rosie. It really can't." He was gripping his drink with soot-stained hands, his shoulders hunched, while looking down at the bar. "I said I'd meet you, but it was a mistake. Everything I believe in is being made illegal by this regime. It isn't fair to drag you into it. Please, you'll be doing me a serious favor by not seeing me again."

"But I don't understand," I said. "Why does this have to end?"

"I don't have a choice, Rosie. There're actually more important things in my life than being in love with you."

"You love me?" I said, incredulous, and Leon looked at me softly.

"Yes, but it doesn't mean anything, Rosie. Not now. There's no room for romantic love in my world."

The waiter brought my double whiskey and I swallowed it as if it were a glass of water.

"I have to go," he said. "Please don't try to see me again. I insist that you stay far away." And he placed his hand on my arm and leaned to kiss me.

"No," I snarled, brushing away his hand and hitting the bar with my fist. "The hell with you." And I staggered out of the bar, feeling like a fool.

Although I was due back in Paris in a few days, I headed to the darkest, dreariest bar I could find. My old Simon's Creek self-loathing returned. I'm no good. Not pretty enough. Not tall enough. I found a gray hair. My breasts sag. I didn't satisfy him. But while I was wallowing in self-pity and depression, I knew I was being dishonest with myself. I knew I wasn't a beauty—but I wasn't unattractive either. I knew that in France I looked French—just as I knew in Germany, I looked like a real Jew. And I knew that although I was considered eccentric, some people thought me interesting.

At the end of my dive into that muddy pool of despair, I understood. I wanted to be heroic in my helplessness. But I didn't have the guts, so I demeaned myself instead. In my imagination, I saw my father looking on with distress. "No, Rosie," he would have said. "You must stop your drinking."

I had become a master of self-deception and self-abasement. Over time I had worn my dislike of myself as armor. It was my statement to the world that I was above silly-girl chatter—that I could take anything like a man.

Just like a man. What in the world was I thinking? Now I can see what was going on. Fear. Fear of the unknown. Fear of being alone. Yet I was hard on Leon—uncompromising, questioning everything. I wanted both the "tough reporter" label and the tradition of marriage and family. I didn't realize it then, but I couldn't have both. That confusion led to my never having children. Now I've transferred my thwarted mothering instincts to my garden.

The rain has stopped, the sun has come out, and a million diamond teardrops are quivering and glistening on my plants.

I don't mind getting my hands dirty; I never have. My friends give me gardening gloves as gifts. I suppose it disturbs them to see my gnarled hands, and the stained knuckles and the dirt under my fingernails. But I always forget that I have the gloves in a shopping bag hanging in the shed—I simply go to work in the garden at the slightest whim. I love the feel and smell of the earth. When I dig up a rock to make way for another plant, I have such an overwhelming sense of accomplishment—as if I'm designing the earth, putting it in order, making it even more lovely than it already is.

Pete Grogan found me at the bar. "Christ, R.B.," he said, "get hold of yourself. You're either going to get yourself fired or die of alcohol poisoning. Ramsey cabled me and asked what was going on. Your cable to him was gibberish. He's seriously pissed off. Quite honestly, pal, your self-pity's getting boring."

"Leave me alone, Pete, I don't need you to be my mother. I've got an impossible one already."

"The hell with you," he said. "You're the most selfish, spoiled woman I've ever met. Do you have any idea what Leon's dealing with?"

I shook my head, and Pete sat down.

"Well, I'm assuming you know that his parents are academics."

I shook my head no.

"What kind of stupid games have the two of you been playing? What do you know about his life?"

"Very little," I admitted.

"That's the strangest thing I've ever heard," Pete said. "What in the world were you thinking?"

I pushed my drink away. "I'm not sure," I said. "In this atmosphere, it just seemed the thing to do. We got used to it. Perhaps it was a way to create our own little safe world, since the outside one has gone berserk. I really don't know. I didn't even know he was Jewish."

"Keep your voice down, R.B.," Pete said. "This isn't the place to be saying that word. His parents," he quietly continued, "were fired from their university positions because they're

Jews. As a result, they've been relying on Leon to support them, and—"

"Sorry to interrupt," I said, "but how can he support them as an engraver?"

"You know, for a bright woman, you're acting alarmingly stupid!"

God, I thought. This is the second time in a week that I've been called stupid.

"Look," Pete said, "Leon's under arrest. Has been for almost a year. But his job's so rarefied that they give him a little leeway. As long as he obeys his masters, he'll be left alone. At least until Churchill and Roosevelt decide what to do."

"Under arrest—he never told me this. What kind of arrest? And why is he engraving swastikas? It seems stupid to me."

"Look—he doesn't have a choice. Because he's one of the best engravers in Berlin, those selfish bastards are convinced that they need him. He's been ordered to decorate all the tableware, candelabras, and serving platters for the high commanders. Hitler's first on the list."

"I saw. They're beautifully ornate, with leaves and flowers. You have to look closely to see the swastikas. But it all seems impossible to me. I don't get it."

"C'mon," Pete said. "Do you think any of those horses' asses would eat off the simple plates of the masses?"

"No, I don't mean that," I said. "That I understand. But how can he work for the enemy?"

"Because he doesn't have a choice, R.B. They pay him a minuscule salary, which keeps his family from starving. And his contacts with the Reich keep everyone safe—at least for the time being. So, now do you get it?"

"Yeah, I get it."

"Well, Ramsey wants you back in Paris for a few days—so you'd better get yourself together. You look awful."

I sensed that Leon was gone forever. I couldn't believe how much I missed him. I wondered why he hadn't asked me to help him and his family. I wondered why the two of us had played our silly game of noncommitment. And I wondered why he had said he loved me; he had never said it before. It all made my heart ache with longing for him. I felt stranded between the safety of being an American and the dark reality that was beginning to take shape in Europe.

* * *

I returned to Paris. Two days later, even though it was the middle of the night, I took a walk to try to clear my head. There was no moon as I strolled along the Seine. The river had become a dark mirror reflecting the shimmering winter stars. I walked beside the leafless plane trees whose shadows were projected on the walls from the feeble bridge lamps. Every now and then a cloud would appear and block the starlight. In those moments the river became menacing and mournful. I saw vagrants trying to stay warm around small fires that had been set against the damp gray walls along the river; I saw night-foragers picking through garbage bins; I saw a man walking with a battered guitar over his shoulder; I saw street-walkers hobbling home on their high-heeled shoes; I heard the staccato clattering of hooves and then saw a shepherd leading two sheep to the market. I saw lurking men, but I had moved beyond my natural fear, and paid them no mind.

I reached Les Halles. The marketplace offered up the splendid aromas and noises of life. It was a balm to the merciless ugliness and despair I was wallowing in. Les Halles was illuminated by bonfires made from broken wooden vegetable crates, along with kerosene lanterns hanging off the horse-drawn wagons and gas-driven trucks. The market was bustling with life and light in the middle of the night. Every so often, the men who were unloading crates of food stopped to throw back a shot of calvados, obviously convinced that this gave them the strength to carry on. Although it was winter and the only vegetables were potatoes and turnips, onions, some carrots, and cabbages, the scene made me hungry. But the huge hunks of bleeding horsemeat in the abattoir section threatened my reverie. Even though I chose not to look, I could not escape seeing the gutters flowing with blood and bilious water.

As I entered a café favored by journalists, I saw Andy Roth sitting morosely at one of the tables, obviously having had a lot to drink. I knew that Ruby was back in England.

"Andy. Are you okay?"

He didn't answer, but I could see his trembling hands, see the weeks of heavy drinking and depression. I felt guilty for having been so tied up with my own troubles. I really hadn't paid Andy much notice.

"Ruby has someone else and wants a divorce," Andy said, and his already rummy eyes looked even more miserable. "I don't want to talk about it, R.B., it's too upsetting."

So neither of us spoke—two sad people, elbows on a wine-stained tabletop, drinking wine without a name.

I was lost in thought when I heard Andy. "This is stupid," he said. "I'm going to Madame Beloit's." And he stood, obviously drunk. "Come with me, R.B. It won't hurt for you to see another side of life—especially from a woman's point of view. It'll make a good story."

Madame Beloit's brothel, La Petite India, was above a bookbinding shop on the rue de Rosiers in the Marais. It was primarily frequented by journalists and men from Les Halles, along with a few tourists looking for a story to take back home. It opened at midnight, closed at seven in the morning, and was run by the firm, bejeweled hand of Madame Beloit.

I tagged along, feeling ridiculous, but also curious. We climbed the stairs to be met by Madame herself. "No women, Mr. Roth," she said in a husky voice. "You know better."

"I'll leave," I said, embarrassed.

"No, I need you to stay. Just sit here." He pointed to a chair in the corner.

"My friend, here," he said to Madame Beloit, trying to stand straight and look presentable, "is a famous writer and it would behoove you to let her sit for a while. Yes?"

"Yes," Madame agreed, with a glint in her eyes.

I took out my notebook and officiously flipped it open.

Madame was a huge woman with many chins, dressed in billowing black taffeta, with white lace over her bosom, and just a bit of nipple showing. Her face must have been pretty at one time and she still had startlingly beautiful blue eyes. Before taking more than five steps into her house, a client had to place the mandatory francs into Madame's fat, outstretched hand. The parlor smelled as if someone had sprayed an entire bottle of Shalimar in the air.

The electric piano was playing "You're Driving Me Crazy," adding a slice of mournful humor to our evening. The room was almost proper in its furnishings, except for small pictures that had been cut out of a magazine and placed in cheap frames. They depicted (I counted) fifty-seven positions of the Kama Sutra.

Lounging on the deep red velvet sofas was an array of women waiting to be chosen by the leering men. They were dressed in transparent yellow or red saris that left one breast exposed, in keeping with the theme.

"That's my favorite," Andy whispered, poking me in the side. "Her name's Effie—reminds me of the Rocky Mountains."

"But, Andy," I whispered, "I thought you were true to Ruby," and he turned and looked at me as if I was born yesterday.

Effie was much taller than a typical Frenchwoman, and thin and wiry—like a ranch hand. "Every time I see her," he said, "I'm reminded of lassoing steers and half expect her to slap her thighs, do a jig, and sing, 'I'm an Old Cowhand.'"

"Come on, handsome," Effie said to Andy.

"No Berlin, Mr. Ramsey," I said firmly, while leaning against the doorjamb. "I won't go back. Go ahead and fire me. I don't care." I waited for an explosion.

And it happened.

But coldly. Seriously. Without space to move. "I don't give a good goddamn what your reason is, Miss High-falutin'. You're going back." And he brought his furious pink face right up to mine. I could hear chairs scraping behind me.

"Let her be!" I heard a reporter yell.

"Yeah," boomed the chorus of employees.

"Don't you dare touch me, Mr. Ramsey," I said quietly, while feeling my lip snarl like a fox's.

He stepped away, grabbed a beer from someone's desk, took a swig, then slammed the bottle on a table, sending glass shards and beer everywhere.

"No Berlin, no job," he shouted and left the newsroom.

One man, Leon, had threatened me. Another man, Ramsey, was threatening me, too. I felt torn in half—as if every man who was important in my life had a pronouncement about how I was to behave, including my father. It was funny. I felt I could do battle with my mother and survive—but the opinions of these three men petrified me.

I knew I had a few days to get things back on track. It was Andy who came to the rescue. "Quietly," he said, "propose to New York that you write a series of six articles, one a week, on Germans living in Paris. It'll make Ramsey look good. And it'll give you six weeks to get yourself together. Now, come on—let's go have dinner. At least when I'm with someone, I actually eat food."

Later, we arrived home to find Madame Pleven, the concierge, fast asleep with her folded arms upon the table, cradling her snoring head. She was supposed to check all the residents as they came in and went out, but it was two in the morning and she had obviously lost her battle with wakefulness. Slipped into a crack beside her bell was a formal envelope addressed to me from the American Embassy.

> *Dear Miss Manon, I need to speak to you. There will be a Christmas party Saturday night at the Embassy. I would appreciate your coming about 9:00 P.M. and we'll find a quiet moment to speak. Formal dress is required.*
> *Sincerely yours, John Clancy, American Consul.*

I had no idea what Clancy wanted to talk to me about. Perhaps, I thought, something to do with Stella's disappearance? Perhaps he wanted to recruit me? I knew that some American correspondents had been convinced to feed information from their private sources to the embassy. But I had never been asked. Sexy and beautiful women were used for gathering information, not someone like me.

Formal dress? That was a joke. Shopping for clothes in Paris had become a grim enterprise. The shelves were not stocked as they had been. Fabric was being manufactured for the army, not the fashion-conscious. People were mending, or refashioning, old clothes. Nevertheless, I needed to find a dress. Ridiculous. I hadn't worn a dress since I left New York. Under the cold blue lights of the dressing room in La Samaritaine, I looked drained of blood—like a cadaver. Every pore, every blemish, was amplified a hundred times. As

I was trying on dresses I became more and more depressed. Fancy clothes and I are not compatible. I settled for a pair of dark gray trousers and a teal-blue silk blouse. After all, I was a journalist, not a socialite. But I would wear Clara's mink coat.

It was snowing, and by three in the afternoon it was dark. I walked to the boulevard to get a bath and a haircut. "Cut off the curls," I told the barber, "I want my hair to look smooth." The barber, Louis, shrugged as he whipped the blue-and-white-striped cloth around my shoulders. "You can't smooth your kind of hair, Mademoiselle," he said. "Your hair's naturally curly from the beginning of its roots. I'll have to shave your head to get rid of the curls."

"Okay," I said. "Just do it, please."

"Shave your head?" asked Louis, and I laughed.

"No, no," I said, "just a regular trim."

When I returned to the hotel, I went to Andy's room to ask if I could borrow a pair of Ruby's galoshes to wear over my dress-up shoes. "Hey, Andy, you there?" I asked as I knocked and pushed the door open.

The room was a pigsty. Clothes strewn about, a bed without sheets, a saliva-stained pillow without a case, an old green and black plaid blanket on the floor. It was freezing. There were empty whiskey bottles scattered here and there, old crusts of bread, hardened pieces of cheese. It was alarming; he had rubbed out his cigarettes right into the tabletop and left the butts there.

Andy wasn't home.

I had not realized that my friend had slid downhill so drastically. He was obviously in deep trouble. I could understand why. Andy's wife, Ruby, wasn't only a stunner, but a flirt, too. I could certainly see why Andy had fallen for her, but could never figure out what she had seen in the bespectacled, introverted Andy—except that he would bring her to gay Paris. It had not been unusual to walk by their door and hear Ruby screeching. Most likely, Andy had gone mute, since this was his nature, which apparently had made her even angrier. I wondered how such a shrew could be so beautiful. It didn't fit. And now she had left him.

I borrowed the galoshes.

It was a bitterly cold night. Arriving promptly at nine at the American Embassy on the avenue Gabriel, I left my coat, and almost forgot to leave the galoshes. I entered the main reception room. All the fireplaces were lit, candles were burning on the Christmas tree, candelabras were ablaze. I was mesmerized by the glitter. There must have been more than two hundred people there, and in that light everyone looked beautiful.

Before I could get something to drink, I felt someone tapping me on the shoulder.

"Evening, Miss Manon," Mr. Clancy said. "Come with me. Let's get away from this crowd." We walked into an anteroom. "Have a seat," he said, and we both sat on an apple-green silk-upholstered sofa. All I could think about was how my shimmering blue silk blouse was so beautiful against that color.

"I want to ask you, Miss Manon, to do me a favor. We need people like you—who go back and forth over the border with immunity—to carry papers for us to the American Embassy in Berlin."

"But," I asked, "isn't there still a diplomatic pouch that goes out each day?"

"Yes," he said, "there is. However, it's becoming obvious that this won't be allowed much longer and we need to establish a trusted network. Will you do it?"

"I don't know, Mr. Clancy."

"Miss Manon," he said, and I could tell he was trying to be polite, "this is really no longer a question. You correspondents know better than anyone what's going on. Seriously, do I need to say more?"

He was right. I did know what was going on, in nightmarish detail.

"I'll do what I can," I said.

"Good, Miss Manon, I knew you would understand. Now, each time you travel to Berlin, please let my assistant, Miss Kovner, know. She'll arrange for you to receive the papers."

Well, there goes my theory about beauty and spying, I thought.

"Now, let's sit for a moment longer. I need to talk to you about another serious matter. Listen carefully. We're warning our Jewish citizens and strongly suggesting that they leave Europe."

"So, what does that have to do with me?"

"Miss Manon," he said, obviously irritated, "I know you're Jewish through your aunt, Clara Silverman."

"Well, I'm only half Jewish," I said, "so I should be fine. And with a name like Manon—"

"Don't count on it, Miss Manon. You know what *mischlingmann* means?" And he didn't wait for my translation. "It means that half-Jewish people, like you, will not be protected much longer. So, please listen to me—believe me. Get out while you can."

"But if you're telling me to leave because I'm in danger, why are you placing me in more jeopardy by having me be your courier?"

"Ah, of course—good question. To be honest, we'll use you as long as you're freely moving back and forth over the border. What matters most is the job you're doing for us. You're a grown-up. You make your own decisions."

"That sounds like cold logic to me," I said.

"It is, Miss Manon. Sadly, it is. But we need trustworthy people—and you're a trustworthy person. Now, I need to get

back inside," Clancy said. "Thanks for helping us, Miss Manon."
We shook hands. "Give me a few moments before you join the
party."

I didn't like any of it. But I really had no choice. I had never
been patriotic, but my weariness about patriotism was being
replaced with an overwhelming desire to do the honorable thing.
How odd. Walking to the door, I paused and looked around
the room for the bar.

No. I was seeing things.

It must be the lights.

No. That couldn't be Leon.

But it was. I was sure.

He had not seen me. What to do? I began to walk in his
direction, making my way through the crowd of people, keeping him in my line of vision. When I was a few feet away he
spotted me and turned to go out the nearest door. The look on
his face was not welcoming. I began to shove against people
until I reached the door and then looked around. There he was
in an alcove, waiting—debonair in a tuxedo.

"What's going on, Leon?" I said. "What are you doing here?
What—"

"Wait a minute, Rosie," he said.

I grabbed him by the arm.

"Let me go, Rosie. I can't tell you anything," he said.
"Nothing at all." He stood straight as a pole. "Turn around
and walk out of here, as if you've just been to the ladies' room.
Just *do* it, Rosie. If I see you in Berlin, you'll hear the story.
Now go. And don't look back."

"I can't, Leon," I whispered. "I love you. What if—"

"No 'what if's,' dear Rosie. Just go."

I turned, left the room, not even pausing for a drink, and
fetched my coat. Halfway down the street, I realized that my
feet were wet from the snow. I had forgotten Ruby's galoshes.

I was genuinely rattled. What was going on? I couldn't figure anything out. But Leon appeared to have forgiven my atrocious behavior at the Hotel Aldon's bar.

On my way home I became conscious of my hunger and stopped at Gillotte's for dinner. The bistro had sawdust floors and generations of dead flies piled on the windowsills. It was a kind of home to many of the unmarried reporters, along with prostitutes and pimps. I liked the joint, but that night I felt out of place in my fancy clothes. I looked around, expecting to see Andy, but he wasn't there. No matter. I had to figure all this out. But the more I thought, the more confused I became. Nothing made sense. I ate quickly and left.

When I got back to the Hôtel Espoir, I changed my clothes and went immediately to Andy's room. It was dark inside and I sensed that Andy still wasn't there. I was alarmed. I went back down to the street to the telephone at Henri's Café. Calling the *Courier,* I got Ramsey on the phone.

"Can I speak to Andy?"

"He's not here, R.B. Didn't show for work. Any idea what's going on?"

"None," I said. "None at all."

"Well, he'd better get it together. If he's not here tomorrow, he's going to be sacked."

I went back to my room. I didn't know what to do. Andy skipped around from bar to bar. Finding him could be hopeless—and I already felt hopeless enough for the evening. I went to bed.

The next thing I was aware of was a loud knocking at my door. It was opened, and Monsieur Pleven, the concierge's bald, asthmatic husband, stepped inside.

"Mademoiselle," he said wheezing through a cigarette, "your boss sent a messenger and said you're to get to the office immediately."

"This is my day off."

Monsieur Pleven shrugged. "It's still night, Miss Manon," he said, and closed the door.

It was a mess outside. While I was sleeping, there had been more snowfall. No wonder everything was so quiet and I had slept so well. Taking the Métro to the George V station, I walked across the snowbound Champs-Élysées in my old Nevada boots, waterproofed with lanolin. There were no cars, no trams. The street lamps cast a soft haze upon the new snow. It felt eerie, not at all romantic—and I felt a stomach-churning trepidation.

The newsroom was gloomy. Ramsey was sitting at his desk, staring out the window. There was no clattering of typewriters, no chattering of copyreaders. It felt as if the world of news had died. Of course it had not, but Andy Roth had.

He had been on a very long drunk and was wandering the Paris streets, incoherent, barely able to walk. Witnesses said that they observed him trying to balance himself on the icy stone railing of the Pont-Neuf and that he had appeared to fall accidentally into the Seine. People tried to help, but he had filled his pockets with small pieces of rubble.

I felt a deep invasion of sorrow, but I knew my grieving had to wait.

"His body's at the morgue waiting to be identified," Ramsey said. "Would you go?"

"Why don't you?" I shot back angrily.

"Too squeamish, I have to admit. Please."

"But what about his wife?" I asked. "Let her see what she did to him!" I was furious at Ruby.

"She's in London," he said, "and the police want him identified as soon as possible. And you know Ruby. She'll take her own goddamn good time."

Andy was waiting on a cold slab of grayish white marble. His hands and face were the same cold white. His wonderful red hair had faded to a nauseating pink. His eyelids were closed. He was frowning.

I legally identified my good friend, Andy Roth.

A week later, I heard a knock at my door. "Come in, it's open."

"Hi, Rosie," stage-whispered Andy's wife Ruby, and she stepped into the room in all her red-headed glory.

Before I knew what had happened, she flung herself into my arms and began to weep. She almost knocked me over. I'd forgotten what a large, strapping woman she was—not at all fat, but substantial and very tall. I led her to the chair and invited her to sit. But she wouldn't let go and began to wail even louder.

"Ssh," I said. "You don't want the entire hotel coming in the door, do you?"

Ruby sat in the chair, brought her knees together, smoothed out her skirt, and tried to pat her unruly curls into some semblance of propriety. "Okay, luv, let's talk about plans to ship the body home. His parents are hysterical and I want to get all the rituals over with as quickly as possible."

"Don't you feel for him at all?" I asked. "You're so removed— even your crying seems fake. Dammit," I said, getting angrier. "Don't you care?"

Ruby shrugged her shoulders.

And I swallowed bile.

The British consul arranged to ship Andy home. Ruby played the bereft widow like a professional. She wore a black veil and carried a black lace-trimmed handkerchief. I rode in the embassy's car with her, following the hearse to the boat at Le Havre. We hardly spoke. When we arrived, the longshoremen, traditionally honoring the dead, stood at attention, holding their caps. The driver opened the car door and Ruby got out.

I waited a moment, thinking he would come around and do the same for me. It didn't happen. I got out by myself and walked around the car to where she was standing. The hearse backed up to the edge of the dock and the casket was lifted out by eight men. She began to walk up the gangplank behind the coffin.

"Wait, I'll go with you," I said, trying to be kind.

"The hell with you," she said. She took an obvious breath and—like a movie star—walked slowly, and with great deliberation, up the gangplank. Ruby was well aware that all the men were watching her, and when she reached the hold of the ship, she gave an extra swish of her hips as a final good-bye.

* * *

My personal toll of dead people grew. On a bleak and snowy day, Stella Mair's body was found buried under the doorstep of a small villa on the periphery of Paris. Because the soil was primarily clay, she was well preserved. But it was obvious that the murderer had trouble digging in the clay; her body was buried jack-knifed in half at the waist, her head wedged between her knees. Although fully clothed, she was barefoot. Stella had been strangled. A rosebush was planted on her grave.

The alleged murderer was a German national named Ernst Vosberg. With blood on his clothes, a swollen lip, and a bloody bandage wrapped around his head, he was brought shackled to the police station. After being tended to by a doctor, he stood before the bench and was booked for the murder of Stella Mair.

That afternoon, Inspector Pascal said that despite what reporters had thought, this wasn't a cold case. "We check every tip that comes into headquarters, no matter how small.

"Due to a conscientious citizen, we found our answer."

On the day of the murder, the accused murderer's neighbor,

Illario Sandro, had been in the process of vacating his house and moving back to Rome. He hadn't read about the missing actress, but many months later a friend told him the story. He wrote to the police in Paris and told them about having heard screams from the next house. Assuming it was a lovers' quarrel, he didn't want to interfere. But those sounds had continued to haunt him.

They finally had an address and set off immediately. When the police arrived, no one was home.

Five minutes later, a man came through the garden gate while playing with another neighbor's dog. The police began to question him. Ernst Vosberg, who gave his name as "Robert Hunter," asked to see their credentials.

The policemen showed him their identity cards. Vosberg went into the villa.

"Here are my papers," Vosberg said, and he leaned toward a table. When the police stepped over the threshold, Vosberg turned to them with a Mauser in his hand and fired several shots.

French police don't usually carry guns; neither officer had one. One officer was wounded in his left shoulder and the other had a scalp wound from a bullet that went through his hat. They wrestled with Vosberg. The policeman with the hole in his hat saw a hammer on a table, grabbed it, and cracked it on the perpetrator's head. Vosberg was momentarily knocked out. Covered with blood, his head was wrapped in bandages and he was taken to the police station. The police searched for, and dug up, Stella's body.

Inspector Pascal called a press conference for the next afternoon at the Préfecture. The inspector requested that I come to see him before the crowd of reporters appeared.

Pascal's office was a closed-in box, filled with the smells of cigarette smoke and old coffee. But it was tidy. The only things on his desk were a brown leather desk pad, a loud wind-up clock whose minute hand made a tiny ping each time it moved, and a green fountain pen that he nervously rolled back and forth.

"Have a seat, Miss Manon," Pascal invited. "I wanted to see you privately. I need you to do me two favors. The first is to identify Miss Mair's body. Do you think you can do it? Otherwise, I'll have to ask Miss Silverman or another family member to return to France, and by the time they get here, it won't be a pretty sight. What do you say?"

God, is this my new profession, I thought—identifying bodies?

"I'll do it," I said. "When?"

"When we finish the next favor. Now come with me," Pascal said. "I need you to identify the suspect. Besides your aunt, you're the only one who has seen him close up in the flesh. The shopkeepers were hopeless; none of their descriptions came as near as yours. By the way, his real name's Ernst Vosberg, not Bobby Hunter."

"A German national?" I said, and Pascal nodded.

"But talk to him in English," he said.

A scoop, I realized. But with Andy gone, I'd have to be careful how I handled this. I followed the inspector.

Vosberg was in a windowless room with two wooden chairs, but no table.

"Hello, Bobby," I said in English as we walked into the room. "Fancy meeting you here."

"I don't know you," he answered in English.

I couldn't detect the American accent.

"Cigarette?" he said.

"No," Pascal said in French. "Ask Miss Manon politely— or you won't get one."

"I would like a cigarette, please," Vosberg said in English.

Vosberg had walked into the trap.

I wasn't surprised. His voice was melodic, smooth as silk,

just as I had heard it all those months ago. And his American English was clear as a prairie night. He certainly didn't sound like a killer. One of his police guards put a cigarette in Vosberg's manacled hands and placed an ashtray at his feet.

"Now stand, Mr. Vosberg," the inspector ordered. "Is this," Pascal asked me, "the man you saw with Stella Mair at the Studio Hôtel on July 17, 1937?"

I stood in front of him. "Look up, Vosberg," Pascal commanded.

Vosberg would not look at me.

I looked at him from the front and then the side, taking my time. I was trying to make him suffer.

"Yes, he's the same man I saw at the hotel with my cousin, Stella Mair," I said in English.

Now Vosberg stared hard at me. "I've never seen this woman in my life."

"Where did you learn English, Mr. Vosberg?" I asked.

"None of your damn business," he replied in French.

Pascal opened the door and we stepped into the corridor.

"Thanks, Miss Manon. You've been a great help. We have the right man, and can formally charge him now."

I watched as Vosberg was led downstairs, on his way back to his cell. When he caught sight of the photographers, he turned to his guard and said, "I would be perfectly willing to pose if I were shaved and dressed in a suit, but not in these clothes."

It's a long time since I've thought about Stella. I think I've sanded down the sharp edges of how I perceived that tragedy. But because of these old notes, my memory's being rudely jarred. I realize that over the years, I've been unconsciously reshaping my history. Translating it. Sanitizing it. Transforming it into fiction. Although I must give myself a bit of credit: I did see that Stella's death was heralding a terrifying future.

I took a taxi to the mortuary. Here I was again, following death. As soon as I walked in the front door, I felt sick to my stomach from the smell of carbolic soap and a hint of rotting flesh. I wanted to put my handkerchief over my nose and mouth, but willed myself not to do it. Before I had seen Andy's body, the only dead people I had ever seen were when I had covered a couple of murder stories in Nevada, but I never saw the bodies close up. I had observed their corpses from afar, merely as curious illustrations of death—and was proud that I could stay emotionally uninvolved. But this was different. Stella had exuberantly represented the optimistic side of my family— the ease of being Jewish—her unlimited curiosity. It was eerie seeing her lifeless body. More than Andy, she reminded me of a figure in a wax museum. Her face was slightly changed. The once bow-shaped lips were now two long pale lines stretching across her yellowish face. Her nose had reverted to the long and thin Silverman shape—almost as if that hereditary charac- teristic on her mother's side had the opportunity to emerge at last.

Would I ever be able to get this image of her out of my mind?

"Yes," I said to the official, "this is Stella Mair."

I made it to the press conference at the Sûreté just in time. When it was over, I rushed back to the *Courier.* "So," Ramsey asked, "what's the scoop?"

"Listen, Mr. Ramsey," I said. "Back off! There's so many details that my brain's spinning."

"Sorry, kid," Ramsey said.

"Anyway, I can't write this, and you know it. How about Pete? He's back in Paris for the birth of his child."

"Yeah, I know—the baby, the baby. Big deal! Because of this, we've had to hire a freelance stringer for the Berlin office, and he's costing loads of money."

I kept my mouth shut, not wanting to create more problems. "So, okay, your idea's good. You write—Pete will edit. But Pete will be given the byline."

"No, I disagree. He writes, I edit, and he still gets the byline." Pete was under a seriously short deadline. It took us time to decipher my handwriting. I'd taken copious notes. Oh, how I missed Andy. He might have been impossible in some ways, but when it came to getting down the facts, he was a whiz. As Pete finished typing each page, he tore it out of the typewriter and passed it directly to me. I took a cursory glance, used my red pencil now and then, and handed the pages straight to the copyboy. The copyboy, rather than taking the chance of putting it in the brass tube that fed copy to the composing room, ran it downstairs to the Linotype machine operator. It took us until 3:30 in the morning to finish the work. The headline news of the expulsion of the U.S.S.R. from the League of Nations had been moved below the fold.

What an amazing day that was. My poor cousin's fate had shoved aside all the news of the world. I still remember the feelings of hubris. Heady stuff for me—a short faux cowgirl from the high mountains of Nevada. But today I question my lack of empathy—my shifting the tragedy to make myself a hero. The notes I'm going through remind me of Alice and the looking glass—what was real?

On my way home from the newspaper office I stopped at a café and had a bowl of onion soup, deliciously sizzling with Gruyère cheese. The warmth of the soup, and my enthusiastic consumption of freshly baked bread and red wine, assured me that I would have a good morning's sleep. I was sad about Stella, but had already become used to the idea of her death. Indeed, I felt relief that we finally had an answer.

As I turned onto the boulevard St. Michel, a newspaper

truck pulled up to the curb in front of Monsieur Villières' newspaper kiosk. While I watched, Villières climbed his ladder and pasted up the banner: **American Actress Found Dead**. When I went upstairs to my room, I cut out the photograph of Stella from the *Courier* and taped it to the wall above my desk, next to a photo of Andy. I wrote a letter to Aunt Clara while they both smiled down on me. Too much death.

Both photos are here with me today. They're taped onto a yellowed onionskin page. Stella was pretty, in an old-fashioned way. Thinly painted eyebrows—dark lipstick on a mouth shaped like an angel's wings—glossy-shadowed, deeply set eyelids. Both Stella and Andy were wearing fedoras pulled down at a rakish angle. The only difference was that Stella had a feather in her hatband and Andy had a sweat stain around his.

Stella's murder was being called "the murder of the century." Her story was getting even more play than the 1919 story of Bluebeard—Henri Landau—and his slaughter of ten women and a young boy. The news media were taking advantage of the drama. And so were Pete and I. But Inspector Pascal had made it clear that he couldn't feed me any more scoops. Because of Ramsey, a few people (supposedly sworn to secrecy) knew that Stella was my cousin.

I was baffled by the fervor created by the story. There were many murders in Paris—why had this one become such a cause célèbre? Why, when the rest of Europe and Asia were teetering on the edge of an all-out war, had the murder of my cousin become front-page news? The only rationale I could see was that the urgency of the world's situation was beyond the control of the people; they felt helpless and needed to have their minds directed away from the dread of what might happen to their lives. I thought it strange that the psychopath

Hitler, who was a bona fide threat, was seen as a vague menace—while Vosberg, simply an ex-con German psychopath, was raised to celebrity status. He was being called *le monster allemand.* The public was fascinated: that monster, who had no papers, crossed the frontier into France, killed a woman—and almost got away with it. It was a metaphor for what the German war machine was threatening across Europe—except that the Germans were indeed getting away with it. Adding fuel to the Vosberg fire were the insidious references in the tabloids to Stella being Jewish. Just as the consul, Clancy, had warned—anti-Semitism in France was percolating up to the surface. Even some of the major dailies were playing the Jewish card. It undoubtedly sold papers.

After the news conference, I returned to the office. Ramsey had moved our desks to a corner near the staircase, leading down to the typesetting floor. A new person had been hired to do nothing but wait next to us and then run our pages downstairs. This new employee was a woman, and a young and pretty one at that. But there was no time for wondering what Ramsey was up to. Pete wrote, passed it to me, I read, and she ran.

Three hours later, we were finished with another four-column lead story, **Autopsy on American Jewish Actress: No Rape**. It ran alongside **100,000 Chinese Ready to Die to Hold Nanking**.

Stella had been strangled with a long white silk scarf—and another white silk scarf had been stuffed into her mouth with such violence that her upper gums were torn away and a tooth was knocked out. The coroner could find no indication that she had been sexually assaulted. Pete and I fought to keep the word "Jewish" out of the headline, but Ramsey was adamant: "Anti-Semitism's good for circulation." We were soon both sick of the whole sordid story. We wanted to write with compassion. Ramsey wanted cold irony.

*

On Sunday I returned to the office. "Jeez, R.B., you're just in time," said the now nattily dressed Ramsey, with his feet up on his desk, drinking a beer. "You won't believe what's going on. While Vosberg's in his cell staring at the wall, thousands of people are flocking to the scene of the crime. It's become a ghoulish tourist attraction."

"Forget the villa," I said. "What's going on with you? Broke down and bought yourself a new suit?"

And then I understood. The pretty young copyreader was sitting beside Ramsey, looking at him with adoring eyes while drinking a glass of milk.

"Gee whiz," said the young girl, whose name was Gladys. "Why would they want to go to such a gruesome place? And who's Bluebeard? I keep hearing his name."

"Listen to her, R.B. Boy, it would be nice to be that naïve again."

"Who's Bluebeard, Miss Manon?" she asked again.

"Please just call me R.B. Everyone else does."

"Oh, no, Miss Manon, I couldn't. You're old enough to be my mother and from where I come from, that's considered downright impolite."

My heart fell to the basement. I was only thirty-two, for heaven's sake. Gladys's remarks weren't just a stab at my pride—they were sobering. I tried to ignore her. So did Ramsey. Gladys looked perplexed. She was simply waiting for me to tell her the answers.

"Bluebeard's real name," I said, "was Henri Landau. The press nicknamed him Bluebeard because of *The Legend of Bluebeard* by Perrault."

"Did he really have a blue beard?" Gladys asked.

"No," I said. "Actually it was very thick and very red. I'm surprised you've never heard this story. In 1919, it was a big deal in the news."

"Well, golly Moses," Gladys said, "in 1919, I was only four years old!"

* * *

I knew it was coming, but didn't expect it so soon. Madame Pleven, the concierge, handed me a cablegram. ROSIE PLEASE ACCOMPANY STELLA TO CHERBOURG STOP CUNARD WHITE STAR BERENGARIA STOP SAILS DECEMBER 21 STOP CLARA.

Hell, I thought, that's tomorrow. I went to the cable office on the boulevard des Capucines. YES STOP LOVE STOP ROSIE.

The next morning, I called Ramsey from the café and told him that I was ill and staying in bed.

I went to the morgue.

When I had seen Stella in Brooklyn, I had thought her too dramatic and talkative. She was charmingly petite and had flitted around like a bird. But I had liked her curiosity and appreciated all the questions she had asked about moving to Paris, although at moments I did grow weary of her intensity. She had wanted to see everything, go everywhere; live in London, live in Rome. Now she was going home forever.

Stella was in a plain pine coffin. There were no formalities. She was waiting on the loading dock. Her name was handwritten on a torn scrap of brown paper and taped to the side. I drove to Cherbourg in the cab of a transport truck and could hear Stella's coffin rattling in the back. When we arrived, the truck turned and backed up to the edge of the quay. Six men, rather than the eight needed for Andy, lifted her coffin and began to move up the ramp. I walked alongside as she was carefully stowed into the hold. All the ship's longshoremen had stopped what they were doing and stood silently, holding their caps across their chests. They waited until I turned around and walked down the plank.

By the time I arrived back in Paris, the weather had turned dismal and my mood matched it. I spent Christmas alone and then refused to join my colleagues for their annual twenty-four-hour drunken New Year's Eve celebration. I mourned both Stella and Andy.

On New Year's Eve, Mr. Hin came to my room with a bottle of wine and a book of his poems. As soon as we turned on Radio Paris, we heard the announcement that a decree had been issued by the Reich: Jews were now purged from the German economy.

"It's getting worse and worse, Mr. Hin," I said. "How can one celebrate at a time like this? All I see happening in the new year is war."

"This is true, Rosie. But let's try to be happy tonight. Now here's a toast: *"Vive la France, et ses pommes de terre frites!"* Long live France and her fried potatoes!

And I replied: *"Vive l'Amerique et le chauffage central!"* Long live America and central heating! And we laughed.

"Now," Mr. Hin said, "I will read you a few poems that were written in a better time—we will drink some more wine—and then we'll listen to a special broadcast: Sibelius conducting his own composition, *Andante Festivo,* on the BBC."

On January 2, I returned to the newsroom. "I've just got word," Ramsey said, "that Aurora Sand, the granddaughter of the novelist George Sand, is a graphologist. She's been asked by the court to examine Vosberg's handwriting. And, this is a quote, 'to see if she can find clues to his nature.' You need to interview her."

I made an appointment with Madame Sand for the next afternoon. I have to admit that I was nervous, feeling as if I were walking into sacrosanct territory. George Sand was a literary heroine of mine. I'd read most of her books, both in French and the translations into English.

The only person I've ever known who has read *La Petite Fadette* by George Sand was Mr. Hin. We used to laugh about how sentimental we both were—convinced that this was why we were such good friends. *Fadette* is an obscure novel that still makes me teary when I read it, after seventy years. Primarily, the tale is about found, lost, and found-again love. Reminding me of Leon, losing Leon, and finding him again. I remembered reading it that New Year's Day in 1938.

Madame Aurora Lauth-Sand was seventy-three years old and still a beauty. She was far more fragile than her mother and grandmother. And unlike her female relatives, she had features that were graceful, rather than coarse. A practicing graphologist for many years, she was hired by the investigating magistrate.

"Come, sit beside me, dear, and have some of this lovely rose tea."

Everything about her was so delicate that I felt like a gorilla. I kept saying, "Excuse me," for I persisted in bumping into Madame Sand's arm, or her silk-covered leg, or the Chinese-red and gold tasseled damask pillow she was hugging. I finally folded my hands on my lap to keep from fidgeting.

"So, Madame," I asked, "can you tell me what you think about Vosberg's handwriting?"

"Oh, no, my dear, it's too early. It wouldn't be right."

"Well," I said, "I do understand a tiny bit about handwriting and I've seen two of his letters."

"Then we are equal," she said, smiling slyly. "What do you deduce?"

"I have to admit," I said, "that last night, before I came to see you, I went to the library. I tried to read Michon's *Système de graphologie*—so I have a thin understanding of what you do. I do remember that he said, 'Show me a "t" crossed by the pen of a man and I'll tell you the intimate nature of his soul.'"

Madame Sand grinned. "And what else do you remember?"

"It was hard going, reading a technical book in French," I said, "but I do remember more about the 't's. The writer said that people who don't cross their 't's are without will. People who are indecisive bring the line only halfway up to the vertical mark. And people with strong opinions cross their 't's with a flourish. And the last one I remember is that dictatorial-type people cross their 't's above the vertical line. Michon wrote that women cross their 't's delicately, with barely a whisper— and I don't at all agree with that. My mother crosses her 't's in the middle with a flourish!"

"Your mother sounds interesting," Madame Sand said. "I would like to meet her."

"No," I replied, "it's best that she remain in America."

Madame Sand laughed. "She sounds like my grandmother!"

Dear Rosie: Poor Stella. It's hard to believe it's over. After services at the synagogue, we walked to the West End Funeral Chapel for her funeral. I wish you could have been here—it was a beautiful service. Please come home. I don't want to lose another beloved relative. Love, Clara

"There's nothing more for you to do in Paris," Ramsey said. "It'll be about a year before the trial begins. You've been reassigned to Berlin."

"You know I don't want to cover the trial," I said. "You'll have to assign someone else."

"We'll see," Ramsey said. "Never can tell. Maybe the Nazis will have captured Paris by then, and Vosberg, our 'handsome devil,' as people are calling him, will have become a general!"

As I promised the consul, Clancy, I took my valise to the American Embassy to be altered. The night before I left, Miss Kovner at the embassy returned it to me. Someone had discreetly changed the lining to be able to hide papers. I tried to find the secret to the hiding place, but the only way I could see my way in was to tear the lining. I left it alone.

* * *

I returned to Berlin and was as nervous as the clattering train wheels. The dismal weather fit my disposition. It took almost three days to make the normally twelve-hour journey to the German border. The train moved at such a slow pace that I was often tempted to get off and walk beside it. We finally reached the German passport *Kontrolle,* where I nervously showed all my papers and was cleared. Once we crossed the frontier into Germany, the train was even slower. We passed many deserted, yet floodlit, railroad platforms. But when we stopped at the bigger stations, a swarm of threatening Gestapo would board and harshly demand everyone's travel documents. I remember the smell of their damp wool tunics. They moved like automatons, reminding me of wind-up tin soldiers, although far more menacing. At every stop they found one or two passengers who were suspicious and dragged them off the train. I'll never forget the smell of fear that invaded the air.

Then on the stretch between Hanover and Berlin, the train was detoured and halted at a siding. Everything was turned off. It was dark and cold, and I was grateful for my fur coat. An official came through the cars and ordered us to pull down our window shades. "It's an order," he barked, "from the *Kommandant.*"

I watched through a gap. In an enormous rock-strewn field, sheltered on three sides by hills, troops of the Reichswehr's infantry were training. Soldiers slithered on their bellies in the cold, wet, dark night toward a make-believe enemy. Then, as if in a movie, loudspeakers blared the sounds of war: cannons, machine guns, tank artillery, screams of men and horses. I knew it was theater, but I was scared. So much elaborate preparation for death, I thought. I spent the rest of the journey longing for both Leon and the open, free, blue skies of Nevada.

I'm still amazed that I had the courage to take my first "journey of resistance." I remember being much more frightened than I admitted in my notes. Even though I put on a tough face, my instincts were to head for the nearest exit to safety. Over those war years I was delegated to carry reams of confidential papers and a wide variety of verbal secrets between the two American embassies. I'm convinced that part of my good reputation as a newspaperwoman was due to my reliability. However, it cost me profound apprehension. Yes, I could be trusted. But no, I wasn't good at acting upon things that threatened my personal life.

Which reminds me of Andy Roth.

If I had gone for help on his behalf—if I had not been trustworthy and kept his secrets—maybe he would have lived a full life. After all, we were avid students of Freud, both of us interested in how, and why, we behaved the way we did. But I had thought that I understood Andy. What arrogance! It wasn't until years later that I could admit that I hardly understood him at all. Instead of us both drinking too much and wallowing in our misery, I should have insisted that he be hospitalized to dry out. Take a break from the booze. Perhaps speak to someone who could help him. I had not yet been disciplined by hardship, by grief. Now, of course, I would do it all differently.

Once I arrived in Berlin, I felt better. I was greeted by the sun—luminously reflecting on newly fallen snow—and fast-moving, billowing clouds. Although I had missed it that year, I liked being in Berlin at the beginning of winter. Birds, coming from the east, migrated through the city toward the west and south. The sky was almost dark with their flying bodies, and their sound in the crisp air was both melodic and out of tune.

The next day was the opposite. No sun. Soot covered the snow. Dreary.

I delivered the packet to Eva Kantor. I liked her. She was a straight shooter, even though she was from Atlanta and not the American West.

"Thanks for the papers," she said. "Please let me know the next time you leave Germany—there's always something that needs to go back to Paris. Did they search you?"

"No, they didn't—and to tell you the truth, most of the time I forgot I had them in my case."

She laughed. "It's most likely the reason you weren't searched. You didn't look guilty!"

I went to see a friend, Stefan Kluge, at his chosen office—a run-down bar on Prinz-Albrecht-Strasse. Stefan was a German reporter for the last liberal newspaper in Germany, the *Berliner Morgen-Zeitung*. He was often in trouble with the authorities for being a little too articulate about his views of the present government; he had chosen this bar on purpose. The Gestapo headquarters were across the street from where he sat. He could watch the comings and goings of officials, along with people being "brought" (dragged) in for "interrogation" (torture). He rarely saw them come out. With purposeful irony, he called it his *Kehlsteinhaus*, after Hitler's eagle's nest in the mountains of Berchtesgaden.

"Here," he said, "is the spot where I'll never forget the enemy. It keeps me alert for my work."

The "work," I knew, included Stefan being a member of one of the many small and isolated groups of German resistance, the *Widerstand*.

"Hey, R.B.," Stefan said. "When did you get back?"

"Just last night—what's going on in the city? It's so bleak."

"It's your gloomy frame of mind," Stefan said, and without missing a beat, added, "I heard that Leon threw you out."

I felt myself turning red with embarrassment. "I don't look at it that way," I said, "but I don't want to argue. Listen, I'm here to ask you for help. I just went to his apartment, but a Nazi officer opened the door and began to question me. I pretended not to understand German. Do you know where he is?"

"He's gone, R.B. The Nazis got him cornered."

"Oh, no!"

"No, I don't mean that they put him in a camp or killed him—at least not yet. They're letting him stay in his apartment, but since you left, it's guarded around the clock."

"Why?"

"Because they've added gold to his repertoire. You won't be able to visit him there any longer. You know he's engraving—"

"I know what he's engraving," I said. "I saw it with my own eyes."

"But," Stefan said, "he's allowed out with permission—you can see him. That is, if he wants. We get together occasionally for a drink."

"Will you ask him, Stefan? Will you tell him that I'll do anything, that I—"

"Take it easy, R.B. Of course, I'll get a message to him."

"How?"

"Stop by here tomorrow evening about seven—perhaps I'll have some news."

The next day, two hateful press conferences, back to back, kept me occupied. Nothing had changed. The same warmongering by the officials—the same threats to non-Aryans. Now, more than ever, I knew there would be war. And I was terrified that the Germans could win. They were well organized with their sophisticated military equipment, while the French were still using horses and cannons. And the Germans were so smug in their convictions that I felt feeble in my rage.

It was raining, and I didn't have an umbrella. I ran from the trolley to Stefan's bar. Dripping wet, I burst in, but didn't see Stefan. I felt my heart drop.

"Hi, Rosie," I heard, and swung around.

"Leon," I said, and threw my wet arms around him. We both laughed.

"Sorry I was so abrupt, so rigid," he said. "This fear is crushing, and—and—" and he shrugged.

Leon looked worn down, almost shabby. His raincoat was draped over the back of his chair and I could see the frayed collar and cuffs. He was wearing a black sweater that looked too large for him; he had lost weight.

"Your hair!" His hair was almost white.

"Going gray overnight's quite the style here," he said. "It's a badge of honor."

The lack of hair color exaggerated the deep, almost purplish, half-moons under his eyes. But his eyes were still filled with intensity. In one way, he was more handsome than ever. In another, his face echoed the anguish of Europe.

"But, you," he said. "You look beautiful—"

"Oh, sure. Since when!"

"You're still a very silly woman," he said, "even though you're so smart."

"Thank you, Leon. But are you all right? You look like you've lost weight. How are your parents?"

"Slow down, Rosie. Let's sit. Look," he said, "you've a very good idea of what's going on. Except that while you were in Paris, the laws have gotten even more severe. The abuse gets more violent and widespread with every passing day. I can't move—I'm a prisoner in my own home. The Reich is using me to get its fancy engraving work done. And as long as I continue to do its bidding, it has agreed to leave my parents alone. You see, Rosie, the enemy needs me—and, perversely, I need them. If I stop, we'll all be sent to a concentration camp. If I escape, my parents will be sent to a concentration camp. It's horrifying. We can't win."

"Are your parents safe?"

"They, like all their Jewish friends who used to live in the fashionable neighborhoods of Berlin, have been forced to 'migrate.'" Leon laughed with scorn. "They've been 'relocated' to the neighborhoods around Linienstrasse and Grenadierstrasse where working-class Jews live. My poor parents. They were once esteemed academics; now they're jammed into an apartment with three other elderly couples. They sleep on the floor. They share a bathroom. There's no hot water."

"But why don't they live with you?"

"Think, Rosie. The Nazis won't let this happen. They're afraid their precious silver and gold will go missing. We have to get out of here, but I can't get my parents to make a decision. They simply don't believe that such evil can continue. I'm approaching old friends and colleagues, and have some plans. But everything takes time. So I steal minuscule flecks of gold and silver tailings, slowly accumulating some valuable metal. But I've a long way to go. The official who oversees my apartment counts every damn dram, every speck of metal. If only my parents had escaped when I arranged it two years ago, we'd all be in Switzerland. But I keep reminding myself that I'm fortunate."

"I don't understand," I said. "How you can consider yourself fortunate? It sounds terrible!"

"Well, because my parents refused to leave, I now have you in my life. And then, if it hadn't been for an old friend, we would all be in trouble. Because of him, we're still here in Berlin and not on a train to some godforsaken camp. It's a strange situation—I'm indebted to him, but I'm stuck, too. If

I do anything wrong, he'll be arrested. And I've known his three children since they were born—I was even a guest at their christenings. You see," he went on, placing his hand on my arm and leaning forward, "he was my friend and classmate in art school. Now he's a Nazi official, and he has put himself in great jeopardy to help me. I know it sounds bizarre, but it's the truth, and—"

"It doesn't make sense," I said.

"He's a friend, Rosie, and a wonderful artist—far more talented than I am. But I agree with you. I don't understand why he became a card-carrying Nazi. They must have something on him—while at the same time they need his artistic expertise. Occasionally, he asks me for help with the propaganda posters he's illustrating. He does the sketch—I do the inking—and then he lays down the colors. It is so confusing, but without him— well—"

"So you still see him?"

"Of course, almost every day. He lives down the hall. He's my boss. His name's Gerard. No, I won't tell you his last name," he said, reading my mind. "It's too dangerous for you to know. If they ever traced anything back to you, you'd be arrested. You have to understand that he's the one person keeping my family from being rounded up and sent away."

"Oh, my dear, my dear," I said. "What a terrible world this is. But I could help you, and—"

"No, no, you still don't understand," he said, sounding exasperated. "You're almost as much at risk as I am. Everyone knows you're Jewish. Your managing editor—what's his name?"

"Ramsey."

"Yes, Ramsey. I've heard from Stefan that he's convinced you're running away from your Orthodox family in New York."

I had to laugh at the absurdity. "He's always suspected I'm Jewish. Now he knows I am. Anyway, I assume that he would be happy to axe me."

"Perhaps in the flesh, because you're such a troublemaker! What my grandmother used to call a *honeypessle*." Leon laughed.

"Oh." I was delighted. "My Aunt Clara used to call me that too! Do you know what it means?"

"Not really," he said, "although it was always a form of endearment. I suspect it means a 'little pest.'"

And we both laughed.

"But back to the real world," Leon said. "You're an excellent journalist, Rosie, already familiar with the ways of the regime. Your paper needs you. And don't forget, from what I gather—Ramsey rides high on your reputation."

"Yes, maybe. But he's such a bastard. I hate working with him."

"No one seems to have choices any longer," Leon said. "Not even you Americans. And I'm sorry to hear about your cousin. Stefan told me that they found Stella's body and arrested a man."

"Yes, and I sent her home to the family in New York. There's been so much death, Leon. So much."

Oh, how I can still feel my body leaning toward him, my lips almost touching his, whispering, "But I won't lose you again, Leon. I can't bear the thought."

We walked through the rain to my room. We were soaked.

"I'm nervous. I feel that this is our first real time together," I said.

Leon came behind me and unclasped the barrette that was keeping back my hair.

He smiled, and while looking at me, holding on to a chair, he took off his wet shoes and socks.

While I, not taking my eyes off Leon's face, removed my wet shoes and stockings.

He took off his soaking jacket and shirt and started to chuckle.

I took off my raincoat.

He took off his trousers.

I took off my black sweater and slacks and started to giggle.

Leon took off his underwear and made a wry face.

I took off my underwear and tried to look very serious.

We stood in the jumble of our discarded clothes and looked at each other.

"This is the first time," Leon said, still not touching me, "that I've looked at you in all your glory. You're beautiful."

"And this," I whispered, "is the first time I've seen you so tenderly exposed."

And, as if we were hearing the same music, we moved together in a sensual dance of love.

I'm not going to describe further the intimacy of our private time together. I may be called old fashioned—but I would rather use my imagination to create the act of sex than have it described to me in blatant Technicolor and heard in stereophonic sound. Imagining is far more stimulating, even to an old lady like me!

But I can say that I've never forgotten that night. It was at that moment that I understood love. Deep love. Passionate love. Lasting love.

Later: "But I have to explain about being in Paris," he said.

"No, no. You don't."

"Just listen, Rosie. Please. Gerard is responsible for me and the other forgers and etchers—"

"I didn't know you could forge," I said, and Leon looked at me strangely.

"Does that make a difference?" he challenged.

"No, of course not," I said, "except that you've instantly become a prized possession!"

"Well, anyway," he said laughing, "Gerard decided to spy on his wife."

"Do you know her?"

"No. He's just remarried. His first wife was also with us at school. She was my girlfriend, first. But soon it became obvious that they were interested in each other. We were young, romantic—everything was tragic. I thought my heart would break. But Gerard was sensitive to my feelings and has always looked out for me. They had both made their living by illustrating for magazines and books. She died after the birth of their third child, about four years ago. This new wife lives not far from Berlin in the countryside with his mother and the children. One way or another, he became convinced that his current wife was having an affair with one of the German trade representatives to the American Embassy in Paris. This man had been a classmate of hers. Gerard came up with a plan. Ostensibly, he was sending her to Paris to buy unadorned silver plates and trays for his artisans to work on. Through a labyrinth of connections, she was to meet someone at the American Embassy who would direct her to a reliable retailer— meaning someone who was willing to sell to the Germans and not register the sale."

"But that doesn't make sense," I said. "What's wrong with the French bureaucracy having this information?"

"Nothing!" Leon said. "It's just that he's paranoid—convinced that some authority or another's watching him. He instructed me to forge two invitations to the Christmas party— one for his wife and one for me. I refused. He got nasty. The next day he had two of the most ominous-looking, black-leather-clad Gestapo goons pick up my parents and take them to their headquarters on Prinz-Albrecht-Strasse. Right where we met earlier today. He made me watch from the corner as they were dragged in, already handcuffed, without even a suitcase between them. 'Do what I say,' he ordered, 'or your parents will go away forever. I'm sorry, Leon. I really am.' The threat was clear and I knew he would carry it out. He released my parents an hour after I began the work."

"But why didn't you contact me?"

"No, it was too risky. There was no way that I was going to jeopardize my parents' safety. Can you understand that?"

Yes, I could.

"So I watched that stupid woman make a fool of herself in front of the embassy's guests. It was amazing. I don't know if you saw her, but she was tall and insisted on wearing her fur coat, even though it was boiling inside. And she had too much to drink, spoke atrocious French, and was flirting with anyone who would pay attention to her. I followed her for three days and got back on the train for Berlin when she did. She wasn't fooling around, thank goodness. I would have hated having to report her. Actually, I wouldn't have reported her, even if she was seeing someone, but I knew Gerard would read the truth in my face unless I were absolutely certain. Thank God, I was."

"Have you ever made fake passports?" I asked.

Leon was silent.

"Okay, okay," I said, "I get it. But I need to ask another question. Is it dangerous for you if Gerard finds out that we're friends?"

"Yes, it's dangerous, but he already knows. That's why not one bit of information can go beyond this room. I have to be sure that nothing's traced to you. I'm aware that I provide a valuable service for him, and it behooves both Gerard and me to keep the status quo."

Now I can see that there were many sides of Leon I didn't understand. A part of him was cloaked, hidden from me—protecting himself. I know this is natural during overwhelming anxiety, but I wish I had been more sympathetic, more considerate.

But in 1939, my life in Berlin did begin anew. Even though the prognosis for peace was grim, my relationship with Leon was filled with light. My writing changed, too. I didn't stab my words onto the page with such anger—I tried to find promise in the continuing talks that were being held between governments. Ramsey thought I was getting soft. I didn't care. I wanted my dispatches to be written with both hardcore honesty and a glimmer of hope. My style of writing became easy to identify. I had unconsciously figured out how to write like a man without losing the heart of a woman.

Along with covering politics in Germany, I was writing my column, "Berlin Journal." Every few days I would search for material by exploring different neighborhoods of the city. I tried to find some promise of a better future. Each time I returned to the pressroom and to my typewriter, I was filled with depression, heavy with foreboding; rarely did I find an encouraging story. But I kept trying. One nice day I took two trams to get to Friedrichshain, an area built for the working class—now an unofficial ghetto for Jews who had been forced from their homes. I was stunned. Makeshift tables had been set up on the sidewalks. On these tables lay everything from used shoes to musical instruments to elegant china and silver to piles of old newspapers. I understood without asking. The vendors were selling their possessions, trying to collect enough money to emigrate. It was eerily quiet. The government had purposefully isolated them—no trams, no automobiles. People spoke in soft voices.

The population was being deliberately starved. The shop shelves echoed, empty. In comparison I lived like a queen and the guilt gnawed at me. And I had to ask myself how I, now a Jewish writer in Germany, could continue reporting on the Jewish condition. I knew I was taking a big chance. I could be sent home by the Gestapo or simply disappear into an SS building forever.

After the day spent in Friedrichshain, I began my column: *Human beings are being forced to sell their possessions for the dream of freedom.* I wired it to Paris. The next day I received a cable from Ramsey. *Cool it with your poor Jews. Nobody's interested.*

I needed to be alone with Leon, away from the overwhelming fear that encircled us. Leon's mood, I could see, matched mine.

"Let's get out of Berlin," I said. "We need a break."

"Wonderful idea," he said, "but not possible."

"Could you ask Gerard anyway?" I said. "Maybe he'll be so happy that his wife's not fooling around that he'll give you a break. God, it's as if you're in jail."

"Exactly—I am in jail! Listen, Rosie. May I remind you that we're not living in your democracy? You make me angry with your optimism!"

"It's not optimism," I said, "it's love. And I'm trying to understand. Really, I am."

"I'm sorry," he said. "I'm being mean to you. But you've got to understand that we're living in an enormous and sinister prison. Look around," he said, and he swept his arms toward the gray-sooted, locked windows in a bar—"this is the definition of fascism. This is what it means to lose one's freedom. I understand you're having a hard time getting used to it, but I suggest you open your eyes wider. And, yes, I'll try asking him."

We met a couple of days later. It was raining. When I got off the tram, I couldn't find Leon in a sea of black umbrellas. Then I spotted an umbrella that was popping up and down, looking as if it were trying to fly away. It was Leon. Laughing, he led us away from the crowd. "Be aware," he said, "I'm being followed."

"Why?"

"Why? It's simple. I requested permission to go away with

you. And Gerard has to make sure I don't leave Germany. The guard will follow me until we return from our holiday."

"So, permission was granted? How did you do it?"

"It wasn't so hard. All Gerard said was, 'Yes, for one night only. And remember—no return, no parents—and you'll be followed.'" Leon anticipated my next question. "My passport was confiscated a long time ago and he won't return it. But he'll arrange for a temporary travel pass. And no," he said, "I won't forge anything. I don't want to take any chances."

"But if you don't have a passport, then what's he worried about?"

"That I may betray him. That I may indeed have forged other passports for my parents and myself. That we may flee. He can't afford to trust me, and he can't afford *not* to trust me. He's putting himself in a precarious situation in allowing me this escapade. Yes, there's a part of Gerard that's still good— but I don't know how long this 'good' will last. The morals of even nice people are being corrupted, slowly but deliberately."

I continued to be stunned by the reality of our situation. And my surprise wasn't over yet.

"This next part is hard for me to say, Rosie. Please be patient."

He lit another cigarette. I watched his face.

First there was anger in Leon's eyes. Then, as if he had erased his feelings, he said, "Okay, here it is. You're going to have to pay for our holiday. I have no money of my own."

I didn't know what to say. I knew this deeply hurt his pride. "Of course I will," I said. "It's not a problem."

I couldn't believe the pressure Leon was under. He looked worn out and I was afraid that I was contributing to the fatigue. But I was also infuriated. "That bastard Gerard. I'd love to punch him in the face for doing this to you."

"Oh, come on, Rosie, act like a grown-up. Isn't there enough violence without your adding to it? Now, may I make a suggestion? There's a seaside town called Sonnenshein on the Baltic where I used to go as a child. Let's go there. It'll be freezing cold, maybe stormy, but we can dress warmly and walk along the seashore."

I could see color flooding his cheeks and knew it didn't matter where we went—as long as we could change the gloomy landscape.

We waited for the train at Stettiner Bahnhof. "Why are so many people sitting in the station's café?" I asked. "I've never noticed this before. No one has any luggage."

"Train station cafés," he said, and paused and looked around, "have become, for the moment, the only safe public places left for Jews to visit friends. We can't go to our own cafés because they've been closed, nor are we allowed to sit in an Aryan one. And even this meeting place won't be allowed much longer, I can assure you."

I sat closer to him, lit a cigarette, and waited without saying another word. The train arrived. It was only four cars long. "This little train," I said, "makes me feel that we're going where no one else wants to go. I like this."

Leon smiled. "Or no one can afford to buy train tickets to a seaside town."

We were alone in the compartment. There was a melancholy mood around us. Our guard, whom we had nicknamed the Shadow, was across the aisle in another compartment. He had a long thin face with vertical folds that made him look as if he had once been much heavier. Dressed in a cheap brown suit, he also wore a black overcoat and a tan fedora that was too big and came down over his ears. I smiled at him, but he glared back at me.

The train slowly left the station.

"Here," Leon said, taking a flask of whiskey out of his pocket. "Have a sip, Rosie—it'll help." Just then the door slid open, startling us.

"Tickets and travel documents," the ticket collector, wearing a tan armband with a stitched black swastika, demanded. We handed him our papers. He looked at Leon. He looked at me.

"Jews?" he said, and turned to leave without opening the documents.

"Wait!" I said. "You can't take our papers."

"He'll bring them right back," Leon whispered. "It's protocol."

Now, rather than being angry, I was scared.

"I think we'll be fine," he said. "They're trying to frighten us. It's their classic harassment. Our papers are in order—I made sure. Try to relax. It's no use making a scene. Actually, it's dangerous."

"I know," I said. "I've been routinely stopped to show my papers. But this is the first time I've been identified as a Jew. It feels odd." And Leon took my hand tightly in his.

Within a few minutes the ticket collector returned, handed back our papers without comment, and walked out. It took the next hundred and sixty miles for me to get hold of myself. The incident reminded me of when I was a girl, but at least then I could fight back with words. Now I was gagged.

KEINE JUDEN ERLAUBT! No Jews allowed, was posted in the hotel's window.

"Wait here," Leon said. So the Shadow and I leaned against the same fence. In a few minutes he returned with a smile on his face. "Come on, you two, it's all right. The proprietors remember my family, and they've offered our friend here one of their nicest rooms."

"But we can't go into a place that's illegal," I said. "Or can we?"

"Yes, it's fine. Because we have a guard, it means that the Reich has authorized our visit. They're nice people and embarrassed to put me in this position. By the way," he said, lowering his voice, "I told them we're married."

Our room was on the second floor and the guard had been placed at the other end of the hall. We were close to the sea. I found the sound of the waves crashing against the seawall thunderous and upsetting. "You'll get used to it," Leon said. "Anyway, it'll give us some privacy from the Shadow." We quickly washed up and went to dinner.

The dining room was three floors above ours. It was run-down and smelled seaside-musty, but it was clean. The view of the water was spectacular—and although it was a stormy sea, it was considerably quieter than in our room. The light reflected off the whitecaps of the towering, gusting waves. Every few minutes it felt as if the raging water would surge over the seawall and flood the downstairs.

The only other people in the room were the proprietor, who was pleasantly friendly, his wife, who was cheerfully cooking and singing, and our guard, who sat on the opposite side of the room, glumly tucked into a corner.

"Quite a night, isn't it," said the proprietor.

"Have you ever been flooded?" I asked.

"Rarely, Madame, but this we risk for the love of our hotel."

And he showed us a bottle of red wine.

"Madame," he whispered with a bow, "this is a wedding gift for you and your husband—and for the memory of better times."

"It's French wine!" I whispered back. "What a wonderful treat. Thank you."

"It will help to warm you," the proprietor said. "There's no coal, so no heat. We put extra eiderdowns on your bed. I hope you enjoy your dinner," he said, and he served our wine as if we were at the Ritz.

Next, he poured a large glass of whiskey for our Shadow—which was quickly accepted, and just as quickly downed.

There were no choices for our meal. We were served a fish stew with turnips and potatoes, along with freshly baked bread. The stew was plain and I kept adding salt and pepper; the bread was filling, and we finished the delicious bottle of wine.

After dinner, we excused ourselves. The Shadow was drunk. "Don't worry," the proprietor said, "I'll take care of him."

When we opened the door to our room, we had to laugh. Piled high, like a bed in a fairy tale, were numerous colorful eiderdowns. We hurriedly undressed and slithered in.

"Ah," Leon said, "a little elf has been here and brought us heated bricks and two hot-water bottles."

It was a different world under the weight of the blankets. We moved toward each other, as people will do when they're feeling safe—when they're no longer weighted down with troubles. Slowly. Caressing in slow motion—not pulling apart, for fear of a cold draft or reality striking the skin—we made love to the sound of the sea.

The next morning we took a walk along the edge of the water. Our poor Shadow. He was wearing dress shoes that looked worn out.

"I can't really enjoy this," I said. "That poor man must be freezing. Let's go back." And we reluctantly turned around.

In the afternoon, we boarded the train in Sonnenshein to return to Berlin. The ticket taker insisted that our guard share the compartment with us. I have to admit that I had become immune to his presence—and although we never spoke, there was a certain comfort in his being with us. Somewhere in my head I had presumed that he was our pass to safety. The ticket collector entered our compartment. This time I wasn't upset. I was so in love, so awed by the turn that my life had taken.

"Pay attention, Rosie," Leon said sternly.

"Off the train! Off!" the ticket collector yelled at us. "You're Jews. You're contaminating my train!"

At first, I was stunned.

"What in the hell do you mean?" I demanded, after finding my voice. "We're legal. We have the correct papers. I want to speak to your superior. Now!"

Events moved quickly. Four men dressed in black, leather-belted coats, high black boots, and black fedoras (without insignias) appeared out of nowhere and gripped us under our arms. We were literally lifted off the train. The more I fought, the more passive Leon became.

I felt both embarrassment and rage. When I looked up for help from Leon, I could see from the look on his face that he was somewhere else and I was no longer in his thoughts.

Passengers were yelling at the officials to get moving. This made me more furious—almost hysterical.

Then I glimpsed, out of the corner of my eye, the Shadow speaking to an official.

Within minutes we were released and allowed to reboard the train. Our guard sat back down across from us. "Thank you," I said. He gave a slight nod and looked out the window.

I felt so alone, even though I was sitting beside Leon. The scenery sped by, and I didn't comment on it. I tried not to cry. Leon was impassive.

We arrived at Berlin in silence. The weekend had been spoiled. How could I have been so stupid?

The guard, without a word, left the train and blended into the crowd.

We followed.

Leon almost commanded, "Let's sit here on the bench." I watched him as he sat. He reminded me of a frightened snail.

"Let's go to a café," I said. "I'm freezing."

"You just don't understand, do you, Rosie? We can't go to any café. Dammit, pay attention to me! Don't you understand that if I'd been arrested, my family would be jeopardized? That every-thing I do reflects back upon my parents? You move through the world with impunity. I can't afford the luxury. You keep forgetting that I'm not a newspaper story. Look at me, Rosie," he said, grabbing my arm. "I'm real flesh and bones, easily bruised. And like this," he said, and he snapped his fingers, "I'm gone."

"But—" I tried to protect myself from his anger.

"No 'buts,'" he said. "I've lived in a state of anxiety most of my life. My parents have always had their heads in the clouds. I saw this coming long ago, but I never expected it to be so bad. I'm rooted here. That's why the enemy succeeds—they understand this. You don't really understand the situation. You can simply get on a train and cross the border whenever you want. I can't move. I'm trapped. Every non-Aryan is trapped. You can scream and yell and carry on. I can't."

By now Leon's teeth were clenched and he was fiercely whispering. "I must be meek and mindful—and obedient. And this makes me roil with rage—and believe it or not, you bring it out in me. So, Rosie, what are we going to do about this?"

What I did was to cover myself in a skin that was hard on one side and soft on the other. The outside showed a tough and worldly reporter. The other side, I saved especially for Leon. It was challenging to keep my opinions and anger to myself, but I tried—and he understood that I was trying.

Today, as I'm sitting in my glorious garden, with the scent of lavender gliding by, I can say that it was Leon who taught me about love. I've never forgotten what I learned. And I believe that's why I've never been able to banish him from my heart. Going through these notes brings out old feelings of longing for him. Am I still in love with Leon, or with the Leon that I created and who now lives in my imagination? There's no language for what I'm feeling at the moment. I'm stymied. I should pull some weeds.

After we returned to Berlin, things began to change for me. My political reporting was being lauded. *Agence France-Presse* and other newspapers were running my columns on a news service contract, and I was placing human-interest stories with the BBC. I finally felt that I had the credibility to write more-detailed and serious feature stories, even as they were becoming more risky to publish.

But I didn't show the stories to Leon. I didn't want to compromise him more than my mere presence already did.

My stories went deeper. They were despondent—profoundly sad. Rarely was there humor. Everyone felt displaced, either physically or emotionally.

"The world as we have known it is gone," Pete warned me over a drink at the press club. "You've got to be careful with these stories. No names. No identifiable buildings. Everyone must be anonymous. Barging into a café, a Jewish-owned store, a synagogue, is plain stupid. You've got to be more clever; otherwise, not only will you be punished, but those good people who are giving you interviews will too. Speak more quietly and carefully, R.B. Everyone's being watched."

I learned to whisper.

But I felt an obligation to write meticulously the stories of the oppressed—feeling as if I were a truth-teller, a crusader for those deprived of their freedom. Soon, there were quiet warnings from the German government to the *Paris Courier*, *Agence France-Presse*, and the American Embassy about my reports. Ramsey and the higher-ups in the New York office were getting nervous.

"You're in the hot seat," Ramsey cabled me. "Don't know how much more of this you can get away with."

The hell with Ramsey. I was no longer concerned with what he thought about me.

I noticed a sinister difference in Berlin. Most Germans now

assumed that it was their duty to inform the authorities of any suspicious behavior—within their families, by their neighbors. They listened for people on the street to say the wrong words. Anybody questioning the regime was taking a chance: embassy people, even foreign correspondents. And the *Abwehr*, undercover agents, infiltrated every part of the city. Everyone was spying on everyone else. It had become fashionable to disdain foreigners. Unless you were blond and blue-eyed, it was best to keep a low profile. This was impossible for me to do. My colleague Pete, echoing Leon, was forever warning me to be careful. Denunciation had become respectable.

It's too quiet outside. I've moved to my office and turned on the radio to the classical music station. I'm sitting at my desk in one of those newfangled office chairs that are supposed to be good for your back. The only problem is that I've lost so many inches in height that I've had to add a thick pillow under me so I can reach the desk and write comfortably. But my feet won't reach the floor—hence, a sawed-off piece of tree trunk is my footstool.

I need to stop sorting these papers for a while. I want a break from my past. I'll work on my column. I'll write something funny. I wish the pages that I write on could laugh with me— it would make me feel that I wasn't alone. I still write my rough drafts by hand. My handwriting has become squiggly. It's funny to look at, and even funnier to try to decipher. But now there's no one to laugh at my remarks. When I was younger, and still worked in the newsroom in the city, I would often look up and say, "Hey, listen to this." Inevitably, someone would reply, "Yeah, R.B., tell us!" And I would. No more. No one wants an old person sitting beside him or her in an active office that is most likely staffed by young men and women. We remind them of having to watch their manners, their use of bad language. I really don't care about bad manners, or bad language, but I can sense the young people's discomfort with me. The reason they don't want to be around old people is that we remind them of death.

But all those years ago, I couldn't leave the human-interest stories alone. I continued to look at the perilous situation of the disenfranchised. This group grew daily—Romani, Jews, homosexuals, the disabled, Catholics, clergymen, nonconformists, communists. Even mixed-race children were considered enemies of the state. These children were the offspring of the black African colonial soldiers of the French army from the Great War who had married German women. There were also a number of black American musicians who, fed up with Jim Crow, had immigrated to Germany in the twenties. Many had married German citizens. Hitler called their children "Rhineland bastards."

For the past few years, I had been friends with a man named Richard Moses, a black American jazz saxophonist. Richard had been born and raised in Harlem, but had moved in 1926 to Berlin where avant-garde music was popular. "I liked the mixture of cultures," he told me. "Mulatto chorus girls from Cuba; Senegalese waiters, with their singsong French and mystifying Wolof; White Russians standing outside bars encouraging people with their funny German accents to come in and enjoy the earthly delights. It was a cool time."

Berlin in the twenties offered him a freedom that he had never experienced in America. People took his music seriously. He ignored the Nazi threat. Then in the 1930 elections, Nazis were chosen by the people to represent them.

By then Richard had married a German woman, Daria Möhring, and lived in Charlottenburg at Savignyplatz. They had two children: Coleman Hawkins Moses, named after the great saxophone player, and Annelie Edith Moses, looking like a little bird when she was born—like Edith Piaf. There was always music in their house: practicing the sax, playing the piano, singing.

"At first," Richard once told me, "there were no racial epithets shouted toward the stage. Or perhaps it was because it took me such a long time to learn German that I didn't understand what was being said from the audience. Hey Rosie," he said, "being naïve gave me my freedom—for a while. Then, as time went on, my German became more proficient and Hitler's ideas became more pervasive. The shouts from the audience became menacing, and I began to dread going to work."

When Leon and I returned from our night by the sea, there was a message from Richard asking me to visit. "It's important," he wrote. Saturday afternoon, I took the noisy, elevated S-Bahn to Richard's neighborhood. I walked for a few minutes before arriving at an enormous block of apartments that had been built in the nineteenth century for the middle class. On either side of the massive wooden carriage doors were two large chestnut trees, now barren of leaves, but still impressive. Inside was the courtyard, and I could swear that I still smelled horses. Going to my left, I entered the ground floor and saw the warning VORSICHT! FRISCH GEBOHNERT. ATTENTION! FRESHLY POLISHED. A lesson in fascist duplicity, I thought. This warning was in every apartment house in Berlin, even if the floors were filthy. I rode the creaking iron cage up to the fifth floor.

Richard opened the door. Since I had last visited the apartment, it had been reduced from four rooms to one. According to an official decree, the occupants had to make rooms available to Jews, who had been forced from their homes to make more comfortable housing for the Nazis' higher echelon. The Moseses' room was immaculate, but showed few signs of warmth. It had been stripped bare of its most comforting items; the blue-and-white ceramic coal stove was still there, but it was obviously not working. There was a gas two-burner stove, two chrome lamps casting a faint, ugly blue light around the room, and four unmatched wooden chairs. The piano was gone.

"It's cold in here," I grumbled.

"No more coal," Daria said, "except what I carry back from the embassy, which gets us through the evening. And, as you can feel, it's not enough." I noticed that they were all wearing their coats.

"Sorry," I said. "That was rude." And they didn't bother to say I was forgiven.

Coleman was now ten, and his little sister Annelie was eight. When I visited in the past, they had been rambunctious and excited about absolutely everything. Now they sat quietly, politely, on their rolled-up mattresses, their little legs not even touching the ground. I sat next to Coleman and smiled at him. There was no response. Their mother hovered, speaking softly to the children, encouraging them to speak to me. Daria was a tiny woman with a pretty, simple face framed by bobbed blond hair. She taught German to the children of the American and British diplomatic services assigned to Berlin. It had been amusing to see Daria standing next to her husband—she was so short and he was so tall. But now, no one was smiling.

I kissed Richard and went to embrace Daria, but she stood aside and shook her head. "Please don't, Rose. If you do, I'll break in two."

As was traditional, I had brought a bottle of schnapps for the adults and chocolate for the children. But this evening, no one seemed interested in eating or drinking. The adults sat on three mismatched chairs. "Where's the table?" I asked, and Richard pointed to the corner of the room, where pieces of the table were neatly stacked.

"We use it to get the coal started," Richard said, shrugging his shoulders.

For the first time that I could remember, I felt strange in

their home. The children were so quiet. Richard kept looking quizzically at Daria, and once I caught her shaking her head no.

I blurted, "Look here, you two. What's going on? Do you want me to leave?"

"No, of course not," Richard said. "C'mon, let's go for a walk and have a drink."

He and I left and silently walked down the street until we reached Savignyplatz. At the corner were two identical bronze statues of little boys facing each other, each pulling a reluctant goat.

"Coleman and I watched these two sculptures being installed in '31," Richard said. "It was funny because he asked me why there were two. 'I don't know,' I said, 'what do you think?' 'It's in case one little boy dies and his sad parents will have another.'"

"Something's happened, Richard," I said, taking his arm. "What's going on?"

"We can't talk here," he said. "It's too cold. Let's get a drink."

We walked to Grolmannstrasse, where there were a number of bars. "This one stays open late," Richard said, and we entered the dark, somewhat dank establishment, groping our way toward two chairs in the back.

We ordered two schnapps. "Tell me what's happening," I said. "I don't understand."

"A fascist group," Richard said, "thought to study the supposed purity of the white race . . ."

"Oh, no, Richard—no," I said.

"Oh, yes, my friend," Richard said. "Oh, yes."

"I've heard about this, but didn't believe such a thing could be true." I was stunned.

"Yes, Rose, it's true." In a flat tone of voice, Richard continued. "Their goal's to sterilize the Rhineland bastards. And they're succeeding. They've already rounded up hundreds of children of mixed race and forcibly performed surgery on them. I've heard that some of the children were kept there, as a scientist would keep a cage of rats. They were subjected to even more suffering through merciless medical experiments. Four months ago both our children were taken from us in the middle of the night. We had no idea the fuckers were coming."

Richard began to cry. "They took them from their beds, still in their pajamas, keeping us away with guns and clubs. The kids were hysterical. We were hysterical. We both threw our coats over our bedclothes and ran downstairs to follow them. They were bundled into a black wagon and driven off, with the two of us chasing that fuckin' car down the street. Of course, it was no use. They turned a corner and were gone. We ran. It took us about twenty minutes, but it felt like hours, to get to the American Embassy, and we pounded on the door. No one would let us in—they must have thought we were lunatics, which we were at that moment. Finally, after I stopped screaming in German and switched to English, they opened the door. Some embassy people were awakened and quickly arrived to hear our story. The ambassador appeared. He began calling people in the German government. Not one of them admitted knowing where the children had been taken, or why. Then he made another call, to whom I don't know. We watched his face during each phone call. On this, the last one, he had a look of incredulousness. He said, 'What? Say that again. I think I misheard you.' He hadn't misheard. Both our kids had been sterilized. It was too late. What you saw in the apartment were two formerly energetic and curious kids, now so traumatized that they barely function."

"How . . . why?"

"I gather," he said, "that it's been going on since last year. The program depends on snitches. In every building in Berlin, the regime has appointed a *Blockwart* to watch and amass information about the tenants' religion, the color of our skins, whether everyone's legally married or not. When this new edict was announced, our *Blockwart* didn't have to look far. He turned our kids in and is proud of it. The motherfucker! Rose," Richard said, grabbing my hand, with tears welling in his eyes, "we have to get out of here. If we can get to France before war starts, maybe we can go back to the States. We've sold everything in the flat except for the bare necessities. We're hoarding money. We legally have to charge our boarders rent— who, by the way, are Jewish and are also being forced to pay off the *Blockwart* every month. And now, not only can't I get work, but there's none anywhere—especially for a colored man. Anyway, I have to stay with the kids while Daria teaches. They rarely go outside. They're scared of cars and strangers on the street. I read to them, do schoolwork with them, practice in front of them, sing to them. But they rarely respond. They hold each other's hands, afraid to let go. We've got to get them out of here and get them some help. They're zombies, Rose. I don't even know them anymore. Can you help us?"

"Yes, I'll try. Of course. I promise. Let's have another round. And please, from now on, call me Rosie." I beckoned the bartender.

Sitting there, hunched over my glass, it had finally dawned on me that the world I desired didn't exist any longer. I realized that my innate sense of freedom was balancing on a pile of political debris. The German gate had slammed shut, imprisoning everyone. Not just the non-Aryans—everyone believing in the concept of free choice. It was clear. Yet here I was, sitting across from a dear friend who was in abject anguish. Not only was Richard desperate to get his family out of Germany— he was suffering such inconceivable sorrow and rage that he could barely sit still in his chair.

"Tell me what you've already done," I whispered, suspicious of the people in the bar.

"We've been working with the embassy," Richard said. "Although they're sympathetic, nothing's happening—and every day there's another reminder of my kids' misery, my wife's anger and confusion, and my guilt. I keep thinking that if we had gotten out before, none of this would have happened."

"C'mon, Richard, how would you have known? Even covering the German situation, I didn't see this coming." But I was lying. I should have known better, too—and now I was also beginning to acknowledge it. I accused myself of being dispassionate, too self-involved. And in my gut I understood that these accusations were true.

Richard was still crying. He didn't try to hide his tears. "I was muleheaded. I wasn't thinking of anybody except myself. Thought I was so fuckin' smart. Thought I was beating Jim Crow. Thought I knew everything. I didn't know shit, Rosie," he yelled. "I stranded and destroyed the only people I love— thinking I was so clever."

Richard stood and screamed at the customers. The heads in the dark café all turned toward him. "Why didn't you just cut off my prick? Why did you make my children suffer for my being a goddamned *nigger*?"

"Sit down, Richard," I said, tugging at his jacket sleeve. "You can't be carrying on like this in public. Sit down!"

It was quiet as a church. Everyone was watching. I hoped no one understood English. And Richard sat.

I didn't know what to say. The depth of Richard's heartache was something I had never experienced.

The next morning, there was a loud knock at my door. I had been deeply asleep and was disoriented for a moment. It felt like the middle of the night, but the morning was dark. It was pouring rain.

"Oh, sorry if I woke you," Richard said, "but you said to be here early so we could get to the embassy before the lines start. Daria has taken the day off."

"It's okay, it's okay," I mumbled, trying to get my bearings. "Too much drinking. Give me a minute, I'll splash water on my face."

We arrived to find the press corps office at the embassy alive with nervous activity. The embassy officers and reporters, including Pete, were huddled around the ticker tape. "What's going on?"

"We're not sure," Pete said. "It looks as if the Krauts are planning some kind of putsch. Our source is talking to the embassy in Paris. We're waiting for information."

I didn't care. I wasn't interested in a putsch. I wasn't interested in grabbing the story—I wasn't even tempted.

"Could you cover the story, Pete? There's something I have to do." And without waiting for an answer, "Let's go, Richard," I said.

We went from one American official to another. Nobody seemed to know how to help, what to do. I began to sense that nothing could be done. By three o'clock, we had been in and out of six offices and had spent intolerable amounts of time waiting on hard wooden benches.

I was afraid to acknowledge what I was seeing.

"C'mon, Rosie, can't you see what's going on here?" Richard said. "Can't you? When we walk into an office and they first see you, they have an inviting smile. Then they see me and their smile becomes a grimace—or a look of fear rolls down their face like a friggin' window shade. And here I am among my countrymen. What a riot! You can see why I wanted to get the hell out of my own country. But now I'm stuck in another where everyone's either afraid of me or repulsed by me. If we can't get out of here," Richard asked, "then how will Leon? He's in a similar boat."

I spun around. "What do you mean?"

"C'mon, don't you know? You're in love with him. You're supposed to know this stuff."

"Goddammit, what *stuff*?"

"Leon's a Jew, for Christ's sake, Rosie. Where've you been?"

"Yes, I know he's Jewish," I said. "And so am I."

Perhaps Stefan Kluge could help. I had heard Stefan make a serious confession during a dinner after much drinking. His situation was treacherous—and no doubt if the Gestapo got word of his transgression, he'd be sent to a concentration camp and so would everyone else in his family. I had sworn absolute silence, and I meant it. But now, months later, I needed to bend my promise slightly.

After leaving Richard, having agreed to meet him the next day with news, I found Stefan at the bar on Prinz-Albrecht-Strasse. I thought him crazy to use this joint as his hangout. Nevertheless, when I entered, there he was, sitting near a window, drinking a beer. After I ordered a whiskey, we engaged in shop talk.

I was waiting for a good moment to ask Stefan my burning question. We chatted about our colleagues, caught up on the political gossip. I began to drone on about how awful the world had become, how my newspaper didn't understand me. Then I caught an ever-so-slight frown on his face.

"Why in hell do you think your life's so interesting that anyone cares?" Stefan said. "Really, R.B., the world's disintegrating and your life means nothing more than a bag of potatoes."

Stefan signaled for the check and then turned back to me.

"You Americans, you're so sure of yourselves. You think everyone lives in your free, big, open spaces. Well, you're wrong. We're suffocating, R.B.—look past your own nose, and—"

"How's your wife?" I interrupted.

Stefan looked at me askance. "You know she divorced me," he said, "and went to the States. Everyone knows that. And good riddance to her. Now I have Estelle and wonder what I saw in the other one."

"Come on, Stefan, I know the truth. You told me the story yourself. I need help."

"You mean you're going to blackmail me? Never thought I'd see you stoop so low, R.B."

"No, of course I'm not going to blackmail you, Stefan, don't be such an idiot."

When he was living in Paris, Stefan, a Christian German citizen, met, and eventually married, a Jewish German woman, Esther Stein. She had lived in France for many years, first as a student, then as a writer for a German-French magazine. In 1935, the Nuremberg laws were passed, prohibiting the intermarriage of Jews and Aryans. When it became obvious that the Nazis were going to be in power for a long time, the couple came up with a plan. While still in Paris, they filed for, and received, a divorce. A few months later, Stefan's assignment in Paris ended and he was sent back to Berlin. A new passport was made for Esther. She left a month later and they reunited. Now they were living in Berlin as lovers, feigning distaste for marriage and children. Esther became Estelle. Stein became Schröder. Dark, curly, "Jewish" hair became blonde hair, ironed each morning to make it straighter. The Kluges had become normal, everyday anti-Semites.

"Wait, Stefan, please. Please hear me out. Sorry about my grousing." And I proceeded to tell Stefan about Richard and his family, including the sterilization program.

By the time I had finished, Stefan looked drained.

"Oh, God," Stefan said. "This is horrible, just horrible. We're all in trouble. We've got to get out of here. Listen, R.B., this means you too. Even the Gestapo thugs at the headquarters across the street must have their eye on you. None of us is safe."

"I know," I said. "I'm trying to get used to being Jewish—but I don't have a built-in alarm system yet."

"But what are you going to do about Leon?" Stefan asked. "In my case, Estelle won't leave because her family's still in Hamburg—still convincing themselves that all will be better. And Leon's parents feel the same way—meaning he's stuck, too."

"I need a first-rate forger," I blurted. "Can you help me?"

"Yes, I know someone," Stefan said. "Leon."

"Won't work. I won't put him in jeopardy. Do you know anyone else?"

"Yes."

Late that evening, as arranged, I met Richard at the same bar.

"Anything happening?" Richard said.

"Do you have dollars?" I asked.

"Yeah, I've dollars that my brother sent me. Why?"

"Do you all have American passports?"

"No, only me."

"Okay, we need to get American passports for everyone. We'll need money. I'll let you know how much, as soon as I know. I need photos of Daria and the children and everyone's date and place of birth. You know, all the pertinent details."

"Rosie, how can I th—"

"No, not yet, Richard. I have no idea if I can pull this off."

When I returned to my room, I found a note slipped under the door. *I'll be away. Back soon. L.*

I had to assume that Leon was doing another job for Gerard, and tried not to worry. A few days later, when I arrived at the pressroom, I was handed a letter from Mr. Hin.

Dear Rosie: We miss you at the Espoir. I wanted to let you know that an American was here looking for you. She said

*she was hoping that you were back in Paris, but Madame
Pleven told her that you were still in Berlin.
Sincerely, Hin.*

My heart sank. Someone I had known in New York? I didn't
want to be bothered with renewing old friendships. But I cabled
the *Paris Courier* to see if my colleagues had any information
about the mysterious woman. Maybe she had gone to the office
looking for me? There was no answer. Just my luck—the Nazis
were jamming the system. I should have known better.
Reporting back to Paris had become almost impossible. If I
was lucky, I could convince an international operator to keep a
line open for me while I dictated to the paper. Otherwise, it
could take twenty-four hours to get an article onto a printed
page.

I felt as if I were being lassoed and hog-tied, just like in a
roundup in Nevada.

* * *

A few evenings later, Nevada came to my door. There was a
knock. "It's open," I said, and turned around to say hello.
"Oh, shit, Ma, what are you doing here?"

I was stunned.

My mother looked stunned too. She stood at the door holding a red-leather suitcase that matched her red wool coat, and
wearing a red pillbox hat with a pink rose attached to the brim.

"May I come in?" she asked.

And then I realized that the woman looking for me in Paris
had been my mother.

"Ma, what happened? Has something happened to Father?"

She nodded and sat on the sofa. She didn't bother to hug me.

It was the winter of 1939, and I had not seen my mother for
almost five years. She was now in her mid-sixties, and her

thick, black, shoulder-length hair was sprinkled with very little silver. Although she had gained weight, she was still eye-catching. Even now, she smelled of the outdoors—the Western sage-smelling air was woven into her clothing.

"Yes, he's dead," she said, and leaned back against the cushions, taking a handkerchief out of her pocket. She simply held it. There were no tears.

I was flabbergasted. I had always assumed that my mother would die first. My eyes welled up with tears. Then I wept. Not for a moment did my mother reach out to me. She sat as if waiting for a bus. It took a while for me to calm down. Finally, I went to the bathroom and threw cold water on my face. I knew I had to collect myself. Knew that my mourning would have to wait until she was out of my sight. Knew that I had to get through this next bit of time.

Taking a deep breath, I said, "Tell me what happened, Ma."

"Your father retired from teaching," she began in a flat, story-telling fashion. "He retired from drinking too. Father Maloney had died, leaving him without a drinking partner, but also without an equal intellect. Your father didn't know what to do with himself. He read a lot and reread even more, especially your mentor, Mark Twain."

"Ma," I said, "I was five years old when Twain died—aren't you stretching the story a bit?"

"Well," she said with disdain, "you used to boast that he was buried on the hill behind our house!"

I was surprised to hear this. I couldn't believe that she had any memories of me.

"But I was just a kid, Ma—awed by living near where he used to live. Don't you understand that kids live in fantasy worlds, and—"

She ignored me. "I think," she continued, "that his monthly letters from you were the highlight of his retirement. He always gave them to me to read. Two months ago, I noticed that he was becoming breathless during our walks. I said to him, 'Paul, you must see the doctor.' He did. And the doctor made an appointment for him to go down to Reno for tests. Since I was finishing up a magazine job, I didn't go with him. I never saw him again—well, I never saw him again alive. A drunken woman, who was in Reno waiting for a divorce, was driving up the mountain, taking the curves at breakneck speed. She forced him off the road. He went through the railing, and rolled more than a thousand feet into a ravine. The driver broke her index finger."

Mother paused. "I wonder how she felt with divorce papers in one hand and a murder in the other."

"Oh, how awful," I said. "How did you—"

"Paul was buried in the Golden Terrace Cemetery," she said. "You remember, Rose, the one on North Lode and Comstock Street. I had no idea if this was all right with Paul or not. When I walked toward the cemetery, I read the sign, *Blessed are the dead who die in the Lord,* and I thought how your agnostic father would have found it amusing to see his final resting place. The grave next to him was Elmer O'Brian's, the famous gunslinger from Silver City, and the next one over was my friend Annie O'Riley, the prostitute from D Street. Do you remember her?"

"She took care of me when Mrs. Cheng was indisposed."

"Yes, that's right, and she used to substitute for me at school when I had a long trial to illustrate in Reno. Then came Father Maloney at the end of the row. It seemed fitting to me. On the day your father was buried, all the field grasses were a shimmering whitish-gold, punctuated here and there with those lovely yellow flowers of sage. Do you remember, Rose? Or was it too long ago?"

"I remember, Ma, but they always made me sneeze."

"Well," she replied, "perhaps it was better that you weren't there. Walking to the grave, brushing up against the sage, released a wonderful aroma in the air. You would have been sneezing throughout the service, bothering everyone."

"Boy, you don't change, do you?" I said. She went on.

"Anyway, I didn't want to cable you the news. I needed to tell you in person. And I've always wanted to return to Europe. So, I stopped to see my family in New York and just kept going."

"Jeez, Ma, you came all this way just to tell me? And why didn't Aunt Clara tell me in her last letter?"

"I asked her not to say anything. I needed to tell you in person."

There was a long silence. "Sorry to be so blunt," I said, "but since when have I become so important? You've never even found time to write me, not even on my birthday." Surprisingly, I choked up, and abruptly got up and yet again went to the toilet. It was only after reminding myself about how angry I was at her that I could face her again. Nothing's new, I thought. How depressing. We're both still the same.

I remember. That was an appalling moment for me. I realized that I wished she had come to tell me that she loved me. To say she was sorry for the violence she had hurled at me. To ask me to forgive her. Even today, I'm surprised at how much I still long for her love.

"I don't understand," I said when I returned. "How did you get into Germany? And why come here when you could be arrested? Haven't you been reading the newspaper? Don't you know that Hitler has a racial purity program—which means you're scum?"

"Well, if that's so," she shot back, "what are you doing here?"

"I'm a journalist. I can get away with it."

"You mean, hiding behind 'Manon.' Well, so can I!"

Oh, God, I thought, the same hair-trigger temper, the same bully. My mother was a professional at making me feel insignificant. The only difference I could discern now was that she wouldn't dare to hit or push me around. But as I was getting older, I had sadly learned how much like my mother I was. One of the reasons Leon had a hard time with me was my own temper. Leon needed comfort. I needed to have my way. Now, here with my mother, I needed comfort. But she needed to have her way.

"I sailed to France, having only your address," she continued. "When I arrived I took a room at a hotel that Clara recommended. I don't know what to say, Rose, I'm just wandering, waiting for a flash of lightning to give me an idea for a future. Now that Paul's gone I can't imagine staying in Simon's Creek. I don't need to stay in America. I don't care about nationalism—I think it's narrow thinking, dumb. I've always been an outsider, and I feel more like one now than ever before."

I was in an emotional eddy, feeling profound guilt for not seeing my father for so long. Now I wouldn't have the chance to say a final farewell. My mother seemed to need me, but the idea of having her around was deeply disturbing. I had assumed that I had severed my ties to both my family and my country. Becoming so involved in my work and my new life had left me rarely homesick. Most every day, I was shifting languages, from English to French to German, even to Mandarin; I assumed I had become a woman of a world larger than Simon's Creek, Nevada. Like my mother, I wasn't chained to any country; now I was hearing my mother say some of the same things, and this confused me.

She was looking around my room. "How nice you keep your room, Rose. Certainly different from when you lived at home—I'm impressed! You must have a boyfriend."

I would not say a word. Leon was none of my mother's business.

"But I don't understand how you got here," I said.

"It wasn't so difficult," she replied haughtily. "Clara wrote a letter to the American consul, Clancy, who instructed an attaché to issue me a visa."

Now, I thought, here she is, sitting with her grown daughter in a tiny, cramped, dreary room in Berlin. There was silence.

She broke the stillness. "I can't believe what I've just seen. I took a tram down Kurfürstendamm. It was horrible. All those beautiful buildings are painted with terrifying graffiti. Ugly cartoons of men, hanging, maimed, tortured, beheaded—dripping in red paint, looking like blood. I couldn't figure out what it was all about and I couldn't ask anyone. The tram I was riding in was silent. People were looking out the windows with no change in their expressions. I got the feeling that they were blind."

"Ma, what's the matter with you? It's anti-Semitic graffiti—Stars of David—men with enormous noses. Don't you get it? The Germans hate us. Want us dead and gone. So now do you know how it feels to be Jewish?" I said. I could feel her anger rising. I couldn't resist adding, "You do know that your family considers you an anti-Semite?"

"How dare you!" she said. "What a terrible thing to say." She stood up as if to leave and stared at me with a hard look. "You're just as cold—haven't changed a bit—always trying to kill my feelings, just like—"

"Oh, for Christ's sake," I said as my anger won the battle. "You can posture all you want. You can march out of here—I really don't care. Your refusing to admit you're a Jew makes me ashamed of you. And I can say this with impunity, because I've also been ashamed of being Jewish—and I learned it from you! And now isn't it ironic, that you're in the best place in the world to find people who agree with you. You'll fit right in."

She sat back down. "My anti-Semitism, as you call it, isn't any of your goddamned business. So try to take a little pity on me. After all, I am your mother."

I began to put on my coat. "Forget it, Ma," I said. "Right now our argument's not important. What's important is that you've got to get away from here. You're taking unnecessary risks. Which hotel are you in?"

"I don't have a reservation," she said. "I thought I could stay with you." She looked around. "Where's the bedroom, through that door?"

"No, that's the closet. I sleep on the couch. Come on, I'll take you to the Hotel Aldon. It's where a lot of journalists stay. You'll be safe there. We'll figure all this out over dinner. How does that sound to you?"

She gave a terse nod.

We couldn't find a cab, so we walked. I carried her suitcase and she followed. It began to rain just as we entered the hotel. Knowing that the Aldon's restaurant and bar were favorite places for reporters to meet, I didn't want to eat there. The idea of introducing my mother to my colleagues was intolerable.

Next door to the hotel was a beer hall that catered to the clerical workers at the embassies in the area. I often went there when I wanted to be alone. Now it was pouring rain as we carefully made our way down five steps into the cold and dingy space. The only sources of heat were a wood-burning stove, glasses of alcohol, layers of warm clothes, and human beings jammed together. Over the bar protruded a motley stuffed black bear, fangs bared—with a Nazi flag hanging from one of its eyeteeth. Written on the chalkboard menu was *Bratwurst und Kartoffel*—that was all.

"Do you know what the sign says, Ma?"

"Of course. Sausage and potatoes."

"I didn't know you could read German."

She ignored me.

The waiter, clad in a large, much-used white apron, came over. "Evening, R.B. Who's your friend?"

I disregarded his question. "We'll have two of those," I said, pointing to the chalkboard, "and two beers—and please, George, don't forget the mustard. "You can only eat this food with large dollops of mustard," I said, turning to my mother. "I have no idea what's in the bratwurst, and it's best not to ask."

We talked. My mother was truly unmoored. She had no idea what she was doing. Yet, like a homing pigeon, she had taken herself across the sea—had put herself in harm's way—all with a tenaciousness that impressed but didn't surprise me.

"A feather. That's what I feel like," she said. "The only problem's that I'm not connected to a body. I feel that I've been plucked and thrown to the wind. I know what I don't want to do, but I don't know what I *do* want to do. I've enough money between our pensions, our savings, and the insurance settlement from the divorcée. I'm fine. Don't worry, I won't be a burden. But if I do stay in France, or—"

"Ma, you can't stay in Europe! There's going to be a war. Why would you want to do this? If France is invaded, and it looks as if it will be, you'll be identified as a Jew. You're crazy to be swimming against the tide—"

"I don't know. I thought that there was a lot of war-whooping, but that everything had quieted down."

"Not at all," I said, "not at all. Don't you read the papers? There are rumblings through the underground of a major move by Hitler in the next couple of days. Germany is infested with *agents provocateurs*. They're looking for people like you. Naïve—not used to the ways of the Reich. If they snag you in a roundup, they could push you across the frontier, send you to a camp, hold you for ransom. None of these actions is uncommon here. You must get out—now. Within days, you might not be able to leave legally. You watch. After next summer's harvest, this entire continent will explode."

"But what about you, Rose? What are you going to do?"

"Listen, Ma, I'm taking it one day at a time. I'm a reporter. It's my job to write about trouble."

"Aren't you afraid?" she asked. "I would be."

"No, you wouldn't," I said, smiling. "You'd be just as interested as I am if you lived in the midst of this craziness. Listen— I think Hitler's planning to swallow France. He's been building nests of traitors throughout the country, using the Paris Exposition as a front. You saw it, I'm sure. The German Pavilion's grim, menacing bronze eagle perching on the plinth, trying to overwhelm that meaty, stalwart Russian bronze couple marching toward glory. And—"

"You sound just like your father, Rose. I always knew you got your love of words from him. But I didn't understand, until now, that the way you put them together is like his too."

"Thanks, that's a compliment, Ma. It's so hard for me to imagine him gone. Now I understand why I didn't get a letter these last two months. I had just assumed it was the postal system."

I felt awful. My father gone. Even with his bouts of drinking, he was the parent I loved. I looked up from my beer and saw that it was still raining outside. God, Berlin's gloomy in the winter, I thought. Perhaps I should ask to be sent to southern Spain. There, at least, I could cover Franco's despicable war in a warmer climate.

"What are you going to do?" my mother asked.

"Stay here and cover this insanity," I said.

"Why don't they assign you somewhere safer?"

"Because I know the politics here. It's amusing that I've become invaluable in a country that's trying to get rid of every one of my kind."

Why, I thought, do I have to prove anything to my mother? I felt like a kid again.

"Don't worry," she said, as if she were reading my mind. "I

won't be staying with you. As your friend Freud says, it wouldn't be healthy."

"How did you know I've been reading Freud?" I asked. "Oh, yeah, Papa read you my letters." And I smiled at the image of my father sitting at the kitchen table reading aloud my news-filled, often boastful letters.

The food arrived. It looked gruesome but we were both so hungry that it didn't matter. We watched the rain and were silent as we ate and drank.

"How's Mrs. Cheng?" I asked, trying to be polite.

"She's dead," my mother said bluntly. "Too much opium, over too long a time."

This news made my eyes well up with tears. "Oh, I'm so sorry to hear this—she was such an important part of my life."

"Maybe she was," my mother said, "but it was a long time ago. I can't imagine why you have tears for her."

"You don't sound like you care, Ma."

"Once a life is over, it's over. It doesn't help anyone to mourn. It causes too much unhappiness. Look at this," she said, and she gestured to the room. "People are just eating or staring. No one's speaking to each other. We're all sitting in a bucket of gloom. How do you stand this city? There's no light. No light in the sky. Nothing but grim blue lights in the houses. Everything's so dark."

I had to smile. "Well, remember, you come from Nevada and its big blue sky. You're spoiled. Even now in Paris, the city of light, it's been dark since three in the afternoon. For half the year, Europe's dark; it's the newest metaphor for the mood of the people. Ma, I want to ask you about Aunt Clara."

"Oh, okay," she replied as if being imposed upon. "Since Stella's death, she's closeted herself away from the family."

"Why?" I asked. "It wasn't her fault."

"Well, she thinks it is. And she's changed. Leah told me that she no longer attends Friday night dinners. Children have stopped coming to her shop to help with sorting the buttons—she thinks they're terrified of her face. She's become an old woman. Her hair's a startling white. Clara's vitality," my mother said, "seeped out of her as she waited in that hotel room for Stella. 'Why didn't I see that he was evil?' she said to me. 'Why wasn't I suspicious of a dapper man hanging around a hotel lobby? I knew better. After all, I wasn't born yesterday.' But I also know," my mother said, "that although she's a spinster, Clara's a genuine, honest-to-goodness romantic. She admitted that she thought Bobby Hunter was charming, and could see that Stella was attracted to him. But she also admitted to me, horrified, that she was attracted to him too. She said, 'Miriam, I know it's ridiculous, but I made up a fanciful story in my head about running away with him. I think this is why I didn't step in and follow my protective instincts. And this is what makes my guilt so hard to tolerate.'"

"Poor Clara. I can understand her response to Vosberg," I said. "He's very handsome."

* * *

Someone was knocking. Oh, no, it's my mother, I thought, pulling on my clothes as I unlocked the door. But there was Pete Grogan, looking as if he had seen death.

"Get your coat, R.B., come with me. Hurry."

I did what I was told.

"What's happening?"

"Right after midnight," Pete said, "the Reich gave permission to its citizens to go berserk. Listen. And look," he said, and he pointed to the east.

I could hear the booming roar of machine-gun fire and see flames lighting the horizon. We ran toward the fire. Then we saw the bedlam and stopped in our tracks. Pete grabbed my arm. "My God," he said. "It's an inferno." Plate-glass windows of shops and apartment houses were flying in the air, crashing to the ground. It felt as if every piece of glass was slivered with fury. Because there was no wind, clouds of smoke were perched on top of each burning building. In between the buildings, perversely, as if Mother Nature were laughing at our idiocy, we could see the stars.

"We need to stay out in the open," I warned. "Look like part of the crowd."

We were pushed and shoved and handed bricks to throw, which we both managed to avoid doing. Beer-hall thugs, schoolyard bullies, nasty, squinty-eyed men who had been recruited to the *Schutzstaffel* were beating Jews who had been dragged from shops and apartments identified by the Stars of David on their doors. The synagogue in front of us was burning. Jewish men were trying to shove their way in to save the Torahs. I saw two SS men who, with theatrical manners, allowed some men in—and then closed the doors and nailed them shut. The men were burned alive while trying to save their ancient texts. We watched, stunned. The smells were overwhelming— burning wood, broken bottles of everything under the sun, burning flesh—

"ROSE!" And we turned toward the sound.

It was my mother in her glaring, bright-red coat and her hat with the rose, now askew on her head. She was forcing her way through the throngs, seemingly impervious to their horrific screams. Then we saw an SS man grab her by the arm and start to lead her away.

"You go straight toward her," Pete said. "I'll go around to the rear."

There was a wall of ferocious humanity blocking our way. Then I saw Pete behind her. He had my mother by one arm, and an SS officer had her by the other. I could see that she was screaming but couldn't hear her over the roar. Finally, after pushing and shoving my way through the crowd, I was next to her.

"Goddammit," she was yelling in English, "let go of me."

"Do you want to start an international incident?" I heard Pete yelling in German. "Let go of her now." I pulled out my press pass and showed it. The soldier was momentarily flummoxed, and let go.

"Ma," I yelled. "We have to get out of here!"

"Ma?" Pete said. "What—"

"I'll tell you later."

Using the mayhem as our cover, we took hold of her arms and propelled her down a quieter street. We knew where we were going.

"Rose—" she said.

"Be quiet, Ma. *Please* be quiet."

The American Embassy was in eerie darkness. A huge crowd of Nazi sympathizers surrounded the closed building. Rocks were being thrown. The doorway sentinels were nowhere to be seen. I banged on the side door and the peephole was opened. The undersecretary, Mr. Greenleaf, immediately recognized me. The door opened quickly and closed even faster behind us.

"Oh, no," my mother cried out, "my coat's caught in the door!"

"Take it off, Madame," Greenleaf said. "It's not worth taking the chance."

I showed her to a sofa in one of the anterooms. "You're safe for now. Try to get some rest," I said. "I have to go to a press conference, and then write and file my story."

And a terrible story it was. We reporters were herded into the Reich Ministry of Public Enlightenment and Propaganda, where we were invited to sit in the comfortable pale-blue satin-covered armchairs to listen to uncomfortable news. We sat in straight, precise rows as a German press attaché recited his information. Many of us, knowing this would be our last time having to listen to his lies in person, were very quiet. The world had just spun out of control. I didn't know about the others, but I was stunned, numb with dread—afraid to think about Leon. We were informed of the news. Then we were escorted back to our embassies.

Without checking in with my mother, I went to the embassy's press office to file my story by cable. Using a telephone was out of the question—there were too many life-and-death calls to be made—and I didn't want to engage a line.

HITLER'S INFERNO
By R.B. Manon

BERLIN, November 10, 1938—*Today I've experienced hell. I've seen the hideous faces of madness, heard the screams of people being burnt alive. I can attest from firsthand observation that the citizens of Germany have lost their minds.*

Then, as if this were a normal day, the government held a news conference. The news attaché boasted that in all of Germany at least seventy-five thousand Jewish businesses have been looted and burned. "To add to our list," he continued, "two hundred sixty-seven synagogues have been torched; at least ninety-one Jews have been killed in Berlin and its neighboring areas; and more than twenty-five thousand Jewish men have been arrested and sent to 'relocation' camps. We are well on our way to cleansing Germany of the Jewish filth." And he abruptly left the room before we could ask questions . . .

How in the world did I ever sit there and listen to that repulsive man? Now, I wouldn't think twice about standing up and telling him what I thought. Of course, hindsight is so much easier. But maybe we ancients should be running the world. We do care less for convention—and we do have distinct memories of good and evil. And we, the collective of octogenarians, may not remember yesterday, but fifty years ago is a breeze.

I remember my mother saying that nothing really matters. One of her favorite responses was "Who cares?" But I need to be wary. I need to remember about the health of the world. After the horrors I've seen in my lifetime, I could slip into her negative shoes all too easily—and they would fit.

Mr. Greenleaf walked into the room. "Ladies and gentlemen," he announced, "we've just been informed that all American citizens will be evacuated. Please prepare to leave."

I found my mother. "I'm sorry. Please forgive me," I heard her say, as she tried quietly to slip off the sofa she was sharing.

"Not a problem, dear, I'm awake," the woman next to her said. "Just trying to digest all that has happened. Have to write a report. Hi, R.B.," she said, and turned to my mother. "You're lucky, Mrs. Manon, that you have R.B. here to protect you. By the way, my name's Eva Kantor, secretary to Ambassador Taylor. No, sorry," she corrected. "In the middle of the night, the ambassador was recalled to Washington in protest for last night's hideous rampage." And she rose from the sofa, put on her shoes, and left.

Pete rushed into the room. "Morning, Mrs. Manon," he said. "R.B., I have to speak to you. Come into the press office."

"God, what's all this R.B. stuff? Why don't you just call her Rose?"

Pete was stunned for a moment. "We call her R.B.," he said, with ice coating his words, "because we respect her work and being a woman in this business is tough. Now, come on, R.B.," he said, amplifying my initials.

"Don't worry, Rose," my mother said. "I'll be fine."

"Leon's waiting outside," Pete said as soon as we turned around to leave. "I've just caught sight of him. He must be crazy! He's in the midst of that furious crowd. Hurry."

Facing me outside was the incarnation of evil. Screeching hordes of people. Snarling and howling dogs. The SS were keeping the mob from attacking the embassy. I saw Leon and signaled him to go to my left where the door was. He walked with assurance across the demarcation area and through the door, just as if he belonged there.

He was shaking. "The world's gone mad," he said, and we embraced just as my mother entered the room.

"Well, well, what do we have here?" she said.

"Leave us alone, Ma. Go away." She turned with a huff and left.

"Your mother?" Leon said.

"It's a long story, Leon. I promise I'll fill you in later, but now we have to make plans to get you out of here. Come. Let's sit down. I didn't know you were back in Berlin. Where were you? Is everything all right? How did you know I was here?"

"Always the reporter," Leon laughed. "Questions. Questions."

His voice was extra low and I had to ask him to speak more clearly.

"I got back last night," he said. "Then, early this morning, hearing the noise, I opened my door and realized that the guard outside my apartment was gone. I went to your boardinghouse. All the lights were off, but I could hear people scurrying about, banging into things, whispering anxiously. The porter told me that you'd left in the middle of the night."

"But how did you know I was leaving Berlin?"

"The Reich's radio station," he said. "They've been boasting about last night and how the French and the British delegations are running from Berlin with their scraggly tails between their ugly legs. I assumed you would be evacuated too."

For the moment, all I could do was hold his hands and watch his face. He was so bony; his face was so drawn. Even his fingers were thinner.

Then I snapped back to reality. "You must come with me to Paris. You can't stay here any longer."

"No, I'm so sorry, but I can't," he said. "I can't leave my parents. They need me, you know that."

"Come. Let's try to figure this out."

Within minutes, the dilemma of Leon and his parents had been presented to Eva Kantor. "Well," she said, "we can supply the travel documents but I can't promise that they'll work. You may all have to go through German customs before boarding and then be vulnerable to police checks at the border, and then again upon arrival in Paris. Is the letter 'J' stamped in your *Kennkarte*?"

"Of course not," I said, sounding as if it were too absurd to consider.

"Yes, it is in all of ours—since the first week of October," Leon said.

I looked at Eva, trying to discern her feelings. "Will their cards work?"

"Perhaps," Eva said. "But they'll still need legal travel documents. I'll do what I can, but I can't promise. Here," she said to Leon, handing him a scrap of paper. "Write down your names and dates and places of birth. And R.B., as we discussed, you must get your American saxophonist friend and his family here. Everyone needs to be issued the legal papers. We have about ten hours to get this all done."

"I don't know if I can convince them," Leon said after Eva left. "I just don't know."

"But you've got to persuade them. Please, Leon, I can't leave without you."

"I'll try," he said, "of course. Now, this is what I think we should do. If they agree, they'll be with me at the station. We'll wait on the platform. Don't approach me unless you have all our papers. If you can't get them, ignore me. I'll know that I'll have to try to find another way. My parents are elderly, both in age and in energy. If you *don't* see two old people standing with me, it will mean I'm not coming with you. Now, I have to get going."

I walked him to the back entrance where the guard unlocked the door. "Good-bye," he said. "See you on the platform. And, perhaps, as we get moving toward the border, you'll tell me about how your mother got here. I have a feeling it will sound like one of those cowboy stories you love to tell." With that, he slipped through the door. I watched Leon through the window as he hurried away. He didn't look back.

"Ma, I need to talk to you."

"Whatever about?" she said with a stab of irritation in her voice.

"Ma, listen to me."

"All right, Rose, I'm listening. What's wrong?"

"We have to leave."

"I understand. Poor Rose," she said, "you look as if you've been up all night."

"Have been," I answered curtly. "Now pay attention. There's going to be a mass exodus from Berlin tonight. We're being officially evacuated. The German authorities will be so taken up with what happened last night that we can use this brief pause to get out of here. We need to be on the midnight train. And I'm also taking a family who are friends of mine, and—"

"What about that man I saw you with—the one you didn't even bother to introduce?" she interrupted. "After all this Jewish business, I can't believe you've fallen in love with a Kraut!"

"He's Jewish," I blurted.

"Oh, God, why a Jew, Rose? Haven't *they* caused enough trouble in our lives?"

"I suggest," I said, in a very low, measured voice, "that you get out of here immediately, or—"

I took a breath, knowing this wasn't the time to confront my mother.

"Forget it," I said, trying to contain my rage. "I've already heard from other reporters that the first train out this morning was overflowing and there was pandemonium. Nazi troops had lined the platform—many had snarling dogs. It was obvious that there weren't enough soldiers to keep order. Tonight will be rougher. We'll be on the train under the auspices of the American Embassy, and with a letter of permission to travel from the German authorities. Even if people are hanging out the windows, we've been assured of passage. The soldiers at the American Embassy will accompany us. But we must hurry, and—"

"Okay, I understand," my mother said, "but can I get my suitcase? And what's happened to my coat?"

"I'll try to get your things later. You must sit quietly and wait for me to return. Please, Ma."

"I'm not stupid, Rose," she said, and I looked at her skeptically.

"Yeah, but remember, you're in foreign territory. I'm not."

"All right. All right," she said. "I'll be quiet. But what do we do if we're challenged on the train?"

"We may not be. But, just in case—under no circumstances are you to speak German."

"I don't speak German, you know that."

"Well, you speak Yiddish, and that's very close."

"Whoever told you that? It's too ugly a language for me to bother with."

"Clara told me—why should she lie? Don't you understand," I said, trying to ignore her nastiness, "that we have to believe that we're invisible? Under no circumstances are you to say anything, in any language, about my press credentials or about our being Jewish. It's really important that you pay attention to what I'm telling you, and—"

"Okay, Rose, okay. Stop being such a dictator. I understand. But—what about your Jewish friend? What are you going to do about him? Does he have a family he'll be dragging behind him? If so, they'll be feeding off you for the rest of their lives."

God, I thought, will I ever be free from this monster?

What was wrong between us? Why couldn't we find common ground? At that point, I couldn't see my way past my anger at my mother. I was having a hard enough time clumsily finding my way toward a life of love.

The Moses family had been included in the order to leave. I went by foot to Charlottenburg. There was no other way. The trams weren't running, there were no taxis—the only moving cars belonged to the SS. The streets looked like the sepia photographs I had seen of the Great War. Broken glass was everywhere—indeed, the streets, perversely, sparkled. I had to sidestep smoldering timbers—hold a handkerchief over my nose and mouth—take the long way around to get through streets blocked with debris. People were moving in every direction, many with suitcases and rolls of bedding. It was eerily quiet. One street's sidewalk was lined with dead bodies. I had never seen carnage like this before. People were averting their eyes, but moving forward. I wanted to scream for help— at least to cover their bodies—to bestow dignity upon this awful place. But I knew no one would listen. So this is what war is like, I thought, and tried to pull armor over myself. I was going to have to learn.

I did learn. Over the years of my career, in wars between political parties, between tribes, between countries—any sort of callous killing—I was often there, covering the story.

And today? All these years later? I wonder where my heart had been—I wonder why I had not tended my emotional garden.

The previous night's stars were gone. There didn't appear to be a sky. What was above my head was a solidly painted ceiling of a dreary grayish-brown. I wondered if this was what Dante's purgatory looked like.

It usually took twenty minutes to get to Richard's house; now it took more than two hours. When I arrived, I wasn't surprised to see the vandalism. The elevator wasn't working; I climbed five flights. Some of the doors on the landing were splintered, some had gaping holes, some were standing open, as if the person knocking had been invited in. And I could see that the apartments had been ransacked. Jewish families, I guessed. When I knocked on Richard's door, I heard silence. But I sensed they were inside. "Richard, it's me," I yelled. "Open up! Richard, please let me in."

I heard one latch, then another, and the door was opened a crack.

The family was petrified. Their bags were packed, as if for a quick escape. Good, I thought, they're ready to go.

"We've been afraid to go outside. The kids are ready for an insane asylum. Our tenants fled. What's going on, Rosie?"

"I'll tell you later. We don't have time to spare. Do you have your new American passports?"

"Yeah, we got them from Stefan, but he wouldn't take any money."

"Don't worry about that," I said. "Your dollars will come in handy once we get to France. Now, let's go."

As if they had rehearsed, each member of the family put on a coat, picked up a bag, and walked, single file, through the door.

"Oh, God, what has happened to our neighbors?" Daria asked.

"They're all Jews. God only knows," Richard said.

I led them out into the murky daylight, joining the exodus of people walking back the way I had come.

"Where's everyone going?" Richard asked.

"I've no idea," I said, "but we're going to the embassy."

I took turns with Richard carrying Annelie. Daria appeared to be moving in slow motion, dazed, stumbling. She would be leaving behind her parents, her past, the safety of familiarity.

"Are you okay?" I asked.

"No, Rose, I'm not okay, but I can manage," she said, even though tears were streaming down her distraught face.

I was desperate for a cigarette, but I was holding Annelie on my hip.

I tried singing a cowboy song that I remembered from childhood: *Come sit by my side if you love me. / Do not hasten to bid me adieu. / Just remember the Red River Valley, / And the one who has loved you so true.*

"Such a sad song," Annelie said. "Do you know a happier one?"

"Sorry," I said, "can't think of one right now. Do you want me to sing it again?"

Annelie shook her head.

It was much worse than I had written in these pages of notes. Perhaps I was too close to take in the details—or couldn't tolerate seeing what I was seeing. But now I remember more about our struggle to reach the embassy. We stepped over dead bodies while trying to shelter the children's eyes. At certain places we had to cover our noses because the stench of burning flesh was overwhelming. I don't think we spoke. Maybe I didn't sing to Annelie. Maybe I made it up, trying to be dramatic. I don't remember. The only sound I do remember hearing was the keening of a woman who was standing in the middle of the street, with her gray dress torn at the shoulder, shoeless.

Exhausted, downhearted, we arrived at the embassy. It smelled like a library on fire. In the many fireplaces, the staff was burning files. Everyone was moving efficiently, as if they had rehearsed this many times before. There was an amazing calm in the place. I found my mother feeding one of the fireplaces with papers.

"Ma, this is my friend Richard, his wife Daria, and their children, Annelie and Coleman."

My mother didn't rise. She had an incredulous look on her face.

"How do you do?" Richard and Daria said, and held out their hands to shake. Mother shook only Daria's hand, but barely.

She's impossible, I thought, deeply embarrassed.

"Come," I said to the family, "let's get you settled. We have a long night ahead of us."

I took them to an anteroom outside the pressroom. There were two long brown leather sofas. "Make yourselves comfortable here and try to sleep, or at least rest. I'll let the kitchen know you're here. I don't know what to say about my mother," I apologized. "She has a way of perpetually embarrassing me."

"Don't worry, Rosie," Richard said, "we're used to it."

"Well, I am too, but I still hate it."

Now there was no time for reflection, but I knew the blow-up with her would happen sooner or later, and a part of me was already writing the script in my head.

When I finished in the embassy's pressroom, the Moses family was fast asleep. My mother was nowhere to be seen.

"Christ, she's going to cause me more problems," I said to Pete, who was also being evacuated to Paris.

"She's in the newsroom burning papers," he said. "She's happy as a lark. Perhaps you should just leave her here."

"Oh, how I wish I could!"

An hour before it was time to leave, I found her. "Let's go, Ma. It's time."

Eva Kantor had everyone gather in the main meeting room.

She stood on a chair. "Please listen carefully, all of you. We were able to get all your travel documents ready." And there was a relieved murmur in the room. "We'll pass them out after I finish speaking. Now. You'll all get on the midnight train—that has been assured by the German government. But you'll be lucky to get a seat. Please take turns. I know, considering the situation, that this sounds silly, but you still have to set a good example while representing the American government. Check that you have all your important papers and take as much money and jewelry as you can easily carry. You're allowed only one small valise—and I'm very serious about that. If we see you with more, it will be confiscated. We can't promise that this is going to be an easy ride. Anywhere along the way, German officials can board the train and cause problems. Try to be diplomatic. Don't anyone reveal your religion. Pretend you can't speak German. When you disembark in Paris, you'll have to go through customs. This may be tricky. There will be passport officials sitting at tables near all the exits. Take your time. R.B. Manon will try to find this particular official—a placid-looking man. He has very little hair. What he does have, though, is gray and he combs it over his head. Also, his ears have tufts of gray hair popping out of them like wires, and he has a small moustache." Everyone laughed at her description. "We were able to get a message to him to look out for you. If for some unforeseen reason, he isn't there and you have to go through normal channels, don't try to explain anything—simply give the officer your papers. Stick together. Mr. Greenleaf and Miss Manon," she said, pointing to us, "will lead you through. Good luck."

"But what if we can't get past the passport control in Paris?" one of the men asked.

"Stand aside," she said, "and Mr. Greenleaf will contact the embassy."

As soon as I could catch Eva's attention, I asked about the

documents for Leon and his parents. "Got them," she said, and handed them over.

It was after ten in the evening. Time to go. We were traveling in diplomatic automobiles, with all the authority the embassy could muster. No sneaking. In all, there were fifteen cars, carrying ninety-six adults and five children. Each car had an American flag tied with twine to its antenna. A small staff would be staying behind.

In single file, we walked out to the cars. American soldiers created a barrier between a smaller but still angry crowd and the wall of the embassy. An undistinguished-looking woman, whom I had never seen before, was counting the appropriate number of people into each car. My mother was in front of the Moses family and was placed in one car, while the Moses family and I were placed in the next one. She turned around looking for me. I pretended not see her.

I still couldn't believe the chaos I saw on the streets. Even at this late hour, elderly Jewish men and women were being forced to sweep up the glass. Under the dictatorial eye of the SS, they had no choice. I was nauseated with grief. The German Jews were sweeping the streets so the American Jews could get out safely. It was heartbreaking—they had no similar road to freedom.

The convoy departed under a ceiling of thick clouds that was still hanging just above the streets. We drove past mounds of sodden books, some still smoldering. We drove past groups of people huddled together trying to stay warm and dry. The whole world was gray. There wasn't a spot of color to be seen anywhere. We drove past complete devastation. People looked like their own shadows. It appeared to me that they had already abandoned their real selves to destiny.

Anhalter Bahnhof was mobbed with desperate people. There were people yelling, babies crying, packages being handed up to passengers through the windows. Most frightening of all were the Alsatian shepherd dogs straining at their leather leashes, frenzied by the crowds, teeth bared—waiting for instructions. Huge spotlights roamed over the platform.

As soon as I stepped out of the car, I looked for Leon but couldn't see him anywhere. "Keep moving," I kept repeating to the embassy people, while my eyes fanned the crowds. "Keep moving, please."

A path was made for the Americans. Greenleaf, wearing a pearl-gray homburg, headed the line. I was on the edge, urging people forward. Suddenly, I saw someone grab Greenleaf's arm. "Papers? Now!" A young official, puffed up like a peacock, in a brand-new gray wool uniform with shiny buttons and a serious gun holstered on his thick black leather belt, led Greenleaf to a table.

"Your travel documents," he commanded. Greenleaf fumbled with his briefcase. The soldier watched, bored. Finally, Greenleaf pulled out an impressive-looking document. The official took his time reading it, looked at Greenleaf with a disdainful expression, and stamped it: *Anerkannt*, Approved. Without checking our papers, the soldier pointed, and then herded us down the platform to the last cars of the train.

I was trying to honor my responsibilities to the embassy people while at the same time looking for Leon.

The noise was unbearable. The crush of people was suffocating.

Then I heard my mother shouting, "There's your *Jewish* friend," and she pointed directly at Leon, obviously with his parents.

His parents!

An SS officer looked toward where she was pointing. Richard moved surreptitiously to block his view while I waved the tickets and papers for Leon to see. His parents, I thought with joy. They're all coming!

Then I heard my mother screech, "They're trying to kill me!

Help! Rose!" I turned. She was being dragged from the train steps.

I ran toward her.

"What are you doing?" I screamed in German to the two new soldiers, one with a roaring dog. "She has her papers!"

"Out of the way," one of them ordered, and pushed me aside. "No one spits at me without being punished!"

"She's an AMERICAN! Ma, say something. Tell him you're sorry," I screamed over the din. "Tell him right now, or they'll arrest you." But she sneered at me.

"I mean it, Ma, this is it," I was shrieking. "They can do whatever they like with you—there's no law here that protects you!"

And like a marionette, she smiled at the blond, blue-eyed soldier and said in English, "I'm sorry. Please excuse me. I was so frightened—I'm—"

The SS man with the dog obviously didn't understand her, and yelled, "Get her."

The dog lunged toward my mother, grabbing her bright red coat.

"No," Mr. Greenleaf, now using his German, hollered, "let her alone. She has immunity! She's an American!"

The SS man called off his dog and my mother sank to the platform in a faint.

Stiff with rage, they each viciously kicked her. And with precision, they spun on their heels and left.

But, for me, the circumstance was horrifyingly clear. I had to take care of my mother. She wasn't moving.

Mr. Greenleaf was yelling for me to help.

The train was beginning to move.

"Rosie, I'll help you!" It was Richard.

"No, Richard," I screamed. "Get back on, please—your family."

"Leon. Go get him!" Richard shouted as he lifted my dead-weight mother.

But it was too late.

It was 12:03.

The train was leaving the station, precisely on schedule. Mr. Greenleaf grabbed me by the arm and pulled me into the vestibule, and the door was slammed shut behind me.

The horrified look on Leon's face forever engraved itself upon my memory. The train picked up speed. I had betrayed Leon and his parents. I had sacrificed them for my mother.

I understood that my responsibility was primarily to her—but I also knew that I had broken my own heart. It was over. I had no choice. I had made a decision. The Moses family—a packet of essential papers that Eva Kantor had slipped to me—and, of course, my mother.

She had won again.

These memories are too much for me. I need to walk. Taking my cane, I set off down the dirt road, passing beneath an umbrella of maple and oak trees. I'm surprised at myself. I can taste bile, taste my dislike for my mother. I spit on the road and then remember how, in Brooklyn, my Aunt Clara used to spit in the gutter and embarrass me. That must be why my mother spat at the soldier—a family trait, a Russian tradition?

"This is ridiculous," I say out loud to the air. But after all this time, I still feel despair. And after all this time, I'm still angry.

The scene at the train station is as clear to me as if it were yesterday. Tell him you're sorry! I must have been crazy. Why did I think such politeness could be heard in that mayhem? Absurd. Most likely, they heard the word "American," and had been warned to avoid an incident. But the truth, ugly as it is, is this—she did sneer at me. And while I was trying to protect her, I was manifestly conscious of her dislike of me.

I had to make a determined effort to lead the apprehensive group of Americans down the corridors of the train. All I wanted to do was to fly over the heads of the scrambling hordes of people and, like the figures in a Chagall painting, soar toward the stars and Leon. I kept reminding myself to move straight ahead, not permitting myself to look to my right or my left. Each step I took forward was one step farther away from Leon.

The Moses family was lucky. They found an almost empty compartment and made room for me by putting the children on their laps. "Where's my mother?" I said.

"She found a seat in the car behind us," Daria said. "She's fine. The passengers are tending to her. She'll be black and blue, but nothing's broken. I'm so sorry, Rosie. Is there anything I can do for you?"

No, I shook my head. The only thing I could do was weep into Daria's shoulder. And she had the good sense not to try to calm me.

Everyone in our compartment was quiet, listening to my sobbing, allowing me to be. Beside the Moses family, there was a Jewish family of four—unmistakable because the father and his two sons wore yarmulkes. The family looked frightened, but still the man offered me a swig from his flask, which I gratefully accepted. Richard soon took control and organized the group. The two big boys were told to sit on the floor, one leaning on the door into the aisle, the other against the outside wall of the carriage. Then he made small beds for Coleman and Annelie on the luggage racks.

As Germany rushed by, I stopped crying and stared out the window. I was lost and wandering in my sorrow. The two older boys were wide awake, each reading his own copy of *The Last of the Mohicans* in Yiddish. In English, Richard whispered, "I think that as long as they can keep their attention on the story, they'll feel safe." The children's mother was awake, too, all the while keeping a keen eye on everyone; the father read the *Berliner Morgen-Zeitung* and turned the pages as if they were made of the softest cotton. Daria and the children soundly slept.

In the morning, the train's corridors were still jammed with passengers unable to find seats. The passengers, none of us familiar with this kind of discomfort, were trying to be polite. Nonetheless, we had to crawl over each other to get to the toilets—which soon overflowed. The smell was awful. And added to this was the rank smell of unwashed bodies and damp woolen coats and food. At one point my mother waylaid me when I was in line waiting to use the toilet. "Are you okay?" she asked.

"I should be asking if you're okay," I said.

"Yeah, just bruised," she said, obviously happy to change the subject back to herself. "Imagine the nerve of that soldier pushing me as if I was a bale of hay! I know that I shouldn't have spat at him, but he made me so angry."

"You're lucky not to have been detained," I said. "Even after all you've seen in the past forty-eight hours, you don't believe what's going on here, do you?"

"I know, I know. Don't lecture me. And I know you're avoiding me. But at least we should be happy that we got out of Berlin in one piece, don't you agree?"

"Yeah, Ma, we're lucky. You had better get back to your seat before you lose it."

"I've already lost it. Been in the corridor for a while now."

"Well, take mine," I said, and pointed to an empty place next to Richard.

"No, that's okay, I'm fine."

She started down the corridor and then stopped—she had not finished speaking to me.

"Are you okay about losing your boyfriend? I saw him with two little old Jews. Who were they?"

I couldn't speak. I was struck mute for a moment, just looking at her.

"Those were his parents," I said. "Do you have any idea what just happened out there?"

"Well, yes, of course," she said. "I just saved you from a life of taking care of people who didn't have the brains to get out when they could. You'll thank me later, you'll see."

And with that, she turned before I could say a word, moved an elderly man between the two of us, and walked off.

It's getting chilly. I'm thinking about the first frost, the killing frost—when the plants wilt and fall to the ground. They turn from green to yellow to gray and become mushy, slippery in their death throes. Sometimes, if I want to save a plant, I'll bring it indoors before the freeze. I've learned that I can revive a plant that's on the brink—but it's a fragile moment. I've experienced more than thirty killing frosts in my mountains. And each time, I think of that night on the train. It's become a ritual for me. I now understand that each year, a part of us dies. Our leaves and flowers are absorbed into the earth. But our roots are still here, dormant, waiting out the cold time. Some of us blossom again. Some do not.

The next evening, the nightmare intensified. People yelling in their sleep. Inconsolable children. Stunned adults. In the early morning, we began to get organized. Some tried to clean the two toilets for ninety-eight people. Finally, the man who ran the Teletype machine at the embassy and one of the attachés unscrewed the toilets and pushed them out of the train. Now we had two holes that were scary to use, but it was far better than before. Women knitted while groups of men played pinochle in the aisles. In our compartment, we took turns reading to the children, including the two older boys. Food was shared. Water was rationed. Each time we stopped at a station, ten designated people left the train, ran into the buffet, and tried to buy everything they could carry.

In the middle of the afternoon, Mr. Greenleaf, following his instructions, collected everyone's papers. Although we had all been told that this would happen, I had to help him convince everyone that it was all right.

The train stopped at the frontier. An official said, "Everyone off the train and form two lines. One for men. One for women and children."

The Jewish family in our compartment was petrified. I couldn't bear another tragedy. "Mr. Greenleaf, we have to protect these people," I whispered.

"I'm sorry, but we can do nothing," he said. "They got on the train, I'm sure they have the papers to get off."

"Give me all your entry papers," I said to the father, and he handed them over.

"We're going to put their papers with ours," I said to Mr. Greenleaf.

"No, R.B., please, you can't."

"Oh, yes, I can," I said in the nicest voice I could conjure. And I took the papers and slipped them in, just as the *Passkontrolle* official approached.

First, Mr. Greenleaf handed the official two letters. One was from the American Embassy in Germany, and the other from the appropriate Reich office. He read them, scribbled his initials, and handed everything back to Greenleaf. And with his fluttering hand, he dismissed us, all of us.

The train arrived at the Gare du Nord in Paris at eight in the morning, two days late. I was bedraggled, exhausted, short-tempered. Not Richard and his family. They were excited.

But the other family in our compartment was nervous. "Stay behind me," I said to them. "I'll try to get you through."

First in line, with the nervous assortment of Americans and the German family behind me, I was searching for the trustworthy official. None of them fit the description of the man with the mustache and the funny ears, so I intuitively chose the most benign-looking man I could find. I handed him my passport and leaned down to hear what he was saying. The official whispered under his breath, "I shaved it off"—and stamped my passport. "Stamp the one of the man behind me. Please," I pleaded. And he did.

As each person was freed into Paris, I watched as he or she stood astonished at the exit. Green trolleys, automobiles, people on the streets. Blooming red geraniums in the windows. Normal life. Even the sun was shining. I could hope that Coleman and Annelie would now begin to heal. Their parents were smiling. My mother was, too. And she was the first to speak.

"I'm going back to the Studio Hôtel, Rose. I'll be in touch in a few days."

"Let's make a definite time," I said. "I'll meet you Saturday night at eight at your hotel."

And my mother left—without saying good-bye to anyone.

Next was Pete, whom I had not seen the entire trip because he had been shuttled to another part of the train. "See you later, R.B. Don't forget we have to check in with Ramsey tomorrow," he said, and he left for home.

"Come," I said to the Moses family, "you'll all stay with me while we sort things out."

Really, the only thing to figure out was where to get the rest of the money for their steamship tickets, and in the end it was easy. I collected contributions from my friends and colleagues. And then, when I informed Mr. Clancy, the consul at the American Embassy, about what had happened to the children, there was no holding back the flood of help. It was settled. Richard and his family were to have about three months in Paris, waiting for emigration papers for Daria and the children.

I wrote a human-interest story about the children who had been sterilized in Germany. "I'm worried," Ramsey said. "Worried that we'll lose our readership. Who wants to be told shit like this?"

But I was too distressed to care about Ramsey and his concerns. I was grieving. Here I was, safely back in Paris. Without Leon. My father dead. Stella dead. Andy dead. And I was living in the same city as my mother.

Once, when I was a little girl, there was an explosion in one of the nearby silver mines. It was so powerful that I was thrown from my bed. Everyone ran outside and watched as a geyser of water rose into the air, taking with it a neighbor's wagon and smashing it onto the road, where it splintered into pieces. Now, I was feeling the same emotions—anxiety and awe. What I cherished most had exploded. But even though I was intact, I felt impotent, knowing that I had few choices.

There was no magical way to rescue Leon, but I knew that I could not give up. I had to keep reminding myself of my familial obligation to my mother; my ongoing duty to deliver the secret papers to the embassy; my need to ensure that Richard and his family made it to safety in America. Only when I went through that list did I calm down and begin to think about another planned escape for Leon and his parents.

Meanwhile the Moses family was enjoying the relative calm of Paris. A couple of days after they arrived, I found little Coleman and Annelie rolling a ball down the corridor outside their room. Occasionally, there would be a small yelp of pleasure and all the adults would look at each other and smile.

"What are you going to do when you get back to New York?" I asked Richard. "Will your brother look out for you?"

"Most likely he'll do what he can," Richard said. "But I think

I've figured it out. There're a number of Negro swing bands performing all over the country. I'll audition for as many as will listen. If that idea doesn't work, then I'll try to join the army as a saxophonist for one of the Negro marching bands. That should keep us safe."

The Moses family taught me about familial love. Their son, Coleman, is such a wonderful man. I adore being with him. He's inherited his mother's short height and his father's good looks. He's a bit odd—but who wouldn't be, coming from the circumstances of his life?

He made the table that I'm sitting at now. One day, when he was in his forties, he came to visit, as he often does. I was working at my normal desk, a card table, whose four legs rested on rubber disks, with matchbooks underneath to level everything on my old floor. He had always given me a hard time about the desk.

"Rosie," he would say, "let me make a desk for you."

"No, dear," I always replied, "this is fine. I'm used to it."

One day, he didn't ask. He went out to the old barn, found some nice planks of wood, and went to work. I heard sawing and sanding and hammering and a good amount of cussing, but I stayed inside, not willing to nose about and cause trouble.

Finally, it became still. I watched him from the porch as he stained the wood with a big brush that had seen better days. Before it was even dry, he had it on the wheelbarrow, in front of the door.

"Can I help?" I asked.

"Yes, hold the door open, and I'll wrangle it inside."

"But what about getting it upstairs into my study?"

"Rosie" he said, "I've been wanting to talk to you about this. I've watched you," he said. "You can barely climb the stairs. It worries me. Wouldn't it be better if the room off the kitchen could be made into your study? That way, the only time you would have to climb is when you go to bed."

"You're such a dear," I replied, "But I have to go up and down all day long. It's good exercise for me. If I don't move around, I get as stiff as one of those boards you used to make my lovely new desk."

"Well, I strongly suggest that you stop being so hard-headed," he said. "You're alone out here. You're almost eighty-five. What will you do if you fall?"

"Most likely die, my dear, but that's okay."

"Well, it may be okay with you, but not with me," he declared.

I realized that my being so pigheaded was upsetting to him, which didn't make me proud of my behavior.

"You win, Coleman. Now, how are we going to do this?"

"You're not doing anything," he said, and laughed. He lifted the table, carrying it in front of him like a medieval shield. After much moving around, my new worktable was placed before the windows. Now I can sit and look out at the gardens and fields. And sometimes, since I lead such a quiet life, I can see red fox, and deer.

On Saturday, I met my mother in her room at eight o'clock sharp. "Would you like to have a seat?" she asked.

"Ma, you sit on the chair, I'll sit on the bed."

I was still reeling from the hasty departure from Berlin; from the close calls we had with the Nazis; from observing such horrific violence; from my mother's nasty response to Leon and his family; from the long and treacherous train ride to Paris. And, most importantly, I now understood that she had pulled her spitting act to divert my attention away from Leon—to destroy my chance for love.

"So," she asked, "are we going to have a six-gun shoot-out?" Her hands were fidgeting on her lap. "I'm ready if you are."

I'd been rehearsing what to say. Among the many stinging

lines I had come up with were: Do you know that you're the most selfish, narcissistic person I've ever known? Do you know that I gave up the love of my life for you? And do you understand that you don't deserve my loyalty? Here I was, a grown woman conjuring up the ugliest barbs, the most poisonous rebuttals. A litany of grievances. But I had to ask myself what good could come of a geyser of rage.

"The truth is," my mother said, "I don't want a shoot-out. I'm craving peace and quiet. I really don't want to be bothered by family matters."

Ah. In the end, I'm just a "family matter," I thought with wry amusement. My mother was secretly hoping for a reprieve. Although I felt gagged with anger, I made a conscious decision to give it to her. I was terrified of saying out loud what I was feeling, because those words, once said, could never be taken back.

We lived at opposite ends of the city. I was still at the Hôtel Espoir in the Latin Quarter, and she found a small apartment only two minutes away from the Bois de Boulogne, on the edge of the city in the sixteenth arrondissement. At least I wouldn't run into her on the street.

What a mess, I thought. I've come across the sea to live my own life, and what happens? My mother moves here. It's ridiculous.

As agreed, we stayed in our separate corners of the city. I pretended that my mother wasn't there. But I knew through the embassy grapevine that she had begun to establish acquaintances. She was invited to their functions, introduced as "our brave American, Miriam Manon, from the vast state of Nevada"—who had escaped from Berlin at the last moment— by the skin of her teeth.

"How's your mother?" Richard asked one night.

"I don't know. I'm assuming she's well. I've heard from

people at the embassy that she's been doing watercolor and pencil drawings of the wildflowers of the American West. Clancy bought an entire suite for his office, so the news quickly got around the American community that it was chic to purchase her drawings. Happily, I think she's too busy to cause trouble."

But even though I felt that I had my mother in an emotionally safer place, my anxiety was intensifying. What had happened to Leon? I had not heard a word.

My room at the Hôtel Espoir was a crowded and noisy haven for Richard's family. As many of the old tenants had left, having been arrested or moved to a different country, it wasn't difficult for me to find another room. Because it was only two doors down, I decided to take Andy's. I replaced his smelly bed and cigarette-scarred table with furniture from other vacated rooms, but took possession of his abandoned books. He had three different editions of *The Iliad*; volumes of pre–Great War poetry; many of the Balzac and Zola novels; a frayed edition of Goethe; and a dog-eared copy of our much-discussed and debated Freud. When I opened the Freud, I found it filled with handwritten notations. Andy's handwriting was crabbed and hard to read, but I had always been able to decipher it. I wished I had not opened it. It was like entering a tumultuous, ugly scream. But read I did. Poor man, he suffered far more than I ever imagined. I was struck by my friend's intellect, his complex neuroses, and the power of his sexual fantasy. Andy's imaginary world had been filled with a passion for words and for redheaded women. I was surprised at how much I missed him. We had lost the loves of our lives for different reasons, but I suspected that our pain was buried in the same place.

In my old room, Daria moved things around, trying to give the family a sense of space. We created a ritual. Each morning the children would open the windows and loudly wish

Madame Canari "Bonjour." And Madame Canari would shout "Good morning" in English, and everyone would laugh.

Daria taught the children from nine in the morning until noon, and then again from four until six. The routine clearly gave back to the children some of their happiness. Richard, meanwhile, sat in on jazz sets here and there, met musician friends, and talked about the old days.

"Really, Rosie," he reported back, "it's as if we're old men talking about another world. People are nervous. Some are deeply frightened. Everyone I know is either cooking up ideas so they can safely stay here, or planning an escape. I feel kind of funny around them because I'm so clear about the threat and they're pretty naïve. I'll miss you. I'll miss Paris. But I'm relieved that we're going home."

Three months after arriving in Paris, we all boarded the train for Le Havre. I watched, yet again, the escaping passengers and the holiday passengers. There was such a deep difference between the two groups—it was almost obscene. And Daria and Richard sensed it right away. They held the children's hands, not allowing them to skip up the gangplank.

* * *

Not a word from Leon. And none of my newspaper friends could help. Indeed, most of them had left Germany and were scattered over Europe, still trying to make sense of what was happening for their respective newspapers.

Time dragged by. I felt that I was caught on the apex of a suspension bridge, and didn't know which way to go. War was certain to erupt any day. Horror stories about the treatment of Jews were escaping through the barbed wire. I had tried various Jewish émigré agencies in Paris to help me find Leon, but they were too busy. They were frantically trying to get Jews out of France. But I persisted. Each day I made the rounds of different agencies and patiently waited my turn to speak to someone. One day I'd had enough. I stood in one of the dingy offices—cracked tan or gray linoleum on the floor, scarred old furniture—and shouted at the receptionist, "Goddammit, can't anyone help me?"

The receptionist slowly rose, came around her desk, and stood before me. She was a small, nondescript, middle-aged woman with her gray hair pulled tightly back into a bun. Each time I had seen her, she had been wearing the same brown and black tweed suit with flat, brown-laced shoes.

"You, Madam, are one of thousands of people looking for lost family and friends. What makes you," she said, poking me in the arm with her finger, "think your case is more important than that of the person sitting next to you?" And she pointed to a bedraggled-looking woman. "She's trying to find both of her children and her mother. Can you beat that? Now, go back to your America—your America that won't let the rest of us in. You'll be safe there. Forget here. It's over."

"How did you know that I'm an American?"

"My dear, I was chair of the linguistics department at the University of Berlin."

While I was stuck in Paris waiting for another assignment, I returned to the political desk. I also continued writing my column, now called "Paris Chronicle." These short essays were not particularly newsworthy, but they addressed the individual stories of émigrés. Their attempts to escape from France to a friendlier country. Their feelings about being uprooted. *Agence France-Presse* continued to buy everything I wrote. Even the BBC Empire Service was reading my work on the radio. It was becoming apparent to me that my style of writing was changing. My eye was becoming sharper. My descriptions were clearer. My emotional responses, crisper. Losing Leon had paradoxically unleashed in me a new way of using language.

As it grew warmer in Paris, the days became heavier. People's anxieties were building; plans for escape were more seriously discussed. But residents were having a hard time getting up and moving out of Paris. It was a disaster, this national ennui. And I continued to search for news of Leon—but with no success.

There was no escaping the apprehension. Depression came rolling toward me like a storm. My loneliness and my fears for Leon were causing periods of insomnia. At the same time, I kept reminding myself that it wasn't just *my* world that was bleak; the entire world was suffering the same poverty of hope.

August. Paris was hot and muggy and empty of many of its inhabitants. The extreme heat had furled the chestnut leaves. The Seine was running, but so low that sandbars had appeared in the river. The normally luxurious grass in the parks had turned yellow. People were clustering in shady areas, sharing them with the pigeons, the ravens, and the city's cats. Even the subterranean wine bars were sweltering with damp, creeping with mold.

Every two weeks, I wrote identical letters to Leon, to Stefan, to the bartender at the Hotel Aldon, even to Gerard (without a last name, but care of Leon's address). They were always returned—most having been opened and sealed again with tape. On each envelope was written, *Nicht mehr an dieser Adresse*, No longer at this address, in formal handwriting. Each of my letters said the same thing: *Please be so kind as to send me news of Leon Wolff. Thank you. Rose Manon, c/o* The Paris Courier, *rue de Berri, Paris.* While the efficiency of the German bureaucracy amazed me, it made me furious that the bureaucrats were aggravating my own helplessness.

"Mr. Ramsey, I want to be reassigned. Being in Paris isn't where I can do the paper the most good."

"Well, how about China?" he said.

"No, too far. How about making me a roving correspondent?" I asked. "I could follow trouble. You could send me anywhere at a moment's notice."

Ramsey shook his head and lit a cigar. "Well, that's all well and good, kid, but now that you're known as a Jew, that leaves out Germany, Poland—"

"Yeah, I know what it could leave out. But look at it this way: I don't have a family. I don't have roots anywhere in Europe. I can move around easily. My American passport doesn't have a Jewish stamp. My last name isn't a Jewish one. And 'glamour' isn't a word that's attached to my lapel."

"I'll cable New York," he said, "but you'll most likely have to wait until the Vosberg circus is over."

I reminded him, "We are going to get into that same ethical question again."

"Pete will cover it with you, like before," Ramsey said. "It's your cousin, after all. Anyway, the ethical question doesn't matter anymore. We'll be at war soon."

* * *

The start of the Vosberg trial created a commotion. There were reporters from the largest newspapers, along with famous writers from most European countries, the United States, and Great Britain. I was startled when I saw Colette arrive outside the court in a sleek black car. The chauffeur got out and opened her door, and there she was in all her splendor. For me, even though I had met her a number of times, seeing Colette was like seeing Greta Garbo and Edith Piaf all in one.

Soldiers of the *garde mobile* were standing sentry around the building to keep the crowds calm. Outside the courtroom, thirty telephone booths had been installed. Inside, the specta-tors faced the judge, two white-bibbed lawyers for the accused, the prosecutor, and a jury of twelve men. Of the jury, six men had mustaches, two wore glasses, six were almost bald, and one man had unruly curly hair, while all the others were brilliantined, with their hair flat to their heads.

The courtroom held more than a hundred people. The stalls at the rear were reserved for members of the general pub-lic. I felt sorry for them. There were no seats and everyone would have to stand all day. But they appeared happy to do this, some with their arms resting on the wooden barrier that separated them from the journalists' seats, with their backsides jutting out like shelves. A small gallery to the right of the bar of justice, which had an ornately carved rail, was reserved for people with influence, including Colette, Janet Flanner, Mau-rice Chevalier, Aurora Sand—and even Lord Tennyson's great-niece. I found it amusing that someone in the court had stretched many yards of bluish-green cloth across both the gallery and the stalls to hide the legs of the women—shorter skirts were in style.

I knew what was going to happen next; I could feel the rumbling behind my back. I saw a flash of magnesium. Then mayhem broke loose. The photographers were clamoring for space. They were standing on top of chairs, balancing on rails, shouting for the jurors to look up, accidentally dropping their cameras, swearing, knocking over furniture. As this was going on, one of Vosberg's two attorneys, Renée Jardin, with her hen-naed hair in curls, was idly chatting with her legal colleagues.

Vosberg's other attorney, the star defense orator Moro-Giafferi, was a chubby little man with the face of an owl and an operatic, beautiful speaking voice. His vanity, I could see, was hilarious. Like a peacock he strutted about, dramatically waving his lighted cigarette in an amber holder. *DÉFENSE DE FUMER*, no smoking, was posted on all the walls. But most everyone was smoking. Every window in the court was closed. I was dying of the heat. Damn the French and their anxiety about fresh air, I thought—they were convinced that an open window would make them sick. Moro-Giafferi, although from Corsica, also had an aversion to fresh air. He would sneer at anyone who complained—making a point of wrapping his brown wool scarf around his neck yet again. The only relief was that some of the people in the gallery were eating oranges, and the smell reminded me of sunshine and health and fresh air.

It began to quiet down. For the photographers' benefit, Vosberg was led in. The photographers were allowed five minutes, and the room was ablaze with lights. Vosberg kept his head down. Then the prisoner was led out into the hallway between the courtroom and the prison. The presiding judge, Maurice Levi, ornately outfitted in his scarlet velvet robe, white bib, and red velvet cap, made a pronouncement: ten cameramen would be allowed to stay in the court. There was a loud collective groan and the photographers were marched in single file to the corridor. I could see through the doorway that they were tossing coins to see who were the lucky ones.

When the prisoner was brought back, his chains had been removed. Pete and I were only five or six feet from him. I watched Vosberg intently, and at one point the prisoner looked directly at me and smiled wanly. The audience swung around toward me. Jeez, I thought, this attention's all I need. But I did, strangely, feel special, and then detested myself for having that feeling. I could sense that Pete was struggling not to smile.

Vosberg was wearing a well-tailored blue serge double-breasted suit with a glaring white shirt, a blue-and-white striped tie, and highly polished burgundy shoes. I noted that although he was cleanly shaven, his face was a deathly white, and he had dark circles beneath his sunken eyes. Vosberg was a man of two faces. In profile, he appeared gentle; with his turned-up nose he had the look of one easily tormented. Then, in full view, he showed himself as the tormentor. I could see why I had had such a hard time recreating his face for the police artist.

It's startling, but I've just realized that the pages about my mother's appearance in the courtroom are missing from the trial notes. Did I do this on purpose? Why? After all, when I saw her, it was a dramatic moment. I held the notes, while pacing my garden—roughly brushing up against a large pot of lemon-balm-scented geraniums. That strong aroma brings me to my senses. I walk back into my office and look through a pile of newspaper clippings. Here are my notes about my mother, separate from my trial notes, and kept together with a rusty safety pin. I wonder what I was thinking? Was I so distressed by her presence that I didn't want to be reminded later on? And why did I change my mind and keep the pages? I have no idea.

While the judge was whispering to some officials behind his hand, I looked around the courtroom. I couldn't believe it. There was my mother in a far corner, sketching, along with five other pencil artists.

I was outraged. How dare she intrude upon my territory? I did know that she had a good reputation as a court illustrator in Nevada. But I never, never once, considered that she would bring this profession to Europe.

She must have felt me staring at her, looked up, and caught my irate glance. Giving me a minuscule smile, she went back to work.

I watched her through the thick haze of cigarette smoke. The putrid-green painted walls. The lack of fresh air. The high windows obscured by soot. I had to admit to myself that she sure had guts.

But I also remember feeling that I was seeing myself in a mirror—my mother was my reflection. Like her, I also had guts. Like her, I had a strong talent. But at that time, there was a big difference. I was in mourning—and she was thrilled with her new life.

I suspect that my obituary will claim that I was an accomplished, fearless war correspondent. It's only partly true. I saw myself as pathetic—longing for Leon—longing for love. To do my job, I had to force myself to be tough, never allowing my colleagues to see weakness. Most of the time I succeeded. But seeing my mother in that courtroom confused me. Part of me understood that she had every right to be there—she was certainly talented enough. But I was being pummeled by yet another unspoken, childish tantrum.

I was spinning. How could this have happened to me? No other reporters had their mothers in their public lives. Even the French reporters I knew seemed to have sprouted out of nowhere. As far as I knew, my writer-colleagues—except for Andy—never let on that they even had mothers. And here I was, an only child, being followed halfway around the world by mine.

Colette had always fascinated me. She was a part of the French literary world that I so admired. Sartre, de Beauvoir, Gide—I fantasized about being their close friend. But all I was to them was the French-speaking American correspondent at the *Courier*. The Paris literary scene was a most complicated private club. I could smell their success, taste their triumph—and I wanted some for myself. But I was frightened silly by the possibility of not being taken seriously, of being rejected.

End of the day in court. Where is she? I asked myself, and looked around the room. My mother was in a circle of people. I tried to get closer. Wouldn't you know it? There she was, speaking with Colette. They appeared to be besotted with each other. I heard Colette say, "Come, dear, I'll drive you home."

Pete and I filed our story by eleven. "Why don't you come home with me," Pete said, "and have a nightcap? You can see the baby, since she never sleeps anyway."

"No thanks, Pete, I need to take a walk. But it's nice of you to ask. Can I take a rain check?"

"Sure," he said playfully. "But if you wait too long, by the time you see the sweet thing, she'll be a rotten teenager."

The hot spell had broken and it was quite a cool evening. Along the banks of the river, vagrants were making their fires and unfurling their bedrolls for sleep. Flocks of sheep and goats were settling in for the night too. I could hear the thudding of their bells. Two elderly men, both wearing farmers' galoshes, one in a blue beret, the other in a matching blue jacket, were finishing hoeing a row of cabbages under the yellow light of a streetlamp. Except for the occasional sound of a horn, I thought, I could be in the country. Leaning on the rail, I lit a cigarette and contemplated my mother.

She had obviously applied, and someone had hired her, to illustrate the trial. Who? I supposed it really didn't matter, but it made me uncomfortable. Knowing my mother, I wouldn't have been surprised to learn that she had contracted for the job while in New York. She had to have known that I would be upset, but in her usual fashion had ignored the emotional consequences.

The next morning I waylaid her in front of the court building. "Ma, wait, I need to talk to you."

"Rose, leave me alone," she said.

"But why are you following me everywhere?" I asked. "It's embarrassing!"

"Excuse me," she said, "what makes you think I'm follow-ing you? After all, *Collier's* offered me this job. Did you expect me to turn it down?"

"Listen, Ma, we have to figure this out. You're in my way. I'm the only grown woman—who happens to be a journalist for one of the most important newspapers in the Western world—whose mother's following her around covering the same story. Can't you see how uncomfortable this is? Hell, some magazine like your *Collier's* will see us as good material for a friggin' human-interest story."

"Oh, for heaven's sake, Rose, it's not that bad. And anyway, there's nothing to be done. I'm committed to covering the trial—and I'm determined to fulfill my obligation. So why don't you just ignore me? Stop glaring at me across the courtroom. Then no one will sense that we know each other. I'll make you a promise," she continued angrily. "I won't acknowledge you at all."

Not wanting to get into a screaming match outside the court, I turned and walked off. I knew when I was beaten.

But I watched while Colette's car pulled to the curb. She jumped out before her driver did, yelling, "Miriam, Miriam, allo!" The women kissed on both cheeks and Colette took her arm. I overheard her say to my mother, "Dear Miriam, let's have dinner tonight."

I met Mr. Hin for dinner. "So, Rosie, how is the trial going? And how is your mother?"

"My mother sits there and draws and has the attention of the people in the balcony directly above her. It's amusing to lis-ten to them commenting on her drawings—some even going so far as to point out possible corrections. I can see that it makes her testy—but have to admit that it pleases me!"

I changed the subject. "Vosberg's truly mad. One moment he seems to understand what he's accused of and almost shows remorse—and the next moment he's feeling sorry for himself and acting as if he's a tragic character in a Shakespearean drama. There's obviously something seriously wrong with him, but he's hard to read. He doesn't fit any psychiatric definitions that I've ever read about."

"He appears to be engaged in a Noh play," Mr. Hin said. "He's acting out different complicated characters and wearing an assortment of masks."

"Oh, you're so right," I said. "Not only does he physically keep changing, but he displays different emotional character-istics that appear to do battle with each other."

"Meaning?" Mr. Hin asked.

"Well, he can be suave and make you feel that he's trying to seduce the jury and the judge. And in the flick of a moment, he's scowling at them as if they smell of garbage! I'm glad today's over."

"By the way," Mr. Hin said, "have you heard from Richard or Daria?"

The Moses family had made friends with Mr. Hin. As the chil-dren became less fearful, he had taken them to the park to play. I loved seeing the three of them on a bench, the children sitting on either side of Mr. Hin while he read them stories. The only problem was that he couldn't read English and they didn't speak French. So he had made a game out of their teaching each other. Mr. Hin would try to sound out an English word. They would help him and explain what it meant. Then he would teach them the word in French. Sometimes Mr. Hin would, on purpose, mispronounce a word and they would dis-solve into delicious laughter.

"I haven't heard from them," I said, "but I'm sure they'll write as soon as they get settled."

"Well, I hope we hear soon," he said. "I think we're in for a long siege of isolation. Ships carrying mail are not important any longer. Storage space is being taken up with war-related goods."

We were quiet for a while. I thought about what he had just said. I was learning more and more facts about how a war is managed—having never considered, for example, the delivery of foreign mail during a crisis.

"How long do you think the trial will last?" Mr. Hin said.

"I hope not long. I asked to be reassigned as a roving correspondent, but Ramsey said no. Not now. Besides, I suppose I owe it to Stella to see this ordeal through to the end. But I'm not relishing being in the same room with my mother. And I don't like writing about a hopeless psychopath who apparently killed my cousin."

"But Hitler's a psychopath, too," Mr. Hin argued. "What's the difference? You write about him all the time."

"He's easy," I said. "I have distance from him. She's in my bones!"

"Oh, Rose, Rose," I heard my mother calling out after the next day's session. I ignored her.

"R.B.," my colleague Bill said, "there's a woman calling your name. Are you getting deaf or something?"

"Thanks, Bill, but I need to ignore her. She's been a big bother."

"But—" Bill protested.

"Oh, for Christ's sake, Bill. Let it alone. Just help me get out of here!"

"Wow, pal. Calm down," he said. "There's nothing I can do—she's right behind you." And with a newspaperman's curiosity, Bill didn't budge.

"Rose," my mother said, slightly out of breath, and gripping my arm to turn me around. "Don't be such a horse's ass. Colette and Janet have asked if you would join us for dinner."

"Wow," Bill said. "Introduce me to your charming friend. She's the pencil artist I mentioned before."

Pure hatred flooded my mind. Then shame. Then futility.

"This is Bill Jamison from the *Guardian*. Bill, this is my mother, Miriam Manon."

"Well, I'll be," he exclaimed. "I've been watching you drawing during the trial. You're good. Really good!"

"Thank you," she replied graciously.

I realized that there was no chance for me politely to turn down the dinner invitation. And, because I already had a professional relationship with both Colette and Janet, I could admit to myself that I was fascinated—now I would have the opportunity to observe my mother. But when we walked to the car, neither Colette nor Janet appeared to recognize me. "I would like you to meet my daughter Rose," she said to them. "She's the cub reporter for the *Paris Courier*." My heart sank with the patronizing attitude.

"No, my dear Miriam," Colette said, saving the moment. "We've met her before. But we know her as R.B. Manon, the major correspondent for the largest English-language paper in France. Her work's well known and appreciated by all of us. Now, let's first go to my house before our dinner."

I sat on the front seat of the black Peugeot; Colette, Janet Flanner, and my mother settled into the back. The car reeked of Colette's perfume. I felt as if we were in a funeral parlor, sitting beside a casket. I supposed the strong perfume covered the musty odor of perspiration after a long time spent in a stuffy courtroom. I tried to crack a window.

"No, dear, I will catch a cold," Colette admonished. And I noticed a glimmer of a smile on the chauffeur's face.

We were deposited at 9 rue de Beaujolais in the Palais-Royal on the Right Bank. I had often walked by this building. Sometimes I saw Colette leaning on her windowsill, chatting with her strolling neighbors. Her rooms faced south and overlooked the sharply sculpted, much-too-manicured gardens. Set in the center of the gardens was an energetic fountain that reminded me of the white egret plumes on some of my Aunt Clara's hats.

"Come upstairs," Colette pronounced. "We need to wash up after such a long day." Colette unlocked the door and we all entered. "You go first, R.B.," she said.

"Please, call me Rose," I replied, and she smiled.

I did as I was told and then combed my hair—and with humor remembered to clean my hairs out of the sink, just as my mother had taught me. But, when I looked at myself in the mirror, I could see only the child I had once been. Distressed by this association, I flung cold water at my face, wiped it with my handkerchief, and lit a cigarette.

In the small hallway outside the toilet stood my mother, waiting for her turn. "Isn't this amazing?" she whispered. "Imagine, two nobodies from nowhere waiting to use the great Colette's toilet."

"Ma, I have to tell you that I'm feeling really upset. Being here with you isn't good for me. I feel like a child."

"You keep saying that, Rose. I don't know how to make you feel better. You certainly don't seem like a child to me. Your hair's even turning gray, like your father's."

I thrust my hands deeper into my pockets. Smoke billowed around my face, and I tried to control the most ridiculous urge to shove my own mother.

"Perhaps you should check your dear Dr. Freud," she said, "and see if he can help you." And she entered the toilet and closed the door.

"Here, dear, here I am," Colette directed from the other room.

Entering the room where Colette wrote melted away my

anger. Although it was stuffy, she was sitting with a shimmering brown fur robe thrown over her legs, leaning back against the plump damask pillows. She had henna-colored hair and long, gray, luminous eyes that were surrounded by kohl and framed by thin arches of brows. Her full face was accented with a little chin and a mouth that was long and red. I knew that it was in this room, *la petite chambre rouge,* that she wrote. It was obvious why it had that name—the walls were covered with a deep, Pompeian red silk. Even the divan was upholstered in a shade of red, a deep carmine. On her desk were her collection of paperweights, a portable slanted writing table, a globe, a magnifying glass, a blue lamp, a jar with her fountain pens, and a Persian blue vase of yellow daffodils. Behind the desk were shelves set into an arched wall, holding books, the telephone, and framed butterflies, spread-eagled and lifeless. There was no clock to be seen.

Janet was sitting on the desk chair. She was wearing her trademark black tailored suit, this one a Chanel. Her monocle, used as an aid for her dark-brown eyes, dangled from a black ribbon around her neck. Her nose was too big for her face. Even though she was only forty-six years old, her bobbed hair was so white that it looked translucent. That evening Janet was suffering from kidney stones. She wasn't happy or comfortable.

"Sit down wherever you like," Colette said to me, "but careful of the cats. Now, tell us what you've been covering in this ridiculous world." I liked her directness and began to describe my experiences in Berlin. The women appeared to be interested.

"There's going to be war—a war that may even exceed the Great War," I said in a firm voice, trying not to sound as if I were pontificating, and they nodded in agreement. I could feel my mature expertise returning to my brain. What a relief, I thought. I'm speaking like a grown-up.

"Do you really think there's going to be a war?" my mother asked, walking into the room.

"Oh, my dear Miriam," Janet said. "After you've been here for a while, and then look back, you'll begin to understand the naïveté of Americans. Of course there'll be a war—indeed, all of Europe's balanced on a seesaw."

"Before we get into a long discussion, or an argument, let's eat," Colette said. "I'm starved. And you," she said, pointing at Janet, "you must not drink wine with your kidney stones. It's what causes the pain."

"Nonsense," said Janet. "And after a day of watching that murderer, I need a drink. Let's go."

On the street, I walked behind the three women. They were all short. While my mother and Colette were rotund, both with bigger-than-normal feet, Janet was thin, with tiny feet that moved her body like a bird.

We walked to a bistro in the passage Choiseul. "This is the night," Colette said, "that they serve a special cassoulet. But I have to be careful. I'm getting fat, because I like my food too much. The new oracle," she complained, "is the bathroom scale." She smiled. "So I don't own one."

We were hungry—and we were so animated by the trial that we talked with our mouths full of food, holding white napkins up, trying to be polite.

My mother took center stage. "Vosberg has an odd face," she said. "Drawing him is difficult."

"I think," Janet said, "that he's exceptionally handsome in the medieval way—his features are those of a Holbein etching, with an alert, inquiring, open, hungry eye, an aquiline nose, and a handsome and sensual mouth. I can see why a woman like Stella Mair would be attracted."

"That's a perfect description," my mother said, "and—"

"Wait," Janet said, holding up her hand with its ever-present cigarette. "I have more to say about our Miss Stella."

I felt my stomach flop and watched my mother's stoic face. I realized that the other two women had no idea about our family connection to Stella.

"You see," Janet said, "I know a girl here in Paris who knew her—had known her since she was a child in Philadelphia. My friend works at the American Express office. She said that Stella Mair was a grabby little American. Still, I do have to admit that it was an awful thing to go out to tea with a new foreign beau and have him strangle her."

"Perhaps," I said, "Stella made friends easily. That doesn't mean she was *loose*. It simply means that she was an honest-to-goodness American girl. Anyway, she came from Brooklyn, not Philadelphia."

"Oh, you're right, R.B.," Janet said sarcastically. "Sure. My friend must have given me information about the wrong woman."

No one at the table challenged her, and I was afraid of embarrassing myself.

I changed the subject. "Vosberg is emblematic of our time. He represents our anxieties. Our anxieties for our daughters—our anxieties for France. He's indeed a treacherous man."

Everyone nodded in agreement.

We had finished—run out of things to say—full of cassoulet and tipsy on red wine. And Janet had turned gray with pain.

"You see, dear, it's the wine," said Colette.

"I must go," Janet said, "I don't feel well. See you all tomorrow."

"The poor woman," my mother said after she left. "She—"

And Colette interrupted. "She's stubborn, stubborn as an ass!"

That night Czecho-Slovakia ceased to exist. I heard from the reporters in my office that the Czechs were so surprised by the sudden occupation that the only resistance they put up was to throw snowballs at Hitler's troops. But I found it hard to find humor in the Czech story. As I walked home from the office, I noticed a waning of human energy and activity. People appeared to slink among the shadows. Noisy conversations and laughter were missing. There was an eerie silence in the air. It was obvious that people were preoccupied with despair for Europe, for their own lives. France was dying. And I was preoccupied with wondering what I was doing in France at all. Stella was dead. This I knew. Leon was still alive—so far as I knew.

I was brimming with both boredom and longing. I had no social life. Each evening Pete and I arrived at the newspaper office with only enough time to file our story. After that, Pete would go home to his family, and I would eat at a bistro, sometimes with a colleague, but most often alone. I wasn't bathing enough; I didn't have the time. My clothes needed to be washed. When I had been with my mother at Colette's apartment, I could tell by her grimace that she thought I smelled. Wine, cigarettes, and coffee, along with hard salami, cheese, and bread, were the staples of my culinary life.

My political and humanitarian views were being relentlessly challenged. I had come from a family of contrasts. Mother was the one who owned and used the shotgun; my father wouldn't touch it. I've always stood somewhere in between—the worst place to be. It left me adrift in a roiling sea of opinions. My father had believed that capital punishment was wrong, but I knew that my mother was rooting for Vosberg's demise. Again, I was caught in between. Then I thought about Leon and his parents, and my entire tough-girl belief system came tumbling down. I chose my father's side.

The next day in court made me furious. I watched Vosberg sit quietly and elegantly, his knees crossed, his face erased of feelings. I felt a repugnance so visceral that I had to hold onto both sides of my seat to prevent myself from leaping forward and punching him in the face. Fortunately, the judge called an early recess for lunch. I was relieved to get away from such ugliness—relieved to go outside into the fresh air.

I looked around for my mother and found her with her new pals—along with Madame Sand. "Come," Colette said to the group, "let's go have lunch. Everyone," she said, "please meet Aurora Sand."

"Oh, Miss Manon, it's so good to see you again," Madame Sand said enthusiastically. I could see that everyone, especially my mother, was impressed.

We walked rather slowly, because of Colette's bad feet, to a café across the street from the court. With great ceremony we were led to a large table at the window.

It took a while to order. Everyone had questions, especially Colette. How was the veal cooked? When was it purchased from the butcher? Was the butcher in Paris? What was his name? My mother and I smiled at each other over the silliness of the inquisition, but the others took it quite seriously.

Out of the blue, as if our being together was the continuation from another meal, Janet said, "I think Vosberg's homosexual."

"Ah," everyone said in unison.

"When he said in his earlier testimony," she continued, "'I was close to her on the sofa,' the American press assumed there was sex. But he used the word '*allongé*,' which means to stretch out, as on a sofa—in French, the word has no erotic significance at all. And the police definitely stated that the autopsy showed that there was no intercourse. I understand, thanks to R.B.'s correction, that she wasn't a stay-out-all-night kind of girl. And it's obvious that her respectable Jewish aunt would have never expected Stella to be impolite."

I caught myself feeling piqued at Janet for having to identify Clara as "Jewish." "Excuse me, but what does being Jewish have to do with it?" I asked. "Would you say 'Christian' if her aunt had been Christian? I don't think so."

For a pregnant moment the women were uncomfortable. Janet turned pink with either rage or embarrassment. I could sense that they were all thinking about how to escape the discomfort I had created.

"I agree with what Janet said earlier about Vosberg," said Colette. "He's unusual for a murderer. He's a romantic. He loves flowers and was even cultivating roses at his villa. And he's certainly handsome!"

I knew I was outgunned and folded my hands on my lap, deciding to be quiet.

"Madame Sand," my mother asked, "what did you think of Vosberg's handwriting? Can you tell if he's homosexual or not?"

"No, I can't tell his sexual persuasion," Madame Sand said. "But I can say he's a sociopath, and I don't put homosexuality in that category. His handwriting shows that he has no moral sense of the value of life. He looks for immediate gratification and doesn't concern himself with the aftermath."

"I wonder," I asked Madame Sand, "why they've redefined the word 'sociopath' to mean 'psychopath'?"

"I'm surprised you don't know, Rose," my mother said in a withering voice, before Madame Sand could answer. "You know a lot about Freud." Her nastiness made me want to crawl away and hide.

"It's astonishing," Janet said, changing the subject, "that someone so intelligent could be so ruthless and cold. How do we reconcile his good looks with his evil nature? How—Oh, God, we've got to go! We're late."

"The check," Colette demanded, snapping her fingers.

The next day in court was more interesting. First, there was a discussion of the gun that Vosberg had used to shoot at the police when he was captured. Gun experts were called. At one point, each member of the jury held the gun—and each and every one of them looked down its barrel.

Then Vosberg was asked why Stella had her passport and all her money in her handbag. "We were planning to elope," he said. "She was going to telephone her aunt to tell her. And—" and he held up his hand, as if he were in school asking permission from a teacher. "I have something more to say." He stood. Vosberg put his hands in his pockets and looked down at his shoes. The courtroom was silent. We were all suspended, waiting.

"I admit it," he whispered. "I killed her. I couldn't help it."

"No!" his two lawyers yelled simultaneously.

"No!" Moro-Giafferi boomed again. "Remove that statement from the record. He's crazy, can't you see?"

The courtroom was in chaos. People were yelling at the judge, at the lawyers, at Vosberg. Everyone had an opinion.

I turned to Pete. "I don't understand. Why's everyone so upset?"

"In America," he said, "if you confess to a crime, the next legal proceeding is the sentencing. Essentially, the trial's over. But here in France, if you confess to murder, the sentence is pretty much automatic. It's death, unless you can prove insanity.

"However, if you don't confess, and leave it to the court, there's always a possibility that you'll be given a life sentence in prison or an insane asylum. By confessing, he's undoubtedly killing himself."

The judge banged his gavel over and over again. The lawyers huddled together.

At last, order was restored.

"Continue, Mr. Vosberg," the judge demanded.

Vosberg's hands gripped the railing. He directed his confession to Judge Levi.

"She wanted to make love," Vosberg said quietly. "She was

giddy and playful and pushed me down on the bed and began to unbutton my pants. I couldn't have sex with her—there's something wrong with me."

"Speak up so the jury can hear you," the judge demanded.

"She sneered at me—she taunted me," he shouted. "She called me a stupid eunuch. She humiliated me.

"And I couldn't resist getting her money. I needed the money. I always needed money. And I knew she was Jewish and that Jews are wealthy." And like some poor waif, Vosberg threw himself back into his chair and wept.

I wanted to scream at him. His feeling sorry for himself disgusted me.

I couldn't imagine what Stella had been thinking. This was a part of her that I had seen only once—the time she returned from her first night with Vosberg and I slapped her. Yet it surprised me to hear that she had taunted him. Truly, I didn't believe him. I agreed with Moro-Giafferi. Vosberg was insane.

Court was adjourned. Pete and I met up for a drink with the *Manchester Guardian* reporter, Clyde Thomas. Clyde was a frog-eyed man who walked with a limp. We always seemed to be covering the same stories. We were discussing the case. And then Clyde started to chuckle.

"What's so funny?" I asked.

"When they were passing that gun around," Clyde said, "all I could think about was R.B. and her growing up in the mountains of Nevada. You were squirming with laughter," he said to me, "but so was one of the cartoonists. Do you know her? Is she American?"

"No, I don't know her, but I did almost lose my self-control. It was hilarious! Where I come from, it's considered an act of stupidity to look down a gun barrel. Only greenhorns would do such a thing, to the glee of old-timers."

In some respects the trial had turned into a comedy. Many of the women who came to the courthouse each day wore white hats. They were called "Vosberg's girls," and they were restless. That afternoon, Vosberg was led into the courtroom, and there was a collective and conspicuous sigh. From one of the back stalls a woman screamed, "We love you, dear Ernst!" The police headed for the gallery. There was much commotion. The culprit was taken by the arm—the other "girls" gave out a united shriek—and before you could blink, a policeman had the infatuated woman outside the courtroom doors.

During this time, Vosberg had his face buried in his hands. There was no more smiling at his "girls." When he finally straightened up, his face was red and blotchy and his eyes were bloodshot. Vosberg had begun the trial neat and trim, and in control of his feelings. Now he looked as if he had been crying himself to sleep.

A few minutes into the day's judicial proceedings, Vosberg slowly stood and dramatically grasped the rail before him. Looking directly at Judge Levi he began to speak with a breaking voice, wetting his lips. "I am ready to die for my crimes. I ask you to try to understand me. I am guilty. I offer you everything I can—my life. But please, do not deny me a last request. I am of the Catholic faith and beg to be forgiven." And he sank into his chair and wept.

The prosecutor rose and bellowed, "How dare you ask forgiveness! In the end you are nothing but a vulgar assassin."

That same day, Hitler sutured three countries to the Reich. "Don't be so gloomy, Rose," my mother said as we walked to the Métro. "You're simmering in your own kettle of bad news. Don't you think that if you could step back, you'd see the brighter side of your life?"

I didn't know how to respond. My mother was living in a fantasy world. She was so self-involved that she couldn't bear the idea that even a war could disrupt her plans. And, of course, she couldn't be aware of my sorrow and anxiety about her— much less be sympathetic.

I was beginning to suspect that my mother was truly happy. Certainly, she wasn't grieving for my father. She seldom mentioned him. And I was embarrassed by her obvious sensuality. I had observed men flirting with her while she coyly flicked her eyelashes and demurely looked down. I found it all bewildering. My mother was being transformed before my eyes and rather than being happy for her, I rued her pleasure.

"You're just jealous," Pete said a couple of nights later over many glasses of wine. "It's like what I once heard my wife say about her mother: I wallow under a dark cloud while my mother waltzes in a starlit night. Anyway, R.B., you're not the flirting type. But it's apparent to those of us who have met her that she certainly is!"

If she could recover from the death of a husband of thirty-six years, I asked myself, why couldn't I get over Leon, a lover of a mere four? But I knew Pete was right. I simply didn't know what to do about it.

I often ask myself why I never married. I must be quite strange, I suppose. Although there were men in my life after Leon, I was far more interested in the adventures of my work than in the complications of a marriage. Leon had faded from my consciousness, true. But the passion I felt in that relationship, I never felt again. So, I thought—why bother?

The next morning, the courthouse was again crowded with observers. Pete and I were lucky to get seats. People were perched on windowsills and railings, leaning against walls, jamming the space. Colette was sitting with the actor Maurice Chevalier and Georges Carpentier, the former heavyweight champion of Europe, in the celebrity section.

Today it was the prosecutor's chance to convince the jury that there could be only one sentence for the German murderer: death by guillotine. The prosecutor had changed into a black velvet robe with red-ribboned decorations dripping from his chest. His contrast to Vosberg was startling. Vosberg looked ragged. His shirt collar was now too large; his usually obsessively combed hair was out of place.

"This," the prosecutor said and paused dramatically, "this man is an incarnation of a devil! He must be destroyed. There is no chance for rehabilitation. No, gentlemen of the jury, even with his weeping and sniveling, Ernst Vosberg is past hope. We demand the penalty of death. Nothing less. We have said all that needs to be said. The decision is simple. The handsome devil must die!"

The courtroom became pandemonium. People screamed, "Murderer! Monster!" Others screamed, "No! Let him live!"

Judge Levi banged his gavel. "A recess of one hour is called." There was more screaming. The observers in the courtroom were teetering on the edge of a riot. The guards began to menace those nearest their stations with their raised batons. Then whistles were blown and people began to rush for the door.

Pete and I leaned against the wall, a few feet from our seats. An hour later, after a stern admonishment from the judge, court was reconvened. Everyone was unusually quiet, as if they were embarrassed by their earlier behavior.

The attorney Renée Jardin began her poetic and passionate plea on behalf of Vosberg—a plea for life in prison. She begged the jury to "try to search for the human being behind the criminal." Vosberg had his hands over his face.

"Vosberg's an unknown man," she continued, "a mystic with a split personality. He does not understand, nor can he control, the compelling nonsense of his throbbing mind." Here she paused, looked around the courtroom, and then stood firmly in

front of the jury. "He is delivered and has begun his moral rehabilitation."

Turning dramatically to the jury, she said, "Enough blood!
Enough killing! There are other penalties that will remove
Vosberg from society. It is you, gentlemen of the jury, who will
discover yourselves, in your hearts and consciences, the penalty
that you know is just."

When Jardin finished, a wild wave of applause burst out in
the courtroom. The judge banged his gavel for order, but the
lawyers, and even the prosecutors, crowded around to con-
gratulate her on her ardent attempt to rouse feelings of pity for
a man who had committed such a gruesome murder.

The next day, extra soldiers and police were on duty both
inside and outside the courtroom.

"Jeez, R.B.," Pete said, "this is like the opera at the beginning of the season. It looks as if every mother, father, wife, and
uncle of the judges and lawyers are jammed into the court."

He was right. Women were dressed in veils, hats, and furs;
men were dapper in expensively tailored suits. All the reporters
lost our seats. We were standing, lining the walls, alongside the
photographers.

Vosberg's other lawyer, Moro-Giafferi, was huffing and
puffing around the room. Pete and I looked at each other and
tried not to laugh. He was obviously revving himself up—getting ready to offer the most stunning oratory of his career.

For almost four hours he thundered. He pleaded. He
preached. He rocked on his heels and stretched his short, massive body out over his wooden pulpit and thrust his heavily
jowled face at the jury. He stamped and raged and banged his
fist and massaged his gray mustache. He bellowed at the prosecutor, making him turn red. With perfect theatrical timing his
words embraced the bent-over Vosberg and made the accused
weep even more.

"Vosberg is mentally ill. He's an instinctive pervert. Instinctive perverts are all the more dangerous if they are intelligent, as they use their intelligence to pursue their evil ends. This type of 'instinctive perversity' is fatal. This being the case," he whispered, and everyone leaned forward, "his only crime was to be born."

His voice was now turning into a steam engine. "And I hear people say—Why not kill him? He killed! Let him die! That is the morality of the talon, the law of the lynch mob, the barbarian's justice. Why then our symbols—our traditions—and why my robe—and why yours, O judge? To murder yet another human being? Vosberg's not crazy, but he's abnormal. He wants to correct himself, but he cannot. His illness is incurable."

Moro-Giafferi turned his back to the audience. Then with a grand gesture, he threw his scarf around his neck and turned back again. "Must justice always be a slaughterhouse?" he cried.

The judge called for an hour's lunch recess. The spectators opened their sandwich wrappers and bottles of wine and beer and, without moving from their treasured seats, carried on shouted conversations across the room. Some people, in the invited spectators' section, were drinking champagne from fluted glasses.

Pete and I sat on the floor and smoked, trying to curb our hunger.

Finally, the judge brought the court to order. The room fell silent. Moro-Giafferi continued his defense. His voice rose at the end of each of his sentences. I was captivated. I realized that Stella would have loved being there. It was a spectacular performance. He mesmerized the courtroom. And then, when his audience was perched on the edge of its seats, he whispered, "I rest my case."

The room was silent.

After instructions from Judge Levi, the jury was sent out of the courtroom to begin its deliberations. Time crept by, but no one gave up his or her seat. Again we smoked. Everyone had to watch as trays of food and glasses of beer were brought, hour after hour, to the men of the jury.

"In England," Pete said, "the jury's not given food until it reaches a verdict."

"That's cruel," I replied.

"It makes them act more quickly!"

At 9:20 P.M. the bells rang and the twelve visibly tired men of the jury filed in. The foreman was nervously mopping his bald head with such a large white handkerchief that it could have been mistaken for a flag of surrender. Behind them came the lawyers, then the prosecutors, then Judge Levi. After a moment, the clanking prisoner was escorted to the dock and his shackles were removed.

Vosberg was instructed by the judge to face the foreman of the jury. The foreman read from a paper. Vosberg was found guilty of the premeditated murder of Stella Mair and would be sentenced to death. At first he showed no emotion. Then he smiled. It was a melancholy smile, colored by resignation.

"No," bellowed Moro-Giafferi.

With a harsh stare, the judge said, "Sit down. It's settled."

But Moro-Giafferi, roaring with rage, tried to interrupt. "No! No! My heart is torn," he objected. "Your decision is cruel. Vosberg is mentally ill! He should be given life!"

The judge, white with anger, ignored him.

He struck his gavel.

"You, Ernst Vosberg, will die by the guillotine."

Observers in the courtroom shouted brutally at Vosberg, "Death! Yes! Death!"

An infuriated Moro-Giafferi whirled and screamed, "Cannibals!"

"Okay, now, let me begin my new assignment," I said to Ramsey. "It's over."

"Nope. You both have to cover the execution. Even the guys in New York insist."

"But I don't want to watch a murder. Get one of your bloodthirsty reporters."

"You're it, R.B."

* * *

It was a cold and clear night with barely a half-moon. Pete and I were grumpy—we didn't want to be there. Neither of us was interested in death. We arrived at midnight. Public executions were still the style. Thanks to the announcements in the newspapers, at least a thousand people—drinking and carousing— had gathered on the streets to watch the execution outside of Le Santé Prison's walls. Every time someone went in or out of the green prison doorway, there were catcalls, cheering, and whistling. The two brightly illuminated cafés nearby were jammed with people drinking wine and eating thick sausage sandwiches. Many people were sitting or leaning against the walls of the prison and nearby houses having picnics. The stink from the urinal was disgusting, but it didn't appear to bother the picnicking observers.

Some reporters, including Pete and me, were allowed inside the prison. Although we weren't permitted to speak to Vosberg, we were allowed to be outside his cell.

Soon, we heard the clop-clop of horses' hooves and the rattle of the guillotine-laden wagon driving over the cobblestones, and we went to the nearest window.

"This is it, R.B.," Pete said, and offered me a swig from his flask. I took it.

The wagon backed up to the gates of the prison. The driver jumped down and balanced a lit oil lamp on a rock under an isolated young chestnut tree that grew out of the prison's foundation. With some helpers, he began to unload the sections of the portable guillotine. As the pieces were fitted together, the lantern threw large, flickering shadows on the silent working men. The guillotine grew by increments until it loomed over the crowd.

It was 3:30 A.M. and the sky was beginning to lighten. Except for the very drunk, most people had quieted down and were waiting, some crowded onto nearby roofs, their heads the same size as the ceramic chimney pots. In Vosberg's cell, the lawyer Renée Jardin held his hand, and together they prayed.

It was 4:00 A.M. and almost broad daylight. The bell in the belfry of the Hôtel de Ville tolled the hour. Milk wagons began to roll over the cobbled streets. Monsieur Desfourneaux, the new Monsieur de Paris, the public executioner, entered the building. A small man, he was dressed in a flamboyant black wool cape with a black felt hat pulled low on his forehead. We reporters were led downstairs and out to a roped-off area outside the prison gates.

It was 4:30 A.M.

The gates swung open.

In a headlong flurry, Vosberg was rushed—flung facedown—strapped to the bascule.

But his neck was badly positioned. It wasn't aligned with the arc of the lunette. Monsieur Desfourneaux had bungled it. One of the more experienced execution-valets hurried over and yanked Vosberg by the ears to straighten him out. A spine-chilling scream arose from the witnessing crowd.

The troops raised their rifles and swords in a salute to the Republic. In the suspended second before the knife dropped, a convent bell rang, sounding like bits of ice hitting glass.

Whoosh!

The heavy, finely sharpened blade crashed down upon his neck and rebounded from its own force and weight. A geyser of dark blood spurted from his neck as the jugular was chopped. Vosberg's famously handsome head fell into a large basket.

The entire procedure took ten seconds.

Before the valets could clean the mess with their buckets of water, more than fifty women, all wearing their infamous white hats—all screeching—rushed forward to mop up Vosberg's blood with their white hankies.

Standing next to us was the lawyer Moro-Giafferi. As he caressed his ivory-topped cane, he turned to us and said, "This man lived like a monster, but he died like a saint."

A saint! My god, what was he thinking? Vosberg was a monster, a predator of women. He had left a trail of lovelorn women behind him.

"Someone will write a book," Pete said.

"Yes," I agreed. "It should be titled *The Handsome Devil*."

"Perfect!" he said.

"Yes, and the writer will dig up every gruesome detail. But it won't be me."

"Nor I," said Pete.

I was sick to my stomach and sick in my heart. "You can write this news story without me, right?" I asked Pete.

"Sure, R.B. Go home."

I did. And I wept. I wept for Stella, for her lost promising life. I wept for Clara, her life forever distorted. And I was sickened by the merciless biblical consent of murder: an eye for an eye. I fought with myself. How could I ever forgive myself for cold-heartedly watching a human being killed? What was I becoming? How could I continue to do this job? I would have to learn how to harden myself, while being deeply sympathetic to people, to tragedy. Could I do this? I knew that it would be a challenge to write more sensitively. But I knew that I would have to try. In the end, looking out my window at Madame's cloth-covered canary cages, I wept for myself. And at last I fell asleep.

Yet I remember that within a week of his beheading—perverse as it may sound—I missed Ernst Vosberg. I missed the drama of the trial—the sense of importance I had felt. I missed having special access to him. I even missed the tension of seeing my mother every day. But I had to remind myself that Vosberg was a real, honest-to-goodness murderer and I was only an occasional murderer of feelings.

The greater populace had shared my horror of the situation. Vosberg's beheading was the last public execution in France. And it was also the last time that the French would legally kill a German citizen. Within months, the Reich would become the savage master of France.

The main office of the *New York Courier* gave me permission to wander Europe, looking for stories. Now I could go back to Berlin. Pete would stay on the German political beat, and I would follow my own fancy. But first I needed to deal with my mother. Given that I would not be in Paris on a regular schedule, I would not be able to look out for her safety. Europe was waiting for another sword to fall, and we all knew that France was next.

After an obligatory cup of tea at her apartment, I said, "You must leave. Go back to the States. It won't be long before France is invaded."

"I'll leave when I'm ready," she said. "Not when some idiotic government's threatening me."

"Ma," I said, "it may be idiotic but it has the power to destroy you."

"Oh, shut up, Rose. What do you know?"

"You're one hundred percent Jewish, meaning you'll be the first to be arrested."

"Jewish, Jewish! My parents may have been Jewish, but I don't accept that ridiculous legacy. And I don't have a 'J' on my passport, so how will anyone know?"

"You look Jewish," I said, "whether you like it or not."

Her face was flushed with anger. She grabbed the edge of a table. "All you do, Rose," she jeered, "is make trouble for me. For the first time in my life, I feel I can do what I want. So get the hell out of here and leave me alone!"

Then, as if I were a coiled rattler, I hissed my words, aimed toward my mother's gaping mouth.

"The hell with you!" I said. "Save your own damned self. That should be easy since you're the most egotistical, narcissistic human being I've ever known. It's too bad it was Papa who died—it should've been you."

And I, Rose Belle Manon—grown-up woman and renowned journalist—slammed out of the apartment.

September 2, 1939. Two diplomatic notes, one from Britain and the other from France, were delivered to Hitler. The notes jointly insisted that Germany withdraw from Poland. Hitler refused to respond.

The final blow happened the next day. Britain and France declared war on Germany.

Remorse? Guilt? It didn't matter. I had to check on my mother, but had no idea how she would respond to seeing me. She might not even open her door.

I rang the buzzer and the concierge let me in. Instead of giving her usual shrug of the shoulders, she beckoned me with a crooked finger.

"Your mother's gone," she said. "Moved out yesterday."

I waited for more information. None was offered. I turned and left.

When I got home, Mr. Hin was waiting on the bench outside the hotel. He appeared older, more drawn and stooped than two days before. He was wearing an embroidered cap that I had bought him as a present to replace his old one—but his clothes were ragged, as if he had found them rumpled at the back of his closet.

"What's the matter, Mr. Hin? Are you ill?"

"I suppose you could say, Rosie, that I'm sick with dread. How are you?" he said, looking at me with nothing but kindness.

"Oh, Mr. Hin, what a mess I've made of things," I said, and even though I was outside on public bench, I began to cry. Mr. Hin put his arm around me and I leaned into his warmth. Since falling in love with Leon, I had become more conscious of needing human affection—a touch of a hand, an embrace, it didn't matter.

No one paid attention to my crying. Everyone was most likely crying in some way or another. Our world was changing too quickly, too harshly. Fear had replaced the Parisians' tenacious adoration of love.

"Rosie," Mr. Hin said, while holding my hand, "Madame Pleven gave me this note for you. It's from your mother—she brought it this afternoon. It's too bad you missed her. Is this why you're crying?"

"Yes. I was cruel to her. It's hard for me to admit, but I can't get over my childish longing for her love. I wish I could. It makes me crazy with embarrassment to admit this to you."

"It's natural, Rosie, to feel this way. If you could admit that you're furious at her—that this is the way she is—that you won't be able to change her—then perhaps you'll be very sad, but will find peace with that acceptance."

I sat up straight and blew my nose.

Mr. Hin handed me the note.

I'm on my way to Lisbon. Colette has the keys. I'll write when I have a chance.

My mother now considered Colette more trustworthy than her own daughter. What a telling choice she's made, I thought. I'm surprised she even bothered to write.

"Well," I said, handing Mr. Hin the note to read. "She certainly drew the line."

"No matter what she writes, Rosie, you know you can't abandon her. She may need you later."

"Don't worry. If she needs me, I'll try to be there," I said. "Otherwise we'll do better with a couple of countries and a war between us. More important for me now is to ask you what will you do when we're invaded. You can't stay in Paris. The Nazis don't like different-looking people."

"I'll be all right," Mr. Hin said. "Don't worry."

"No," I said, "you won't be all right." I felt as if I were talking to the air. "Mr. Hin, remember how they took our friend Richard's children?"

Mr. Hin nodded his head in understanding.

"Well, they'll take you too. And if they don't immediately kill you, they may do experiments on your non-Aryan eyes—or take you away to one of their camps where you'll most likely starve to death. Is this the way you want to die?"

"No, of course not," Mr. Hin said. "I haven't decided how I'm going to handle this. But please know, Rosie, that I have plans. I promise."

"Everybody says that they have plans," I said, "but I don't believe them. We're all living in a tub of honey. Because home has been so sweet, it's hard for us to move on."

Mr. Hin took my hand and we sat quietly for a few minutes.

"I'm going back to Berlin," I said. "I leave in two days. As long as America doesn't declare war on Germany, I'll be all right."

"But what about being Jewish?" he said. "You're taking a big chance, Rosie."

"We're all taking a big chance."

Mr. Hin smiled. "You're right. We are. And I plan to continue doing so."

I knew that he was talking about the Resistance—and I knew he wouldn't discuss it with me.

"Now," I said, "I have to pack my stuff and take it to the office for safekeeping. Since I don't know when I'll be back in Paris, it's silly for me to keep my room. I can always rent one here by the night."

"I know," Mr. Hin said, "that Madame Pleven will keep one for you—and will care for your beloved red geraniums! I'll help you move."

"I'm storing only the things that my trunk will hold. Is there anything of mine that you would like?"

"No, only that you be safe, my dear Rosie. I'll get a couple of men to help move the trunk."

Over the years I had collected clothes, books, pieces of fabric that I had used to make my room look prettier, posters. But I would only keep beloved things. My typewriter would travel with me, along with one suitcase of clothes, including my fur coat. My favorite books, my personal notes and reporter's notebooks, newspaper clippings, my Aunt Clara's letters, my father's letters, photographs, a book of poems written by Mr. Hin—all would be packed into the trunk. I gave my radio to Madame Pleven.

"Oh, Mademoiselle Manon," she almost squealed. "You have given me the moon!"

The next morning, Mr. Hin arrived with two men, whom I recognized as the Serbs who had once lived in the hotel. "*Dobra dan*," they said in unison.

"Good morning to you, too," I said, and they laughed.

They lifted the trunk into the boot of an old taxi and we drove to the *Courier,* leaving Mr. Hin behind. When we arrived, I directed them downstairs to the Linotype room where we stashed the trunk out of the way in a far corner. I had to force them to take some money.

After they left, I went upstairs to say good-bye to everyone. But there was no one there. Because all the newspapers had either closed or become German, the French workers had been fired and the Americans had fled to safer assignments. Only Ramsey was there. He was sitting amidst the mess of the dismantled newspaper office. The newsroom was silent. No presses running, no typewriters chattering away. Nothing. He looked lost.

"Hey, Mr. Ramsey," I said. "Are you okay?"

"No, I'm not okay," Ramsey almost growled. "What a stupid question. Look," he said, and he held out his hands. Fat, with dirty fingernails and nicotine stains, they were trembling.

"Have you been drinking?" I asked.

"Of course," he said. "What do you think? R.B., you've got to help me get out of here."

"But where's Pete?" I asked.

"He's off in the countryside," Ramsey almost snarled, "having a carefree weekend with his family. He told me that he needed one more taste of French beauty before he sent his wife and baby to London and returned to dreary Berlin. Who in the hell does he think he is? And he never even considered me. After all I've done for him! Now I've waited too long. I don't know what to do. And the main office has become suspiciously silent."

"Sounds as if there may be a mix-up in communications. Want me to try sending a cable?"

"No, forget it, I've sent a dozen!"

"Sorry, Mr. Ramsey, I don't know what to say."

Ramsey lit a cigarette. "I guess it's tough luck for both of us," he said. "I'm warning you, Rosie, if you don't figure something out, I'll—"

"This is ridiculous, Mr. Ramsey."

"Get off it, R-o-s-i-e," he snidely drawled. "You'd better go to your well-placed friends at the embassy—or your famous writers. You had better do something to get me out of here. I'm telling you, Rosie, I mean this."

I was stunned. There was no way I was going to bow to such a threat. Ramsey had many more avenues of escape than I did. After all, Ramsey was a white Christian boy from Chicago. Let him figure it out.

"The hell with you," I said. "You've finally gone loco—I'm not surprised!"

And I turned and quickly walked past everything I had once loved—my battered desk and chair, the yellowed, crumbling maps taped to the walls, the pneumatic tubes that rocketed my copy down to the presses. Even the rancid overflowing ashtrays and abandoned spittoons.

"I'm warning you!" Ramsey screamed. "I'm warning you, you lousy kike, I'll get you in the end!"

I was scared. I had no experience as a refugee and no knowledge about living in a city that had been captured by an enemy. Although the final invasion had not yet occurred (and there was no doubt that it would) the city echoed with silence. The sidewalks were eerily empty. Shutters were pulled down over all the shop windows. Most of the cafés were closed.

Paris was no longer a city of dreams. It had become a city in despair. No longer was there the easy, gliding movement of people on the streets—no longer were people sitting in cafés and dreaming—no longer were people resting on park benches, reading newspapers, chatting with their neighbors, feeding the pigeons. Nothing in Paris was lazy any longer.

My education and my curiosity were rooted in the rough-and-tumble frontier of the American West. Having arrived in Europe after the Great War, I hadn't developed the protective sense that native Europeans had. My only experience of war was my battle with my mother. But for a moment I imagined that if I had to leave Paris on foot, I would have unique instincts for survival. Heading south, I would walk across the country, using the stars as my guide, staying off the roads, finding plants to eat, intuiting from the landscape where there was water, all things that I had learned from living in the mountains. Fancy dreaming, I thought. I've probably lost my natural instincts for survival—and I never had a sixth sense about war. A fatal combination.

* * *

While reading these pages has ignited my memory, yes, creating an adventure for my mind, I'm exhausted with sorrow. Friends dead. No family left to carry on the tradition. My cousin David, Stella's brother, died many years ago—having never married. I feel bereft of familial history. Sure, I'm a famous newspaperwoman—but so what? That "so what?" has been my constant struggle.

Come on, Rosie, I tell myself—your life has been remarkable. But I have to admit that I get confused with the truth of the heart versus my everyday life. As a foreign correspondent, I met so many people in so many countries. This choice was my own; I had asked for this job, and had been granted that privilege. But that privilege meant that I would never make deep and lasting friendships. It wasn't until I returned to New York that this could change. But by then I was set in my ways—and the possibilities of intimate relationships frightened me.

My prewar life was so rich, and yes, so complicated. How I wish I could have done things differently. Beginning with Mr.

Hin. I knew he was involved with the Resistance, but he was so enigmatic—so protective of me. I sensed that I was the only person in his life that he was close to. He appeared to have no family, no close friends. Parts of us were very much alike.

Why didn't I push him to talk to me?

I know why. He was the perfect foil for my self-centeredness. He would listen and listen and smile and pat my hand. I would go away bloated with contentment. And what did I mean to him? I have no idea.

In the small pond at the side of my house I planted deep yellow, almost orange, water lilies in his honor. I was creating a place for Mr. Hin to float and look up at the sky. Every few years the lilies have spread so much that they threaten to choke the pond. I used to wade in and do the thinning myself. Now Coleman does it for me, while I direct him from the shore. I am religious about this ritual. It is my penance. I know that by leaving him behind in Paris—by not insisting upon a mutual plan—I again failed someone I loved. After the war I tried to locate him, but it was hopeless. He disappeared into the anonymous mass grave of hatred.

And Ramsey? He landed back on his fat little feet in Peoria. Oh, how I disliked him. Still do—although he died many years ago. But I have to give him credit—he not only escaped, he wrote a book about it. In 1954, he sent me a copy, along with a note.

Dear Rosie: Enclosed please find a copy of my book. I think you'll be interested in how I escaped . . . especially since you refused to help me. Start at page 193 . . . you'll understand why. Remember Gladys, my milk-drinking girlfriend, who thought she could save the world . . .

I turned to page 193 . . .

. . . *Feeling cornered and abandoned, I was at my wits' end. Living in my office at the old* Paris Courier, *I was drinking too much, occasionally remembering to eat. One afternoon, Gladys, an old girlfriend, walked in.*

"I was wondering if you were still here," she said.

Gladys was an American who had married a Frenchman. Her husband worked at the German legation as a translator. She also had a cranky mother-in-law, who lived with them. "I'm always looking for excuses to get away from Madame," she told me. "So, I thought I'd drop in and have a look at my old office."

She looked at me with concern. "Ramsey! Are you ill? You look terrible!"

"No," I said. "But I will be if I can't get out of this damn city."

"I'll help you," she declared. "Don't move. I'll be back in the morning."

I was relieved. Knowing Gladys, I knew that my escape was to be her newest mission.

Sure enough, the next morning she returned with a bundle of clothes and a rattletrap bicycle.

"Shit, Gladys, I can't ride that thing. Haven't been on one since I was a kid!"

"Well, guess what," she said. "Either you learn to ride this or you'll be stuck here.

"Now, Ramsey, pay attention. Here's a beret, a workman's jacket and pants, and a pair of sabots. You're to put them on and leave your other clothes here. Believe me, you don't want to be caught looking like an American. Oh, and start practicing riding the bike here in the office—it's certainly big enough with all those desks piled in the corner.

"Listen carefully," she said. "Since there are no trains leaving Paris, you're going to have to cycle south to Bordeaux. It should take about four days."

"I'll never make it, Gladys—not in good physical condition, and—"

"For heaven's sake, stop complaining. I thought you were such a tough guy!

"From there," she continued, "you can take a train to Biarritz. Find your way to the American Consulate and collect your travel documents. They'll take you safely through Spain and into Portugal. If all goes according to plan, you'll ship out from Lisbon on the liner Manhattan, *back to New York. Now, here's some money. You can pay me back after the war."*

There was more in this chapter about his learning to ride the bicycle, finding his way out of Paris, getting lost. Then came the part I liked the best. Terrible for me to admit, but I hope he suffered more than he claimed.

. . . All of a sudden, I heard a low-flying airplane. Within seconds, it was diving straight for me. I dove off my bike into a ditch.

I had never been shot at before. Bullets were hitting rocks and setting off sparks of fire. The noise was terrifying. Thirty seconds passed, although it seemed much longer. Then the plane revved its engine and made a sweeping turn to the right and away toward the horizon. The bastard, I thought, he must find it amusing to scare the bejesus out of me. Hope he crashes while heading back to Germany.

* * *

Berlin, 1940. The sun was out, the sky so deeply blue. I was filled with hope. No one had reported seeing Leon, but this didn't surprise me. Indeed, the lack of news made me hopeful. I would first check into the Hotel Aldon and then go directly to his apartment.

"Good afternoon, Miss Manon," the hotel clerk said. "Welcome back to Berlin. You have some messages." And he handed me a few pieces of paper. Mainly, they were from fellow reporters welcoming me back. One was from Pete Grogan: *Need to see you. Meet me at the Press Club.*

The chief barman, Joseph, didn't even ask me what I wanted; he just nodded his head toward the back. Pete looked up and I could see that there was trouble.

"Hey, R.B., what's up?" Pete said, as if today were an ordinary day.

"Cut the crap, Pete. I can tell that something bad has happened."

"Yes, to Leon," he said softly, and I sat down. "Listen, R.B., I'm sorry, really I am. But I kept hoping that someone else would give you the news."

"Just tell me what happened. I don't care what you hoped."

"Okay, this is what I heard—"

"Is he dead?"

"I think so. But I'm not positive."

And all I could do was to sit there, stiff and silent.

"Listen, I'll give you all the information. Just give me a chance to gather my thoughts."

It was obvious that Pete was nervous. He raised his hand as if he were in school and asked Joseph for another whiskey. "Do you want something?" he asked.

"No."

"It was last week. Werner Schmitt told me to get to Leon's apartment as quickly as I could. You remember, he's that reporter from Hamburg who is with the Reuters bureau? The one who always wore a clean shirt and a bow tie, even if his trousers smelled of urine?"

"Yeah, I know. Keep talking."

"In the afternoon, Werner had walked by Leon's building

and noticed a number of plainclothes police hanging around the entrance, trying to look inconspicuous. Do you want the entire story or just an abbreviated edition?"

"All of it."

"Leon, as you know, was a master engraver and could copy the most intricate designs. This led to his forging career. He was excellent, could make any document look real. I assume you know that he made the papers for your friend, the saxophone player Richard Moses, and his family? It was because of that job that he began working full-out for the Resistance."

"Oh, God, no," I moaned. "Stefan promised me that he would take it to another friend to have it done, not to Leon. It never occurred to me that he would do the job."

"He wouldn't have told you, R.B, nor would he have told his parents—you three were the heart of his life. You've really got to understand this. Anyway, you weren't the first person he forged documents for. Listen," he said, and he reached across and took my hand, "when you were in Paris, he heard that Esther was in trouble because she didn't have the right papers. Leon recommended a colleague but he botched it, and he felt responsible. Stefan told me that he fixed the problems and simply kept on going."

I moved my hand.

"It's still my fault. And how—"

"No, you're wrong," Pete said. "He was heading in that direction anyway. Let me ask you this. If you had his talent, wouldn't you have done the same?"

"Probably not," I said. "I don't have Leon's courage."

"That's baloney, R.B., and you know it. Didn't you notice," he continued, "how much happier he was in the last few months? I think he had finally got his teeth into a way of seriously helping the cause."

"I thought it was because we were so deeply in love," I said wryly.

I wanted to close my eyes and sink into oblivion. I had always loved tragic novels, imagining myself as the savior of someone in distress. But not this. No, this pain was beyond imagination. And—I wasn't a savior. Just as I couldn't save Stella, or Andy, I had not saved Leon.

Pete kept talking. "His chance of escaping went off the edge, thanks to your mother. Sorry, R.B., I don't mean to be so callous."

"It's okay, Pete, it's the truth."

"I think," he continued, "that he was in the process of devising another escape plan. A few weeks ago, we ran into each other on the street. He looked terrible. He told me that his parents had been rounded up and transported to one of the camps."

"Oh, how awful, how awful—they were so close."

"Yes, it was terrible, but Leon had an interesting response. 'I should have gone with them,' he told me. 'Thrown myself in front of their train—something, anything to take away the pain and guilt that I wasn't taken too. But, honestly, as long as Rosie's alive, I'll try my best to stay alive too.' And then he said something that really struck me. 'I had to give up Rosie for my parents, and Rosie had to give me up for her mother. And since her father was already dead, it comes out even.'

"Someone betrayed Leon. We don't know who it was, although I suspect it was his boss Gerard's wife. Anyway, I rushed to his building, thinking that with my newspaper credentials, perhaps I could stop the momentum. The front door was open and I pushed my way in. A Gestapo officer yelled: 'You can't stay here,' and I flashed my papers without letting him read the details.

"I heard a terrible racket. Doors slamming. Glass breaking. Orders being barked. People screaming. Then all of a sudden, I looked up. It was Leon being arrested by two men. He was fighting back, kicking and trying to get his arms loose. He screamed, 'No, Gerard. You can't do this!' They pushed him down the last flight of stairs, where he hit his head on the marble and banged into the railing. I ran to help him, but was punched in the stomach and put in a stranglehold by an SS man. Leon was alive—that I could see. But there was blood everywhere. As I was being forced out of the building, I looked back and saw Gerard. His face was blank. A zombie. Standing beside him in the doorway was a woman, whom I assumed was his wife. She was smirking.

"As I waited on the sidewalk, pretending to gather myself together so I could leave, Leon was dragged out and was being tossed into the back of a black car. He caught his foot on the running board, and for a moment was free. He began to run. 'No! Don't shoot!' I heard Gerard scream. And, of course, he was easily caught within a couple of seconds. Leon fought furiously, but was handcuffed and driven away.

"I followed him to the Gestapo headquarters, the one across the street from Stefan's favorite watching spot. It was odd because it was the first day of sun in a couple of weeks. Yet, when I look back at the day, it was overcast and gloomy and—

"I tried, R.B. I swear to you, I tried to get him released. But there was no one left in Berlin whom I knew. Are you okay? Should I go on?"

"No, I'm not okay, but keep talking."

"I was warned by the bureaucrat at the front desk," Pete continued, "to leave immediately. 'There's not a thing you can do,' he said. 'It's over for him.'

"The next day Leon was taken to another Gestapo headquarters," Pete said, talking to the table, not looking at my face. "I heard he was questioned and tortured—I don't know the details, I promise. Then he was sentenced to 'death for treason and acts preparatory to high treason.'"

I felt as if I were going to faint and vomit at the same time.

I reached across for Pete's whiskey and took a gulp—and waited for it to settle me down.

Pete waited, too.

I nodded for him to continue. "And I might as well get it all out," he said. "There's more bad news. Two days ago Stefan and Esther were murdered by the Gestapo—they were also charged with treason." The bar was so quiet. The radio had been turned off. We were speaking almost in whispers. But everyone was listening. Poor Stefan. Esther. My grief was physical. I grabbed Pete's hand, desperate for an anchor.

"Are you positive about Leon?" I managed to say.

"There are so many killings now," Pete said, "that everyone seems to have lost track, even the meticulous Germans. Sometimes they post the names of the accused and their dates of execution on the gates of the prisons. But I didn't see Leon's name. So no, I'm not positive. I'm so sorry, R.B. Let me buy you a—"

"Thanks, Pete, but I have to go."

"Okay. I understand. But I have to tell you that I leave in the morning for Paris."

I staggered out of the bar as if I were drunk. I wasn't drunk, but I felt a cold, knifelike fury at myself. And I finally realized that I had nowhere to go. No one to go to. My good friends were covering stories all over the world. I was truly on my own.

As I was walking down those dismal streets, all I could think of was how frightened he must have been—and then I imagined his handsome head rolling into a basket. If I hadn't observed Vosberg's beheading, I would have been able to avoid the image. But no, I saw it all in my mind, second by second. I would never be able to forgive myself for perching like a vulture to watch Vosberg's death.

More than five decades later and my memory is still keen. I need to go to my office and find Pete's last dispatch from Paris. I know where it is. I kept it in a folder along with other pieces he had written, which I thought special. I remember it because he wrote it in my journalistic style. It was his way of saying good-bye.

Berlin. Friday, June 14, 1940. I was at the press office listening to the invasion of France on the BBC. The following cable from Pete arrived in the midst of the chaos: *My last article for the last edition in a free France. For the first time imitating your literary style—hope you don't mind. Ta-ta, R.B. See you in London. Pete.*

The Country of France Will Be No More
By Pete Grogan
PARIS, June 14, 1940—*On this unusually chilly morning, a thin and piercing sound gripped the city. Threatening planes swept in, swooped toward their targets, faded away, and lunged again. The populace of Paris held its breath. Unopposed Luftwaffe dive-bombers pounded France from above while some two thousand panzers roared across the countryside, scattering the disorganized French army. The Germans destroyed everything in their path.* La drôle de guerre, *the Phony War, has turned real.*

Today's invasion ended the publishing of all bona fide French newspapers. Even the famous Paris-Soir *has become a Nazi sheet. All news, from now on, will be controlled by the conquerors.*

The exodus has begun. Three of the five million citizens living in Paris, feeling unprepared, lied to by their government, and driven by panic, are moving toward the south in retreat. I wandered the city, walking through the waves of fleeing citizens. The noise is unbearable—a nerve-racking cacophony of honking horns and screaming from people who have been separated from their families in the rush forward. The streets are jammed with refugees carrying suitcases. Hanging off these fleeing citizens' backs are bedrolls, mattresses, pots and pans. Anything with wheels is piled with belongings—children and the elderly and the infirm, chickens and pet birds are balanced on top. Cars creep along, stalling by the wayside when they run out of gas or have simply broken down. There is such a putrid smell of death and fear hanging over the avenues of escape that I often gagged. France's roads are littered with corpses—littered with people, too weary to continue—littered with wounded and starving human beings—littered with animals, mainly dead—everything soaked with human waste. Everyone looks old, including the children. Everyone is overwhelmed with sadness. The dreaded end of France has begun.

There's a small wood bench outside, right in the center of my herb garden. Coleman built it many years ago, and although it's a bit lopsided, I can still sit among the aromas of my plants, my face reaching for the sun. I have to remind myself, though, that each time I stand I must be careful—I could easily fall. These "elderly rules" drive me nuts.

Strangely, now that I've come to the end of reading my papers, looking at my garden makes me sad. Will I live to plant the wildflower seeds I've collected all summer? Will I be here to see them bloom? I can't bear the thought of not seeing how the garden drama plays out in the next season. Every year there are surprises. One year, an enormous sunflower plant grew at the edge of the field. I didn't plant it. So where did it come from? A visiting bird, I presume.

Many of my lessons about growing older are learned from tending my garden. I know that even though I plant my seeds, not every seedcase will burst and give birth to a new plant. But that's how it's meant to be. One day my body will shatter, and

I, a used-up seed, will return to the earth too—but never to bloom again.

* * *

Fifty-two years ago, I left Paris. Reading these old notes has forced me to remember things that I would rather forget— and also things that I'm delighted to be reminded of. Yes, today, some illusions have been shattered; some are surprisingly honest.

I'm going to take a break. Make a cup of tea. While waiting for the water to boil, I turn on the radio and out comes an exaggerated waltz—Strauss, of course. With a red pillow as my partner, I waltz around the kitchen table, gliding to the music on my old polished wood floors.

I fill the emptiness with memories.

I dance.

I try to remember the truth.

I dance.

I try to avoid the reality of my age.

I dance.

I am afraid of death.

I dance and weep.

It had been six months since Leon had disappeared and I still wasn't ready to accept his fate. I was aware that searching for a missing Jewish person in Germany was a macabre joke. There was no agency for displaced people, no government bureau to assist me. Even if I were to find an empathic human being, he or she would be taking an enormous chance. One side of me, the tough newspaperwoman, would need to overcome the woman-in-love's apprehension. I decided that I had to go to the source.

I arrived at the address. Nervous. Come on, Rosie, I said to myself, you've asked questions of far more important and

frightening people. Pretend this is an interview for the *Courier*.
I climbed the dramatic, sweeping marble staircase, trying not
to look for bloodstains. Gerard's door had a sparkling brass
nameplate: *Gerard von Schmitt*.

"What do you want?" asked a tall, blonde, very pregnant
woman who opened the door.

"Mr. von Schmitt, please," I said in my best, most formal
German.

Without saying another word, she ushered me in.

"Mrs. von Schmitt?" I asked. "My name's Rose Manon.
How do you do," I said, and I put out my hand to shake.

She ignored me.

"Wait here," she commanded, pointing to a stiff-backed,
armless chair. She waddled out of the room, resting her hands
on top of her stomach. So, I thought, this is the woman who
was behind Leon's arrest. Until that day, I had never met an
ugly pregnant woman.

The room, a large vestibule, was stuffed with dark, chunky
furniture. I recognized a chair from Leon's apartment. But hanging on the walls were a number of appealing landscapes. They
reminded me of the painters of the Hudson River School that
I had seen at a museum in New York many years before. Warm,
musty, as if it had rained the night before—the pictures were
muted pastoral scenes of rivers and trees in full bloom. Leon
was right. Gerard was a good artist.

And then there he was, with his wife looming behind him.
I remembered what Leon had said about his looks. He was
handsome, in a Teutonic way, and had a pleasant, open face.

"Mr. von Schmitt," I said, standing and shaking his hand.
"My name's Rose Manon from the *Paris Courier* and I'm looking for Leon Wolff."

"I know who you are," he said. "Leon told me about you."

"Did you not receive my letters from Paris, asking about
Leon?"

"No, I didn't," he said, and he turned and looked questioningly at his wife. "Helene?"

"She's a Jew!" his wife said. "I returned them all. Now I'll call the police."

"No you won't," he said firmly. "Please go into the other room and close the door."

She turned with a huff, walked through the door, and slammed it.

"Have a seat, Miss Manon. I apologize about Helene—her vehemence still surprises me. But you have to know that she didn't turn Leon in. All the artisans who were working for the government were rounded up at the same time. The officials wanted them all kept in the same place, rather than scattered throughout the country. Even though Helene's harsh with her opinions, this event wasn't her fault. Now, you want to know what happened to Leon? Am I correct?"

All I could do was nod yes and put my hands over my stomach and press tighter.

"He's still alive, Miss Manon, and—"

"Oh, thank you. Thank you," I said, and surrendered to tears. Gerard handed me his clean folded handkerchief.

I was stunned. I realized I had felt certain that he was dead. This news was so unexpected that it took my breath away.

"Where is he? May I see him?"

"No, you may not know where he is, and you certainly can't see him. He's lucky to be alive. He was badly hurt when he fell down the stairs; it was a serious concussion. It was only because of his remarkable artistic skills that I was able to get him the proper medical treatment."

"Is there any way," I asked, "that I could use my newspaper or diplomatic resources to release him from wherever he is? People must escape all the time."

"No, Miss Manon, people don't escape. People are murdered without a second thought. There are piles of dead bodies all over Europe. And it's going to get worse. But back to Leon. He's in a concentration camp where he works with other people who have his same talents, and—"

"You mean," I interrupted, "forging documents?"

"Yes, forging documents. Also engraving whatever he's ordered to engrave. Basically, he must do whatever he's ordered, or he'll be eliminated."

"Is the new definition for the word 'eliminated,' death?" I asked.

Gerard let a moment of silence pass.

"The only advice I can give you, Miss Manon, is to hope for the best. In the meanwhile, I'll try to get a message to him that I've seen you."

"Oh, yes, please do that! I would so appreciate it. Tell him that I'll wait for him. Tell him that I love him. Tell him—"

"Miss Manon!" Gerard said. "I'll be lucky to get any word to him, but I will try."

"May I come back to see you again?" I asked. "Would you be able to tell me if he got the message?"

"Absolutely not," he said. "You'll put me and my family in an untenable position. I beg you, please don't. If I can find a way to get you a message, I promise I will. But don't count on it."

I never did see Gerard again—nor did I get a message from him. The United States declared war on Germany and I was forced to leave Berlin.

I barely got out of Germany alive. There were four of us: another American journalist, who worked for United Press International; a mystery writer, who I think was spying for the British; a German who had voiced the wrong opinion and had been seriously threatened, and me. For more than six weeks we suffered a series of harsh and terrifying events. We ended up on the rocky shores of Sweden—and two weeks later we arrived in London. What I remember most is my determination to reach the U.K. I convinced myself that if I survived, so would Leon. The articles I wrote about this two-month journey of escape became my first book.

* * *

And then there was my mother. Once I was settled in London, I knew I had to look for her. It wasn't hard. When I walked into our embassy, I saw one of her drawings hanging behind the front desk.

"Oh, my dear Miss Manon," the receptionist said, "I'm relieved you're here. Your mother's ill. She's in a nursing home in the south end of London."

I had no choice. I went to her. She looked terrible. Pale. Deep crevices etched her face and neck. Sprouting from her chin were thick black hairs and the hair on her head had turned white and had been cut short. It looked as if someone had chopped it with a rough-bladed scissors, paying no heed to style—just the simplicity of easy care.

When she saw me, she smiled. Hmm, I thought, what a nice welcome, for a change.

When my mother arrived in London, she had immediately settled herself in a flat. For the first few months, everything in her life was moving along at its normal energetic pace.

"One day I was walking in Regent's Park," she told me. "I felt a terrible pain in my stomach. It sent me to my knees and I've never gotten up. Someone called an ambulance and I was taken to the hospital. It was only because of the pain that they operated on me quickly; they're so short-staffed because of the war. It's a cancer in the stomach, they said. But they assured me that they got it all and that I will be fine.

I know I look like death, but I think we'll be pleasantly surprised."

Oh, my mother! What an enigma she was, still is—although
she's been dead nearly forty years.

After a few days, I helped her home and stayed to nurse her.
I kept an emotional distance—reluctant to open myself to her
anger—unwilling to show her my old dislike. I tried to be nice
to her, all the while hiding my loss of Leon—the loss that she
had caused. Complicated it was, but I kept myself busy. I would
take long, brisk walks when she was napping during the day. In
the evenings I worked on my book. My last days in Berlin. My
escape from Germany. I was in a hurry, afraid I would forget
the nuances.

Of course, just as she said, my mother recovered and returned
to her old self. That first smile she had bestowed upon me
quickly faded as she healed and gained strength. As far as I
could tell, her illness didn't teach her anything. Her recovery
was remarkable, given the extent of the surgery. I'm convinced
that it was the adrenalin produced by her untethered anger,
and her fierceness about living, that helped her heal. And
within a week of feeling better, she dyed her hair black.

I was kept busy covering the war for the *New York Courier*.
Wherever I could, I would silently slip over the lines of a country's frontier to discover and report on something new.

"Why don't you live with me?" my mother asked. "After
all, you're hardly here and it's silly for you to waste money on
hotel rooms."

"Thanks, Ma, but that won't work. When I'm back in London, I'll try to stay in a hotel close to where you live." There
was nothing under the sun that could convince me that I
should live with my mother.

At that time, in 1942, I couldn't believe her offer. Today I can. Because of her illness, she had crossed over into the specific world of the elderly. She was still angry. It was obvious that I continued to make her uneasy. Yet surviving her illness with such vigor offered her new hope. She grabbed onto life with all her might—setting up her studio—drawing English gardens as if there were no war. She also threw herself into the world of air raids and fires and bombs and human suffering. Sharing the job of block warden with an elderly gentleman, she reached out of herself into a besieged community. There was something about her—something that I had never been able to fully admit to. She liked people and they liked her. And although she had this true talent for relating to people, she was dismal in her ability to relate either to me or to our family in New York.

I had an unspoken peace treaty with her. Through the war, and seeing her so often in London, I treaded delicately—stepping over cracks that could bring back angry memories. Those horrible war years became far more important than our personal war. A perspective was found. We got used to each other.

I realize now that I'm feeling a bit helpless in my old age. But I've always been helpless. We all are. I first glimpsed that concept in my mother. As she grew older and became infirm, she became vulnerable and dependent. This made her furious. As a result of observing her, I'm trying to be the opposite—trying to see age in all its beauty and wisdom. After all, I am sitting on this lovely patch of land, my land, holding a glass of cool delicious white wine that I poured for myself—having made my own decision to sit and look out at the world from my own porch. What could be better?

I'm fortunate. I don't feel empty in my isolation. I don't have to be in a herd of people to find satisfaction. But my mother did. She could never find humility in her situation— she was too angry. But she continued to have a sparkle of cynical, even sardonic, humor that people enjoyed and appreciated. I never became accustomed to her kind of humor, though. I always felt that she was showing off.

"When the war's over," she told me, "I'm going back to the United States."

"To Nevada?" I said.

"I don't know. Maybe. I still own the house—I hope it hasn't burned down or been completely vandalized. Or maybe to New York. But I don't know if I have the bravery for that big a change anymore."

"Ma, in three years' time, you came to Paris, were chased out of Berlin, escaped to Lisbon, found your way to London, recovered from a serious illness—and you say that you're not brave!"

We were huddled in a bomb shelter. The all-clear siren had gone off. The noise of bombs and the shooting of heavy artillery had ceased. It was so very quiet. No one spoke aloud. We all whispered.

"I think," she said, "that we're all being pounded to a pulp by this anxiety, this horrific noise. If I were to draw a self-portrait, I'd be covered with highways of nerves that ended at exploding brick walls; you know, Rose, the kind you see in comic books with big yellow flames and black typography screaming," and she raised her voice, "*Boom! Wham!* I feel as if I'm living under a constant barrage of fear. Even though it's monotonous, cowboy Nevada appeals to me now."

But after the war, she didn't go home to Nevada. She moved close to me in New York City, and there wasn't a damn thing I could do about it. At first, I rarely saw her. Between my traveling and writing, and her busy life, we had little time to get into trouble with each other.

Then my Aunt Clara died. Over the years she had descended

further and further into depression. I still can't understand why the intensity of Stella's death had not been at least a little healed, a little faded with time. But Clara appeared to grip her feelings of guilt with extravagant honor. Now, I suspect that Clara was being heroic in her determination to live at all. But I was hoping over time that her innate heroism would give her the will to continue on in her natural, positive way. After all, she used to declare: "My dear Rosie, we are a family of survivors. We always puzzle things out."

Together, my mother and I went to Leah's home in Brooklyn. Clara had left instructions. No service. No religion. No graveyard. No mention of God. Our time of saying good-bye was no more than a moment's sigh.

I still cherish the pin that Clara gave me with the painting of the young lovers. No matter how hard I try to imagine, I can't see those two lovely people being transformed into Leon and me. First of all, we're too dark. That couple is ivory white with yellow ringlets and soft pink patches on their full cheeks. We are dark people, sallow complexioned, dark rings under our even darker eyes. I have a very old sepia photograph of fourteen members of my family in Russia. In the photo they look like a band of tiny monkeys. They are all sitting or leaning on one another. It is a striking group, to be sure. Not quite real. Every one of them is painfully thin, and has black hair and large black eyes bridged by black eyebrows. They look as if they know what is going to happen to them.

They are all dead. During World War II, they were taken en masse from their village to a hand-shoveled pit on the plains. Forced to form a circle at the rim of the tomb, like perching blackbirds, they were murdered in cold blood.

Now my mother was left with one sister, Leah, her least favorite. Just deserts, I mused. And it got even more complex: When my mother was seventy-three, she was struck with another bout of cancer. I was living in Paris for the year, writing another book. Leah sent a telegram in her inimitably negative style: COME HOME STOP MIRIAM DYING.

I was with my mother for the last two weeks of her life. The first week, she was angry and uncomfortable. No matter what I did for her, it wasn't right. Sometimes she would scream at me to let her alone and just let her die, right then and there. "My life," she said to me one night, "my life, what a joke."

"But, Ma," I protested, "you've had an amazing life. You've been lauded for your work, you had a wonderful husband, you've traveled—you have many friends. What more would you want?"

She flicked my words back into my face. "*Gornisht,*" nothing, she said in Yiddish. "My life has been nothing."

And from that moment, she spoke only in Yiddish. When I would respond in English, she said, "*Red tsu mir yidish!*" Speak Yiddish with me! So I spoke everyday German, which satisfied her.

Thanks to the morphine, the second week was calmer. We chatted, she in Yiddish, I in German. We listened to Beethoven. She requested that I read her Mark Twain's essay "English as She Is Taught." "*Leyn es for af yidish!*" "Read it in Yiddish!" she commanded. I translated it into German and she didn't seem to mind.

I waited. Never was there a word of apology. And I waited. Never was there a word of love.

A few times I tried to talk to her about my feelings. I thought we could have our final round. I suppose I was hoping for redemption, for forgiveness. "*Gey redn tsu der vant,*" she said. Go talk to the wall. My mother appeared to be satisfied with the status quo.

Time moved slowly.

One tempestuous rainy afternoon, she died with a smile on her face.

I still dream about that smile.

Was it for me?

Night's arriving and I'm still sitting on the porch. Not hungry. It's been an overwhelming day of memories. I'm exhausted. But I know that I must push on and finish what I started this morning.

It's time to remember Leon.

Losing him was a laceration that has never healed. But I'll try to remember all that I can. Then, I promise myself, the self-pity, the lingering anger, must finally cease. I'm too old to be mooning over love. I need to accept and celebrate my life as it is. I don't want to die like my mother, miserable with her time on earth. I must accept that I will dream alone.

I wonder if elderly people want to learn the truth? Or is the torment of self-discovery too heavy for an old person's back to bear? Do we bat it away with our gnarled fingers, not wanting perception, simply wanting peace of mind, the absence of anxiety?

* * *

The war was over and all the world could see the catastrophic debris. Even for me, a hardened journalist, what I was seeing was almost too excruciating for words. I think it will take generations of artists to distill and create the sounds, the odors, the emotional and physical sights that were discovered when the maze of barbed wire around Europe was hacked open.

I easily gained access to the camps and refugee centers. There were no words to describe what I saw. But I had to try. I understood that if I didn't put it down on paper, the horror would coagulate in my mind and heart. And it could drive me mad. It was at that moment that my style of writing changed yet again. My fury was crushing. My disgust with humanity threw me into a cesspool of confusion. I tried writing in my normal style, but nothing I put on paper could describe what I was seeing. Without being aware of what I was doing, I began to distill my words to a staccato rhythm. My editors complained that I wasn't fulfilling the necessary word count for my column. I told them, "Too bad."

Of course, Leon was on my mind. But there was not to be an enchanted ending. I would not find him in a refugee camp. There would be no grand and romantic cinematic embrace. No, I would not hold his hand as he was recovering in a crisp and clean white hospital bed. I searched. I couldn't find him. I had to assume that he was dead. I returned to America.

In 1961, Berlin was divided. Each day, more and more of the wall was built around human beings penned in by the mighty, self-proclaimed judges—the judges who were supposed to make their lives better.

Years went by. The dream of Leon continued to live with me—not starkly, but like a rose-colored mist. After I returned to America, I commissioned an artist to paint Leon's portrait from my memory. The portrait's small, about twelve inches square. It's painted in sepia and Van Dyke brown with highlights of the same sepia, but muted. His wonderful face is hanging above my desk. I'm in the habit of wishing him *Guten Morgen* before I begin to work—and *Gute Nacht* before I go upstairs to bed.

* * *

When the Moses family moved back to the States, they settled in Harlem. It was obvious to both Daria and Richard that the children needed to be in a safe environment and around family. And Richard's family was pleased to welcome them all home.

Richard didn't have to join the army. He began playing saxophone for some of the big bands, and gigs in jazz joints. Daria went back to school and earned her teaching degree. Soon she was teaching in the public school system. Between the two of them they were managing to make a good living. The problem was Annelie. She rarely lifted herself out of depression. She wasn't aggressive, or unloving—but she couldn't find light in her life. She tried religion. She tried singing with a choir. Nothing worked. Her parents sent her to therapists, sent her to after-school drama programs, to violin lessons—and she tried. Indeed, she was brave.

But some essential part of Annelie's being was forever broken when the Nazis sliced away her femaleness. They rendered her neuter to make their lily-white men safe from temptation.

One early morning, a phone call came. It jangled me out of my sleep—it demolished my complacency. Annelie had flown out her tenth-floor bedroom window onto the earth of 128th Street.

The family was devastated, but not surprised. Like millions of people in the world of war, they had been struggling to heal their wounds.

I was always moved by how Daria had kept her family in a steady and warm embrace. After Annelie died, she labored to fill the empty space. She, with Richard's blessing, took in foster children. She became more involved in the neighborhood. Once, she complained to me, "I have a terrible singing voice. But if I could sing like Annelie, I would be in her gospel choir. Then I could hold her close to me for the length of the song."

But she failed. Less then two years later, Daria was dead of uterine cancer.

I've always experienced a wild joy at brutal weather. I remember Nevada. The vast horizon—the churning, heavy-bellied clouds—my anticipation of a torrential rainstorm. It still gives me goose bumps. But the thunderous weather of death is different. If you're not careful, you could be swept away to nowhere.

Neither Richard nor Coleman could ever find enough peace to carry on their lives in the way that they had dreamed. They tried the best they could. They became an odd couple. Richard was a tall, although stooping, very dark brown man. Coleman was short, and as pink as his mother. They lived together in the same apartment in Harlem for many years. Coleman hasn't married yet, although I sense his time is coming. I think he's waiting to fall in love with a woman who is too old to have children.

Richard never remarried. Quietly, even peacefully, he died at the age of seventy-five.

"At least he didn't die tragically," Coleman said to me. "That was his gift to me, I believe."

In 1989, I returned to a liberated Berlin. It was to be my last assignment in Europe. I wanted to stay at the old Hotel Aldon and sit at the bar where Leon and I had sat. I wanted to see the room where the Press Ball was held each year, and where we journalists huddled together at the end, waiting to receive word that we were being expelled by the Reich. There was such an aura about the hotel; it had been a haven for international journalists, for foreign spies, for questionable and shady trade delegations. We correspondents always thought of it as the cloak-and-dagger heart of Berlin. It was three doors down from the Russian embassy and rubbing elbows with the British embassy. But, alas, the hotel was gone, destroyed by a fire in 1945. No one had told me about it, nor had I read anything. I was booked into the new Hotel Hansablick, also near the Brandenburg Gate.

A clever American journalist had researched and found that I had turned eighty-three on the day of the fall of the Berlin Wall. As a result, a big brouhaha was being made about my prewar German stories. I now had the reputation of being both a good writer and colorfully cantankerous. Reporters interviewed me. I thought this hilarious.

The first interviewer was a woman reporter from the *Times*. "How does it feel to be so old?" she asked.

"I don't know," I answered. "I think of myself as still young. I'm often surprised when I pass by a shop window and see an old gray-haired lady. I always wonder who 'that woman' is!"

She smiled.

"What do you do with your spare time?" she asked, pencil poised above her pad.

She most likely thinks, I thought, that I lie around and watch television.

"Well," I said, "when I've listened to the emptiness for too long, I take off my shoes, put on sad country western music, and dance around my kitchen table."

That created a sensation among my peers. The headline on the reporter's story read: **Jazzy R. B. Manon Dances the Blues**.

As soon as I had arrived in Berlin I began to look for Leon. The East Berlin Jewish community was minuscule, and I decided to begin my search there. A young reporter, Jake Stein, from the *New York Courier* had accompanied me. Once we got settled, and our assignments booked, I sent him to the Rykerstrasse Synagogue. Since 1950, the synagogue had been the center of activity for the remnants of Berlin's religious and secular Jewish community. I asked him to try to find Leon.

I remember how my heart pounded, how I had to hang on to the table, when I read the note that Jake had slipped under my door: *Leon Wolff, metal engraver, is listed at*

Nürnbergestrasse 42, but has no phone number. Hope this helps, Jake.

He was alive!

Not able to bear the idea that I wouldn't see him, I sent a command by messenger. *Dear Leon, is it really you? Meet me this evening at 8:00 in the lounge of the Hotel Hansablick on Flotowstrasse. Please. Rosie.*

I dressed carefully. Smoothed down my short, still-thick gray (I prefer to call it silver) hair, and put on mascara and lipstick. I didn't want to look too fancy, nor too newswomanly (meaning a tailored suit). Wearing a pair of black loose cotton trousers and a red-and-orange patterned Indian-cotton shirt that hid my skin-sagging arms and covered my wrinkled cleavage, I timed my entrance. At three minutes past nine I walked out of the elevator and turned right into the lounge. He wasn't there. And when I saw the old woman, I knew she was Leon's emissary.

She was dressed shabbily, in what some reporters called East Berlin chic. Wearing a nondescript black skirt and faded blue cotton blouse, she had on thick nylons and run-down, sensible shoes. Her white hair was pulled back in a chignon. Her face was very wrinkled—grooves of worry, of a hard life, I imagined. But she was beautiful, sitting straight as an arrow, hands elegantly folded on her lap. All I could think was that I should let my hair grow.

"How do you do," she said. "Speak German?"

"Of course. Of course!" I said.

And she quietly told me, "I am Ruth Wolff. Leon's wife."

Now, three years later, here I am sitting on my porch, remembering my confusion of shock and relief. Meeting Leon's wife wasn't what I had had in mind.

"Where's Leon? How is he? Tell me, please, tell me—"

"Be patient," she said harshly. "This is hard for me."

"Sorry."

"We met," she began, "in the Sachsenhausen concentration camp, thirty-five kilometers north of Berlin."

"Oh, my god," I blurted. "I was so close to him when I was in Berlin!"

I could see Ruth flinch and told myself to be calm.

"Sorry," I said.

"We both had worked for Gerard von Schmitt," she continued, disregarding my outburst. "But we were in different buildings. So I never knew Leon until later. We were fortunate to be imprisoned where we were, considering the alternatives. When Leon healed from his concussion, Gerard had him sent to Sachsenhausen. And here he joined the lucky ones." Ruth laughed—and she had a lovely laugh. It melodically moved around me as if a light wind. And then, like a door had been slammed, she changed course.

"I won't go into the horrific details of the camp. Since you are a journalist, I'm sure you're well informed. But we fell in love."

"Oh, my dear," I said, "I'm not sure I want to hear this. It's too painful."

"No, no," Ruth protested. "Listen!"

"I can't listen to this," I said. "I thought he loved only me!" And then I was embarrassed by my confession.

Ruth looked at me as if I were pathetic. And then her face changed and she became sympathetic.

"I'm sorry, Miss Manon, please excuse me. I'm being insensitive. Meeting me must be startling. I'll leave," she said, and she started to rise.

"No, please stay," I said, putting out my hand. "I want to know. I *need* to know." I could see her try to relax.

"At any given time," she continued, "there were fifteen to eighteen forgers working in the shop. If someone made a mistake—didn't do a good enough job—tried to sneak food out for others—he or she was either eliminated or severely punished. Our lives depended on how well we worked. Otherwise, we were fed well enough—because we were considered essential to their 'cause.' Leon helped us survive. He would remind us that we needed to enjoy the craft we were involved in. 'Just think,' he would say, 'how beautiful a typographic serif is on an italic letter inked with a quill pen. It doesn't hurt us to make a beautiful forgery. We can't blame ourselves for collaborating with the enemy. We are saving our lives, while praying that these beautiful, official papers will get lost, or be burned, or never used. Honoring this art will keep us in practice for when the nightmare ends.'"

"But Leon?" I said.

"Please, let me continue in my way," Ruth insisted. "Leon and I would talk at the end of the day; only work-related talk was allowed in the shop. And of course, there was always a guard sitting by the door. Always with an Alsatian shepherd— and this frightened me since I'm afraid of dogs. Anyway, to continue—Leon told me about you. And I told Leon about my husband and children."

"Oh, you had a family. What happened—"

"Please, Miss Manon, this is hard for me. Please, I must take my time."

My memory of that evening is of the two of us sitting on dark-green upholstered chairs facing each other, a small table between us. I had a whiskey, Ruth a coffee. But I don't remember anything around us. Although I knew we were in a busy lounge, nobody else in the room was really there. I was fidgeting—she was calm. I smoked more than usual. She didn't smoke at all.

"All of us in the shop tried to help each other," Ruth said. "I think what helped Leon and me the most was that we already knew what had happened to the people we loved. Many others in the shop had no idea, so they had to live with a different kind of anxiety. My husband was a teacher, and we had two small children, my little girls. No," she said, "please don't say anything," and she held up both hands to protect herself from my questions.

"We were all rounded up and shipped to Sachsenhausen in trucks. On the platform, I was quickly separated from them— as I was on the list as an etcher. They didn't survive the night." Again she held up her hands. "And this is all I'm going to say about them. Please.

"After the war," she continued, "through a resettlement agency, Leon and I were given an apartment."

"He lived through the war!"

"Yes," she said.

"Why didn't he contact me!"

There was a long pause.

"Because he married me instead, Miss Manon."

Another long pause.

"Tell me the rest," I said. "It doesn't matter anymore."

"Unfortunately," she continued, "the apartment was on the wrong side of Berlin. Yet again, we were fenced in—this time here, in the eastern section of the city. We simply did not have the emotional energy to get out in time. Nor did either of us really care who was running the country—as long as we could be living in clean quarters and able to eat nourishing food and drink fresh water. Simple, isn't it, in the end?" she said. "Basic amenities. But our problem became one of health. Between Leon's working with metals and his incessant smoking, he became ill, with what we thought was severe bronchitis. But in fact, it was lung cancer. He refused treatment. I understood and accepted his decision. He died in 1979."

She's so straightforward, I thought. Died. Done. Leon gone.

"I'm sorry to bring you this news, Miss Manon."

"Why?" I asked. "Our relationship was over such a long time ago."

Ruth was not comfortable with my question. She was wringing her hands. "Many of us who survived the war," she said quietly, forcing me to lean forward, "have a deep sense of needing to complete our unfinished business. We know our families are dead. We know we've lost everything—but many threads had been left dangling. I don't suffer this need—I have no unfinished business. But Leon did. With you and Gerard."

"Gerard! I shouted. "For Christ's sake. He let Leon be arrested. When I met him, I begged him to free Leon."

"Please, Miss Manon, please, don't yell," she said. "You make me very nervous."

"Ha! Didn't Leon warn you that I was opinionated and noisy?"

I was irritated by Ruth's regal calmness. I was fidgeting like a crazy old hen.

"Is there no justice?" I said.

Ruth sighed, "There is very little. But please know that Leon also loved you. To him you represented an unforgettable vigor and exhilaration for life. All I could offer was the comfort of devotion, of simply being with him."

"I'm sorry," I said. "But I don't understand why he didn't contact me."

"Miss Manon," she said, "you know it is possible to love more than once in a lifetime. For the last part of Leon's life he loved me."

And then she stood, smoothed her skirt, and picked up her purse.

"Oh, no, you're not going," I said. "Please stay and have dinner with me. I promise not to scream and yell."

"No, Miss Manon, thank you, but I must go. This meeting has been hard for me and I need to leave."

We shook hands. There was no embrace. She turned and left.

Finally, in Berlin, in 1989, the dream ended.

For most of my life, my anger has flared like a wild brush fire on the steppes of the Nevada mountains. Some people say that getting old softens your view of the world. Not me. I see the behavior of the world more clearly, allowing my anger to be more precise. Yet, although I still like to argue and engage in intellectual combat, the anger is cooler and I'm not as critical as I used to be.

It is twilight. I have walked around to the west side of my house. I keep a chair there so I can watch the sun go down. Tonight the air is being softly pushed about by a flock of noisy sparrows. I hold down the pages on my lap, tempted to let them be lifted by the wind. What am I waiting for?

THE END

SOURCES

New York Herald Tribune, European Edition, Paris, 1937–1939.

P. Berthelot, *Graphologie*, in *La Grande encyclopédie*, 2nd ed. (Paris: 1886–1902), vol. 19, p. 220.